IT COULD HAVE BEEN MURDER

BY
E.D. RICH

Text copyright © 2024 by E.D. Rich

All rights reserved.

No part of this book may be reproduced, or stored in a retrieval system, or transmitted in any form or by any means, electronic, mechanical, photocopying, recording, or otherwise, without express written permission of the publisher.

E.D. Rich.

Carmel, IN

LCCN: 2024921357

Ebook ISBN: 978-1-300-88353-1

Paperback: 978-1-300-97220-4

Hardcover: 978-1-300-97214-3

eli.duncan.rich@gmail.com

Cover design by Alex Dickson

Prologue

When I was little, Mom, Dad, my sister, brother, and I piled into the car for family outings that now seem routine—not mundane, but not special either. It was a beast of a thing, this car: a canary yellow Cadillac with brown leather interior. In those days, in our small town, the filling station would accept a personal check for a tank of gas. Even then, the car's fuel economy was only nine miles per gallon.

We went to the movies—a proper outing for a family of five. Our small town didn't have a movie theater, but it did seem to be teeming with pizza places. We saw 'The Muppet Movie.' I think for a while, I may have had a crush on Kermit the Frog. He seemed to have a good head on his shoulders, was well-liked, and talented—I mean, he played the banjo, which, in my opinion, is a dying art form. And puppets with legs— completely blew my mind. At the time, puppets were nothing more than socks with someone's hand stuffed in the opening. If you saw legs, they were lying inert on a platform in front of said sock. This frog could ride a bike. Again, mind-blowing.

Two things about the movie, though: The end of the show featured 'The Magic Store' and an aptly named song. Somehow, everything was brighter, sparkled, and gleamed bigger and brighter than before. That's exactly how I pictured adulthood. Someday, I would grow up, and when I got there, a door—maybe like a door to a soundstage—would open, and in I would walk, and it would be The Magic Store, or something like it, but maybe, well, probably without the Muppets. But there would be pomp and great fanfare.

As an adult, though, I can tell you there is no soundstage, there is no door, there is no great entrée to life thrusting a golden halo around itself, bathing you in warmth. *This* is your life. You have finally arrived. Find the fainting couch with your name on it, and all good things will come to you just by the wave of your hand. If this is supposed to be what happens, it hasn't yet.

What was the second thing about the movie? Ah. Well. When my own children were small, I picked up the DVD at Target and was incredibly enthused to share this childhood memory. Kermit and the Muppets were all the same as I remembered, but the cameos—almost every person was dead. The grim realization wasn't offset by the brilliance of The Magic Store at the end, though. It was more a reminder that I, too, am temporary. What movie would my son and daughters show their own children and be reminded of their own mortality?

CHAPTER 1
Kate – *mid-1990s*

"I have an idea," I said. "I think it's a great idea."

"Oh, yeah?" said my roommate.

"I think so," I replied. "I mean, I think it's better than most of my other alternatives. Which, let's face it, no one is banging down the door to offer me a job."

We were lying on top of a blanket on the roof of her car, Sarah and I, sunning ourselves about a month shy of college graduation. Her plan was to get married. My plan was unformed. I would love to say my plan was incubating, but then there would have to be some sort of seed to sprout, or a cell line to propagate, a spore, something.

"I was thinking about becoming a salad maker."

Sarah turned her head. "You do make a good salad, and you do love to feed people, but is 'salad maker' even a thing?"

"Someone told me if you can conceive it, it must exist. If I follow the logic, then there is somewhere, someone in need of a salad maker. We just haven't found each other yet."

"Hmm," she said. "What else are you thinking about?"

"I could temp, work retail, wait tables. Something along those lines. The job market isn't great. Grad school isn't off the table," I paused. "I also like the idea of murder adventures."

She sat up abruptly, dislodging pots and potions of tan accelerator and sunscreen—getting the ratio perfect was key to getting a good glow without a burn.

"Sorry. What?" Collecting herself, she scrutinized me. "I don't understand those words you strung together."

Every time anyone asked me about my future plans, suddenly, salad maker seemed much more plausible and palatable, no pun intended. But why not make murder adventures? Not actual blood sport, though, at least not initially. But planning a murder could be a work of art. It could be an adventure on its own. Carrying out everything but the act itself. Debriefing, just like the Blue Angels after a mission—what worked, what didn't, what could be done differently. Could there be a market for it? Could this be some kind of corporate team-building business? Would I do this by myself? How would I find clients? How would I find a business partner or investors? What kind of person would want to put his or her name behind a business like this? What would I call it? Did anything like murder adventures already exist?

Business plan. I needed a business plan. I also needed to be able to do research without triggering any alarm bells and setting the National Security Council, Big Brother, or the Illuminati on my trail. And I definitely wanted to stay way the heck away from the Dark Web. In my early twenties, during a visit to the Grand Canyon, I realized how small I was in the grand scheme of things, and how little help there was depending on the circumstance. When night fell, we walked back to our hotel room, and there was enough light to illuminate our way, but beyond the rail separating civilization from what was out there, I could have been in my backyard, not standing along the rim of a pitch-black pit, and one unplanned step or clumsy move against the rail made grave difference, all under the same glittering stars and velvety night sky. That was my feeling about the Dark Web. Just leave it the fuck alone. And maybe, well, maybe it might leave me alone, too.

CHAPTER 2
The Pitch – excerpts

I'd like to preface this meeting by stating we are noting that we're only holding five pitch meetings, and we are only inviting five people to our pitch meetings. You are one of the select few. Congratulations. Before we dive into the pitch, though, I want to acknowledge that what we do is highly unorthodox. If this doesn't align with your interests... that's fine. You've already signed the non-disclosure agreement. Now, let's get to why we're here.

We've seen the movies, read the books. We understand the basic anatomy of murder and death from the media we consume. You know there's an event horizon defined by a murder. Death is imminent. In those moments of anticipation, you feel a subtle thrill, a frisson, about what's going to unfold.

We watch the bad guys get caught. There's always an Achilles' heel, it seems, that Johnny Law manages to exploit. But why? What went wrong? Was some detail overlooked? Was there a failure to plan—or worse, a failure to plan for the unexpected? Perfection is unattainable. We must anticipate every tiny grain of sand potentially infecting or contaminating a microchip. The moment even one grain enters that closed system, what's the countermeasure? If there isn't one, the plan is sub-standard. The microchip, once infected, compromised, is headed straight for the scrap heap.

In business, when we fail to achieve a desired result, we look back to root cause. We go through the motions of PDCA – Plan, Do, Check, Act. And our improvements are iterative. However, when it comes to planning a murder, we don't have the luxury of being able to workshop. Everything has to be perfect, and all contingencies have to be considered at every step in the completion of the exercise, and the ability to pivot with complete agility has to be automatic.

Who are we, and what are we proposing, and why do you want to invest? We are Diamond Teams. We are a boutique consulting firm with a solitary product on offer. We plan murders. We do not commit murders, and our clients do not commit murders. We guide our clients through every step leading to committing the murder, ending just shy of actually doing the deed. Our execution is in the detail, the planning, the procedure, the full-scale roll-out of murder without actually pulling the trigger, and finally the debrief sessions.

I have one client who, as a team-building exercise, involved his senior leadership team, and we planned the murder of the leadership team of a rival corporation. They then carried out all the steps necessary to take out their targets. Their success was measured not in lives lost but in the act of performing surveillance, social engineering, and capturing video or photographic records of the completion of the final steps in their project, and evading detection by their targets and/or the authorities.

Each member of the team knew exactly what their roles and actions were in the steps assigned to them. They also knew Plan B if anything went amiss. They rehearsed. They monitored their heart rates to minimize panic responses in risky situations, and they used this to keep cool heads during practice operations. They not only learned about their targets, but they learned about themselves. Imagine if you could recognize a panic response but then convert it into a moment of complete clarity, allowing you the chance to change gears without stopping to think through all the pros and cons of what this action or that action may be. You lose no time because ALL the thinking has been done long before this occurrence of stress.

Since the first client, all of my business has been via word of mouth. We do not advertise, but we need your investment to hire more staff and infrastructure to accommodate the demand for our services. Our profit margin to date is 80%. We have no debt at this time, but we are at a point where capital is needed in order to grow in a logical and meaningful way without sacrificing quality or any of our other Key Performance Indicators.

CHAPTER 3
Kate – *thirteen months ago*

Ask anyone what I do for a living, and they would say, "Um, Kate runs a boutique consulting firm. I think they do something for the government. She explained it once, and I really can't tell you what her company does." It works for me. I'm a wife, mother, dog mom, and business owner. I travel for work on occasion, go to the office a couple of days a week, and have a very closely tied management team and cadre of experts who weigh in on subjects of which my team and I cannot possibly know every facet. Every one of us is meticulous to a fault, but we focus on the details in diverse ways, which elevates us to near perfection. I don't know every hair on your head, but my team or I can come up with almost exactly how many hairs are on your head today. We are good. We are solid. We are well-paid, and we have no attrition. We are always recruiting but rarely make offers unless we come across a rare kindred individual who meshes seamlessly in our organization.

Like I said, I'm a mother, and I look like one. I don't think I've always looked like a mom, but it suits me. My husband is the COO of a Fortune 500 company, and our children are in college. Until a few months ago, my husband knew I started my company right out of college but would have struggled to explain what we do. And I was content to keep things that way. I didn't know what he did every day besides going to meetings, pushing pencils and paper, and saying things like, "Yes, sir. May I have another?" Not to minimize what he does, but what he does, in my opinion, seems insignificant in comparison to what I do. I suppose it could be why looking like a mom works to my benefit. No one seems to think maybe I could be Blind Justice, her cousin, or stepdaughter, not when I'm wearing a puffy coat and earmuffs.

I met Kevin a few years after college. He was finishing his MBA, and I was lying to people in a bar. He believed the lie, which endeared him to me. Lying to people in bars was my superpower in my twenties, and depending on how complex the web I wove, it could be exhausting to keep the ruse going for several hours, but he kept buying what I was selling. I told him I was a contortionist with Cirque du Soleil. He was so disappointed I had been sidelined by a broken pelvis and was no longer able to put both ankles behind my head. "That would've been hot," he commented. "I've never been with a girl who could do that."

He kept asking when he could meet my circus friends, and by the time we had gone on our third date, I had to confess I had never been a contortionist and had never been in Cirque du Soleil. "I knew it," he said, "but I wanted to see how far you would take it. I admire your commitment. You doubled down when you pulled out the leotard on our last date."

Six months later, we were married. He kept climbing the ladder at work, and my business had already taken off by the time we had gotten together. It was a challenge to keep a lid on just how much success my business had, though.

Before we ever started dating, my business, not quite a year old, I had too much work to be able to do everything myself. I enlisted the smartest person I knew, who was also someone I had known most of my life and trusted implicitly. Kevin knows I have business partners, but when we first got together, I hid them away like I hid my circus friends. By the time of our wedding, Kevin had met Sam and her husband Chris. Chris was my first client and my second employee.

Sam is the person who could tell you exactly when Schrödinger's cat was dead or alive. She would know with certainty, and if she even felt 0.1% uncertainty, no one ever knew it. To listen to her talk, anyone would think she was a theoretical physicist—she's actually a CPA—as she discussed the nature of decaying radioactive particles. She taught me how to sell the lie, any lie, to anyone, anywhere. Bringing her into the business was the best, most important thing I ever did as it relates to my livelihood.

We had reached a turning point, both of us considering succession planning. This business—our business—had been our baby, now almost grown and ready to stand on its own. As a trio of two moms and a dad, all we could do was set a course for success and trust that our team would continue to carry forward our mission, vision, and values. Even good things can take a toll, and while I wouldn't say I was completely worn down, but maybe a little tired, and maybe I wanted to take the training wheels off and let someone else take the reins, to keep things going as well, or even better, than we had. The timing felt right. There was always the possibility of Chris staying on for another few years—or even ten or fifteen—because he truly loved the work and tended to be somewhat visionary.

CHAPTER 4
Diamond Teams, LLC: The Screening

Page 1:

At Diamond Teams, LLC, we recognize the sensitive nature of our work. We realize its importance and necessity. We understand that you, our client, have come to us in good faith. Everything we do or say is of a proprietary nature, as are all communications and interactions between us. That may seem redundant, but clarifying everything in plain language helps both parties understand the seriousness of our relationship.

If you feel you cannot honor the requirements of maintaining the security of any part of our relationship or services you wish to engage, then the application process ends here.

Page 2:

If you feel confident you can honor all the provisions of the Client Services Agreement, you may continue the application. If your application is approved, you will be required to place $200,000 in an escrow account, held in the event of any breach of confidentiality as outlined further in the agreement. The duration of the escrow account is determined on a case-by-case basis, also outlined in the Client Services Agreement. The Client Services Agreement will be made available to you if your application is approved by Diamond Teams, LLC.

You are required to submit to a credit check before continuing the application process. If you are unable to make the escrow commitment, then the application process ends here.

Page 3:

Prior to completing the application, you are required to submit to a criminal background check. On the following pages, you must authorize all searches to verify your identity.

If at any time there is any unanswered question regarding your criminal background or personal history, the application process ends here.

Page 4:

Your mental health and health status are of paramount importance to Diamond Teams, LLC. To that end, we have engaged a mental health professional to complete a one-hour interview with you to evaluate your mental fitness.

If the evaluation yields favorable results, you will receive an invitation to complete the Diamond Teams, LLC application. If any aspects of the evaluation give pause or concern, then the application process ends here.

Page 5:

Congratulations. You have successfully completed the Diamond Teams, LLC Screening and have been approved to complete The Client Application. If your application is approved, we will provide The Client Services Agreement, along with The Diamond Teams, LLC Scope of Work document.

Page 6:

Congratulations. Your Diamond Teams, LLC Application has been approved. You are required to sign The Client Services Agreement, along with making your escrow account deposit.

As described in The Screening, the duration of escrow funds placement is determined on a case-by-case basis, which will occur after we work collaboratively to sculpt the desired deliverable for you. Every aspect of our Product will be outlined in The Diamond Teams, LLC Scope of Work document.

If Diamond Teams, LLC defaults in any way in fulfilling our obligations, 20% of any monies in escrow will immediately be released. You are still bound to any and all security, privacy, and non-disclosure provisions outlined in The Client Services Agreement.

CHAPTER 5
Assassin – the game

The Rules

1. You have an Assassin kit equipped with:
    a) Laser pointer
    b) Water pistol
    c) Digital stopwatch
    d) Sharpie
    e) Post-Its
2. Laser pointer is to give your target a heads up you have found and are hunting them. DO NOT POINT THE LASER POINTER IN ANYONE'S EYES.
3. Water pistol is to stun your target for 30 seconds. Target cannot move for 30 seconds. Digital timer to be used to mark the time. DO NOT USE YOUR WATER PISTOL WHILE IN A MOVING VEHICLE!!!

4. You neutralize your target by placing a Post-it with your name on it somewhere on their person. Target would also sign and date the Post-it.

5. You are responsible for turning in the Post-it after you have neutralized your target.

6. Your target can also neutralize you. Don't be sloppy.

7. If your target has an active target, you will now assume the newly orphaned target.

8. If your target does not have an active target, you will be assigned a new target by us.

9. You are not required to use the laser pointer or the water pistol. You are allowed to play a totally stealth game.

10. DO NOT DESTROY THE ITEMS IN YOUR ASSASSIN KIT. YOU HAVE TO RETURN EVERYTHING AT THE END OF THE GAME.

CHAPTER 6
Sam – *early- to mid-1990s*

Over Christmas break, Kate and I decided to gather our main and peripheral friend groups for pizza at Kate's parents' house. We explained the rules of the game.

"The game is Assassin," Kate said while passing out half-sheets of paper with the rules of the game.

"Everyone gets an Assassin kit," I said, handing out Zip-Lock bags filled with a laser pointer, water pistol, small digital stopwatch, Sharpie, and pad of 3x3 Post-its. The group seemed to warm to the game, but they had no idea what to do with the items in the Assassin kits, with the exception of the water pistol.

"Here's how it works: you are going to draw a name from the coffee can. You are then tasked with assassinating the person whose name is on the card you draw," Kate explained.

"The way your Assassin kit works is as follows," I said. "Pay attention. I'm going to go through this once, and you have to remember this because someone is also hunting you. The laser pointer is used simply as a warning to alert your target you have located him or her. It's a courtesy. They now know they have been found and are being hunted. They have the option of doing nothing and letting you kill them, or they can run."

"The water pistol is for stunning your target. If you manage to hit them, they are frozen for thirty seconds. That's what the stopwatch is for. Both assassin and target may want to use these when a target is stunned," Kate then added, "You do not have to stun your target, though. It's an option for you. What you DO have to do, though, to complete an assassination is place one of your Post-its on your target, and the Post-it has to have your name on it."

"If you have been assassinated, you have to write the date and time on the assassin's Post-it. All assassination Post-its must be returned to me," I said. "If you have been assassinated before dispatching your own target, you will turn over your target's name to the person who assassinated you."

Kate wound things down by telling the group, "It's ok if you have questions. This is the first go-round with the game, and we know it may not go off as smoothly as possible. I do not need to tell you: You CANNOT stun your targets from a moving vehicle. However," she sighed deeply, "here I am telling you anyway. Water pistol activity from a moving vehicle will result in immediate removal from the game."

"And, guys," I threw in for good measure, "don't be an asshole and point your laser pointer at someone's eyes. It's just mean and unnecessary, and it makes you an asshole."

Kate held up a poster board. We had written everyone's names on three-by-five index cards. Every card was taped to the board, and the board was labeled on one half: ACTIVE ASSASSINS. The other half was labeled: NEUTRALIZED TARGETS. All the players were still on the ACTIVE ASSASSINS half of the board.

"Yikes!" Kate interjected. "This may be the best twist of the game. If you are a target, and you have a chance to turn the tables on your assassin and you manage to tag them with one of your own Post-its, then you can remove the person from the game. Same rules apply. You have to report the neutralized party."

"Again," I reiterated, "all reports and Post-its are to be delivered to me. I am the record keeper of everyone's exploits. And if you're thinking of being all pre-emptive and taking out everyone on the board, don't. It would make you an asshole. You can take out your target or the person hunting you."

There were a few finer points we shared. The game would last no longer than one week, unless there was only one person standing before the cutoff time. Kate and I were NOT in the game. We would only enter the game as a substitute for someone else (i.e., if someone got the flu or something). No one would know if we had entered the game except for the person who had the sickie's name.

Once names were drawn, the game would begin at 8 a.m. the following day. There were twenty-five people playing over Christmas Break.

We started a new game right after the school year ended. The second game had 122 people. The third game, during Fall Break of the following school year, had over two hundred people, and we charged everyone $10 to play, which didn't seem to deter anyone. Our parents and siblings had to help assemble the Assassin kits. They thought it was fun for about the first 30 minutes, and afterward—not so much.

We had to dial things back after the Fall Break game because there was a lot of water pistol abuse. In addition, it was no fun managing all the Post-its coming in all the time. We had to tape six poster boards together to accommodate all the index cards. We felt like bookies, or what we thought old-timey bookies felt like when they kept all the bets in a ledger. Kate kept saying in her silly old man gangster voice, "Call me Bugsy, see. But don't set no coppers on me. You got me, kid?" I had to tell her to stop because she just sounded weird and not like a gangster, and no one, not even her parents, really understood why an antique gangster.

By the time Christmas Break rolled around again, we had decided only the first seventy-five people could play, and once out of the game, all Assassin kits had to be returned. We kept the $10 fee and refunded $5 if players returned their Assassin kits.

CHAPTER 7
Kate

Always, always, always—I love an adventure. Everything about the word sends a thrill through my very being. When someone talks about anything not going according to plan, I think, "Adventure!" and am seized by a visceral attack of excitement and delight. I'm not anti-plan, and I do not crave chaos. You have to have a plan in order for there to be an adventure. There has to be a rule from which one can deviate. Without a plan, there is no deviation, no adventure. Sad face.

The first time I heard 'death by misadventure,' the idea of an adventure going completely wrong, ending in death, the very idea was appalling. Someone had failed to plan, or at least they had planned improperly, and the adventure got away from them.

Imagine having a fragile, brittle, beautiful golden egg put in your hand. It's the only one in the world, the last remaining tenuous filament to the dodo bird. Add a tissue-filled box, a backpack filled with nails, and a flak jacket with soft, fleece-lined deep pockets. The job at hand is to take the egg from Portland, Maine to Portland, Oregon by any mode of transportation. Does it make sense to put the egg in the backpack and ride a bike cross-country? Does it make better sense to put the egg in the box, then in the pocket of the flak jacket, and travel by plane, train, or car? If someone dies by misadventure, they have chosen the backpack-bike plan, and it's not a good plan. It's not even a good contingency plan. If the golden egg winds up in a backpack full of nails at any time, the end for the egg is misadventure, and the person who put the egg in the backpack full of nails is an asshole.

The nails are a contingency plan if someone tries to steal the egg from you during your cross-country trek. There are options with the nails and the backpack, and a backpack full of nails could be a good weapon, indeed. But it is the worst possible cradle for a delicate egg.

Over time, the unnatural deaths that fall into the death by misadventure category have become more plentiful and include some accidental deaths, suicides, and some homicides; however, to my way of thinking, misadventure is for the Darwin Award nominees and recipients and the assholes. Bad choices, bad or no planning, bad brains.

Even with all that, can an adventure exist with the end goal being murder? Yes. Does the murder have to occur? No. Can the focus be on the planning and execution? Yes. Can the planning be gratifying? Yes. Can planning a murder galvanize a team? Of course. What does planning a murder look like? Why not equip someone with a water gun, paintball gun, or laser tag gun and have them lie in wait for their quarry? It is shiver-inducing to think of how many things could go wrong. That's not a plan. It's maybe a plan for disaster. We learned a lot from the Assassin games in high school.

To do everything right requires thinking like a predator. Who is the target? What is the target's routine? What sort of plans are embedded in a target's day-to-day existence? Prepare a predator-prey SWOT (strengths, weaknesses, opportunities, threats). I came up with this after taking a class where we did strategic planning, and it became clear that this little tool had profound applications.

What is the motivation for the predator's selection of the prey? What's the preferred method of removing the playing piece from the board? Is more than one person needed for the operation? Has a research plan been completed that includes disposal options that will lead to a clean getaway? What are the fallback plans? What are the measures of success and failure?

Failure occurs if the predator is hurt or removed from the board, or if the police show up at the predator's front door with questions. And then there's the obvious indicator of failure: the target winds up hurt or removed from the board (The Game of Life board, if you get my meaning).

Murder adventure was an evolution of the Assassins game from high school and involved an entire process with my company (which was just me for most of the first year) planning a murder and training the client to do everything without committing the act. Preparation could involve home invasion, social engineering, catfishing, theft, and myriad other approaches, tools, and ideas to remain one step ahead of getting caught. We would coach individuals and/or teams to plan and mobilize in such a way that success would not be defined by reading an obituary in the Sunday paper but by the prey never knowing they were in the predator's sights. The best adventures ended with the prey feeling like maybe something was a little off for a few weeks but then returning to the usual calm.

CHAPTER 8
Sam

"You have reached Diamond Teams. Please leave the following information on this secure voicemail message: Your screen, application, or client number. Your liaison will return your call within 12 hours."

Everyone going through any part of The Process with Diamond Teams, LLC, received a number. A random number generator was attached to each point in The Process. As a potential client advanced through The Process, a different number was generated, and any previous number was then rendered expired, never to be used again. All potential clients were assigned a liaison and would never deal with anyone but that liaison. Every liaison selected a handle when joining Diamond Teams, LLC, and annually, a liaison had the opportunity to adopt a different handle. Each liaison kept as small a caseload as possible to mitigate any circumstance of chance encounter with anyone going through The Process.

Diamond Teams maintained two small administrative offices, one on each coast. Almost all team members worked virtually, and every effort was made to pair a liaison with potential clients from different geographic areas in the country. All onsite meetings were held in rented, borrowed, or time-shared offices. Potential clients typically had to travel to any of the onsite meetings or interviews. There was an absolute prohibition on bringing any electronic devices into any Diamond Teams, LLC meeting. All documents were retained by the company and could only be viewed by the client via an onsite meeting. Once a document was signed, it was digitized and stored. The paper record ceased to exist within moments of the conclusion of the meeting.

The secrecy and security lent a clandestine feel to every part of the interaction between a potential client and the Diamond Teams' liaisons. The cachet was part of what led to the success of Diamond Teams. There was no advertising, never had been any advertising. There were no breadcrumbs on any social media. Any mention of Diamond Teams outside of client referrals would cost someone $200,000, the amount placed into the client's escrow account. To date, not one client has forfeited an escrow deposit because of social media slip-ups. In an era of over-sharing, this was nothing short of a miracle.

Kate started Diamond Teams, and I joined her after a year. At first, I was part-time, just an extra set of hands, I suppose. Eventually, we realized we had to bring on a third person. Finding the right fit was a thousand times more difficult than the client vetting process that we were developing, or so I thought. We spent time thinking of everyone we had grown up with, people we knew we could trust with virtually anything. People who had moved far from where we had grown up. Kate and I lived 1,500 miles apart, which worked well from a geographic planning standpoint. We needed to find someone else who was also around 1,000 to 1,500 miles away from each of us. As Diamond Teams grew, we made the strategic decision first to have one person in every US time zone. However, murder adventures were more popular than we had anticipated. Who knew that the country was full of people with a lust in their hearts for ending their fellow man? We then aimed to have one person in each geographic region. We still haven't realized the geographic spread goal because we are very, very selective in who we hire.

As a safety measure, Kate legally changed her last name to her maternal grandmother's maiden name. After I left the accounting firm to go full-time with Diamond Teams, I legally changed my last name to my paternal grandmother's maiden name. It made sense at the time, and I am so glad that we took the precaution all those years ago.

CHAPTER 9
Chris – *mid-1990s*

Kate and Sam had been best friends all through high school. They were smart girls and cool, but they only knew that they were smart. That was one of the best things about them. They were always real, always thinking, and never embarrassed about turning things about in their heads every which way.

From the very first moment I met Sam, I knew I was in love with her. In my marrow, I knew we would wind up together (and, oh, my God, I know how schmaltzy and gob-smacked teenage boy that sounds). Of course, since we were in high school and she had big plans for college, there was this thing called life that we each needed to live a little bit, and then, who knows, maybe we would reconnect, or maybe she would see me in a different way than just a guy friend who enjoyed the privilege of sharing her company. We tell ourselves all kinds of stories to make our day-to-day existences not quite so mundane or pathetic, and with teenage angst, I'm definitely leaning on not being pathetic. I never wanted to be the moony-eyed guy pining after the girl who has no idea that she is my universe.

Kate always knew that Sam was 'that girl' for me, and she didn't push or offer unsolicited advice. I think we may have been sixteen or so, but Kate once acknowledged that I had all these feelings for Sam and said, "It's not my place to tell you what to do, but you'll know what to do when you're supposed to do it. And if this thing is supposed to happen, then it will. Don't worry. Things have a way of working out." Then she asked if I could give her a piggy-back ride, climbed onto my back, and proceeded to give me a noogie. I think the noogie was a distraction technique from the seriousness of her philosophizing.

But, on a Thursday evening, just after I had returned home from work, Kate called. Totally out of the blue. I had graduated from college a semester early, which made my parents so happy they took themselves to Hawaii with all the tuition money they had saved. No joke.

From what my parents told me, Kate had graduated maybe a month prior to her out-of-the-blue phone call and was back in our small hometown, living with her parents while she was starting a business. Sam, Kate, and I all went to different colleges, but the four years between high school and college graduation did not lend themselves well to keeping in touch and maintaining relationships with the same intensity as when we were in high school. I would be lying if I said I wasn't pleased to hear from her because of her Sam connection.

"Chris, I need your help, and I trust you to be my first client, and you would get my services for free," Kate said. "And no, I'm not a call girl or escort or whatever. This is not a sexy-time call."

"Wow. OK." I took a beat before responding. "So, it's great to hear from you, and I can't begin to tell you how relieved I am that you're not a sex worker."

"Yeah, no," she chuckled. I could hear her tapping her fingers or something on her end of the call. She was nervous about talking to me about making me her client and giving me some kind of free services. "Remember the Assassins game we played in high school?"

"Of course," I said. "How could I forget winning the inaugural round?" They gave me a gift certificate to a local taco place, and I think I may be able to have free tacos until the end of time.

"What if you could play it today, and you pick one person that you want to eliminate? You are the only player. Your target never knows that you're planning to assassinate them?" she asked.

I hedged for a second. "Are you asking this in a practical sense or in a philosophical sense?"

"Completely practical," she said, sounding sober and... sane.

We were both quiet for a moment. Not knowing that you were in a game, that you were an unwilling participant, that some 'other' was watching you with the intent to eliminate or neutralize you, even if it was fake. I needed to process this before I could give a sincere answer to Kate's question.

"Can I have a day or two to think this over? I would love to give you a flip answer, but I think that morally and ethically, this isn't a straight line," I said. "One more thing, though, how does the game end? I think that's important for me to have an idea of how all the pieces come together to be able to give as fully informed an answer as I can."

She spoke slowly, knowing what she had said had some shock value, and, rightfully, I was shocked. "Since they don't know they're your target, you don't end by putting a Post-it on them. You would use a cell phone, digital camera, or throwaway camera when you complete the step in the assassination that is analogous to pulling the trigger or applying the Post-it, or I go with you sort of as a sherpa."

The next day, I called her back. "I'm in. I'll be your first client."

I knew that she would have already begun creating a process for vetting clients and for planning the assassinations. She called them murder adventures. "Let's face it," she said, "you're potentially skulking around in the dark, possibly following someone to get your evidence photo, and your adrenaline is spiked. It's an adventure. I would call it a misadventure, though, if you get caught. I don't want to deal in misadventures—ever."

I told her I wanted to assassinate Sam. I thought that if something didn't go to plan, Sam would be more forgiving since we had been friends for years. Kate agreed that Sam would be a suitable candidate because if she had to dial someone in, Sam was the best. And, also, Sam already knew about Kate's fledgling business.

I had to take a week off work, and Kate and I met up in Atlanta, where Sam was living at the time. Sam didn't know the timing of when the game would start. She only knew that she was a piece on the board. We surveilled Sam, kept notes on her work hours, eating and social habits. I even went through her trash. We discovered that she went out a lot, and that since it wasn't the busy season, and she hadn't taken the CPA exam yet, our timing was better than we could have imagined. Kate took notes throughout the entire process. I would look at her, noting her furrowed brow because she was seeing vulnerabilities that could not exist if I were a paying client. She talked about risk management, minimization, and elimination under her breath several times every day we were in Atlanta.

After three days of active surveillance, on morning number four over croissants and coffee, Kate produced two glossy booklets, one for each of us. She was like magic because I had no idea where and when she would have been able to produce something like this. Maybe she didn't sleep. "This, my friend, is your bible. This includes every single step for how you will neutralize your target. You need to read this backwards and forwards and commit everything to memory. I don't know if I have thought through every contingency, but you need to memorize all that, too. You HAVE to know every place where there can be a kink in the chain, and you have to be able to fix the chain as quickly and smoothly as possible without losing any of your momentum. You have failed if Sam knows you're here, or if she spots you, or if one of her neighbors spots you, or if someone sees you being creepy and calls the cops."

It wasn't a big book, but the font was tiny. It took me over an hour to skim the first time through. Kate said, "Go to the pool today or go to a bookstore or something. We begin rehearsing for the assassination tomorrow." She made a tick mark in her booklet, closed it, dropped it in her handbag, and took her coffee and my croissant with her.

CHAPTER 10
Kate

The Client Application

Part I – Screening Inventory

- Confidentiality Agreement
- Non-disclosure Agreement
- Credit Check and Financial Solvency
- Criminal Background and Personal History Check
- Mental Health Evaluation

If a potential client passes through the first checks in the screening process (Part I – Screening Inventory), it's like they earned a golden ticket to Willy Wonka's chocolate factory. Everything is arduous for the potential client. Part of the rationale is to weed out potential clients who just don't have the patience to go through the process. We have lost some potential clients due to their impatience and intolerance in our methods, and we have lost potential clients who thought the screening was too invasive, and we have lost potential clients who were assholes and failed the screening.

On the flip side, though, we have had so many clients who genuinely believe it necessary to be invasive and thorough, to ensure that we're not giving a green light to the assholes. After all, who would trust a murder adventure company that put a loaded gun in the hands of Billy the Kid or Al Capone or some other asshole?

Part II – Desire for Services

- Who referred you to Diamond Teams, LLC?
- What do you know about Diamond Teams, LLC?
- Why do you wish to engage with Diamond Teams, LLC?
- What do you hope to achieve with Diamond Teams, LLC?
- Are your goals of a personal or professional nature?

The meat and potatoes, Part II – Desire for Services, is the golden ticket, the actual application. Because we don't advertise, we want to know what brings a potential client here, and who recommended us. We contact the referral source personally and usually learn more about the potential client than we could get from all the steps in the screening process. If it's possible that someone might be an insufferable asshole, i.e., kicks kittens, doesn't call loved ones on their birthdays, has pushed someone into traffic, does not wash hands after using a public toilet, always cuts the cake and chooses the biggest piece, etc., that application goes into The Asshole Pile, saved in case we have a potential client in the future who doesn't have a target in mind but wants to go through the exercise. We have a whole bullpen of assholes, and The Asshole Pile is actually a file on our server.

Part II is completed by hand. We then send the answers to a handwriting expert to evaluate to obtain additional insights into a potential client's personality traits and state of mind. There have been a few potential sociopaths and psychopaths identified, even though the current school of thought is that handwriting analysis as a diagnostic tool for psychopathy is inconclusive, with the caveat that larger sample sizes (more psychopaths) are needed in order to make meaningful insights and conclusions.

After all of this due diligence, though, the most critical make-or-break part of The Process is The Interview. Depending on the potential client's chosen track, the interviews differ significantly. When I first incorporated the interview, I admit, the questions were amateurish. I felt like I was the moderator on The Dating Game or The Newlyweds or something. Maybe that one game show where the celebrity contestants had to fill in the blank to match what the Regular Joe contestant wrote on a placard. The questions were not terribly insightful. Then I went to therapy and several therapists, and friends from college who were getting master's degrees or PhDs in psychology and also divinity, and bartenders—who happen to make excellent therapists. Eventually, I landed on a retired profiler from the FBI. It wasn't all 'Silence of the Lambs,' but it was eerie as fuck and made me think that everyone had some kind of nefarious plan for me just under the gossamer surface of their beings.

During the initial funding round of five pitch meetings, yes, a good chunk of the money was going to be used for expanded staffing, but I also had to pay that FBI guy, I call him 'Profile Man,' a ton of money to raise the hood on the car and explain the engine underneath. I begrudged being gouged, but what I gleaned was worth a thousand times what I paid. In retrospect, it seemed like a lot of money, but when I look back, it was a pittance, but enough to demonstrate my own commitment to my business.

Eventually, the Profile Man became one of my first investors, and I will be eternally grateful for his investment, time, expertise, and mentorship.

CHAPTER 11
Chris

Becoming client one and employee two or three (depending on if you count Kate as employee number one) was a lifetime ago but, even today, feels like it was yesterday. Right now, I have spent almost half my life working with Diamond Teams. It's like the saying: When you love what you do, you don't work a day in your life. I am fortunate to work with my wife and her best friend, who has become one of my best friends. We all share the same values, and we have been working together for so long now, sharing ownership of a business, that Kate may as well be a member of our family.

In the early days, though, when Kate first called and made her request to me to be her first client, I had no idea how important the call would be for me, both personally and professionally. It was a pivotal few weeks, and I'm not overselling when I say those weeks impacted even the most remote corners in my life.

Kate had been working tirelessly to build her business plan, policies, procedures, forms and forms library, testing requirements for liaisons, clients, finding investors, building up her proof of concept, and then beta testing. As client one, that made me her beta tester, and it made Sam her beta test target. In retrospect, there is no one else that I could possibly think of taking on either of those roles at the time. Kevin would have been all right, but he wasn't in the picture yet.

The prospective client screening process is hugely different now than it was at the beginning. We were using screening tools that didn't make sense for what we needed to be able to predict or to generate insights into the personality and thought process of a client. I think during the beta testing, I took no fewer than twelve different personality/psychological batteries/inventories, and I don't think there's any test that is perfect for what we do, but we try to capture as many dimensions as we can into the psyche of our clients. We began using other determinants as our process evolved, and we also hired experts to review the testing, interviews, handwriting samples, etc.

The process now was nearly a clinical thing, as sterile and regimented as it had become through its evolution. We controlled the setting. We kept the office space as clean as possible and wiped everything down following every encounter. We aimed to leave no trace behind in any environment where we acted in a Diamond Teams capacity. Every office space we occupied was swept daily for any listening devices.

We controlled clothing. Anyone who gained approval as a client received a uniform for each day of the week that they would be working with Diamond Teams. The uniforms were simple: chinos and an oxford shirt or polo shirt. We allowed the clients to choose which shirt. We also provided athletic shoes and socks. In case someone needed to run, we wanted to have the correct footwear. We placed air trackers in the hems of the pants and in the soles of the shoes. When we dropped clients at their hotels for the night, the expectation was that they would stay put for the night. If they changed clothes and left, we lost the ability to track the client electronically, which is why we had tracking installed on the hotel room keys. This was a genius idea that one of our children had while watching some show on Nickelodeon. I took the idea to our I/T guys, and they reached out to some developers they knew.

We controlled technology. We instructed every client, both personal service clients and professional service clients, to alert their offices that they would be off the grid for the duration of their projects. We allowed clients to communicate with their families at night. We monitored communication and data on the clients' cell phones while their projects were ongoing. Clients were not allowed to bring their cell phones with them during the day. We generally frowned on clients bringing their laptops because the feelings of being sequestered and total focus on the project had to prevail throughout the murder adventure.

We controlled time in the form of action-packed itineraries. Refinements to the itinerary occurred in the very earliest days of Diamond Teams. We knew that the clients had to be kept busy throughout the waking hours of their days and all activity had to be meaningful, and pertinent to their projects. When we put together the itinerary template, every item included the 'why' for being on the list. If clients didn't know or understand why they were engaging in a certain activity, their buy in to our process would be lost.

The 'why' was something on Kate's radar way before it was a buzzword in every company in America and public speakers and pundits were asking us all to ask ourselves what our 'why' was. What we asked our clients to ask themselves:

- Why are you interested in a murder adventure?
- Why are you willing to pay Diamond Teams' fees?
- Why are you coming to Diamond Teams?
- Why aren't you doing something similar on your own?

- Why do you think Diamond Teams can help you?
  - How do you foresee the resolution of your murder adventure?
  - What does successful completion of a murder adventure mean to you and why?

Then we followed with the 'what' questions:

- What are you hoping to achieve with Diamond Teams?
  - Why are you hoping to achieve this?
  - How do you think you will achieve this?
  - If you do achieve this, what does it mean to you?
- What are you expecting to experience through a murder adventure?
  - How do you think this experience will change you?
- What will you do if your target files a complaint against you for not being stealthy enough in your surveillance?
- What were you told about Diamond Teams and murder adventure before you contacted us?
  - What is it about Diamond Teams that intrigues you?
  - Why?
- What are your impressions of our screening and vetting processes?
  - Why are you allowing us to dissect your life?
  - How does it make you feel, knowing that we are accessing critical data points in your life?

We've heard the onion analogy and peeling back the layers of the onion and by asking 'why' five times (or was it six?) will eventually reveal the true answer, or the truest answer at the time. We wanted to dig down to a potential client's most basic and honest motivation for embarking on a murder adventure, and to get consistent answers, we would ask the same question in different ways, but look for answers that didn't contradict one another.

We worked with so many psychiatrists, psychologists, Profile Man, and other experts to avoid the situation we were now in with that fucking asshat, Guy Brown. I fucking hated that guy for fucking with the job I love.

CHAPTER 12
Kevin – *1 year ago*

Today is our wedding anniversary. Kate was called away due to a work emergency. It's strange that there are emergencies in the realm of boutique consulting firms. What constitutes an emergency? Someone was incapable of consulting? Someone's PowerPoint blew up? I'm not being fair, I know that. I'm projecting. I put everything work-related on the back burner to plan something special for our anniversary, but I'm sitting here at our kitchen table doodling on a scratch pad of paper. We leave pads of paper all over our house. Kate has terrible ADD, and she has to write things down as soon as she thinks about them, or else they're lost forever. She can be telling a story at dinner, get caught in a loop about a specific detail, and then her whole story is derailed, and she has no idea what it was she had been trying to communicate.

In comparison, I'm very humdrum. I am organized and predictable. She often sets a clock based on my routines. One day she said, "Kev, honey, if someone wanted to kill you, you would be so easy to pick off. You never deviate." She is absolutely right. I get comfort from routine.

I like to see everything lined up in a row. I love a list. When I see the grid on TV of all the channels and scheduled programming, it makes me happy. That kind of higher level organization amazes me, and they manage to get commercials sandwiched into all of that with organized regularity.

A friend of ours does freelance work for the NFL. Every Sunday morning, she goes through a run-down of all the businesses and individuals who want to advertise on the digital boards and the giant screens in the stadium during the game. Each slot is for a certain amount of time on a certain location, and the pricing is based on placement, size, and units of time. Makes all the sense in the world. However, who knows how long a football game will last? Sometimes they go long, and sometimes, the game is a complete blowout without many penalties, etc. Every game, though, has more advertising purchased than can possibly fit into the average-length game. Her challenge is to try to get as much of the advertising posted in the stadium as she can, honoring what was paid for, and knowing that there will be some ads that are never seen. For the advertiser, it's a game of chance. The ad may be shown, or it may be punted to the next home game. AND even if the ad is given priority for the next home game, there are still the 1100-pound gorilla advertisers who demand that with their continued advertising revenue and support, their ads should always take precedence. I could not do that job and maintain my sanity. It would end with my not ever being able to watch a professional football game again.

Kate's job, though, gives her satisfaction. She works for herself, and I think she has government clearance or something because she can never tell me what she's working on. Sometimes when she has to go out of town, she is able to tell me where she's going, but I never know much more than if it's a routine client meeting or a team meeting. The work emergencies have been very few and far between throughout our life together.

When we started dating, she had a pretty great CD collection. We have since gone the digital route, and kept back only the sentimental CDs. I'm not even sure we have a CD player anymore. She had The Foo Fighters' first CD. I borrowed it, and I knew that if this girl dug this music, she was one of my people. For our anniversary, I made a video of all the milestones in our relationship and paired it with Foo Fighters' songs that marked the occasions—the signposts of our lives. Sitting here thinking about it, the video is good, but maybe the commitment to a single band is a little over the top. I mean, there are so many songs and artists. One of her favorites, though, is "Walking After You." Kate says it's about a stalker. She has told me on more than one occasion that if I ever dump her, "I'm going to stalk the shit out of you." She's not a large person, but when she levels the serious gaze and tone on me, I know in my bones that she isn't exaggerating, not even a little bit.

While I'm doodling on the scratch pad, though, I shade in the cow that I'm drawing. I am no artist, and the only thing that I can draw that is somewhat recognizable is a cow. All my cows have heads pointing to the left. If someone tried to attribute a right-facing cow to me, then I did not make that drawing. My brain shorts out when I try to change the cow's orientation. As I'm shading, the depressions on the paper from the prior sheet come through.

- Poison.
- Anaphylaxis.
- Gun.
- Knife.
- Shiv.
- Garrote.
- Slip and fall.
- Faulty brakes.

To say this is alarming is completely underselling what I'm seeing. If she had been playing Family Feud and the topic was methods of death, then the list makes sense. Although, if one hundred people are surveyed, how many will come up with "garrote" or "anaphylaxis"? I tuck the paper into my wallet and will be sure to ask if she's all right and why she's listing unnatural causes of death.

Tonight promises to be unremarkable. Some microwave dinner. Checking email, and perhaps changing some of the music on the anniversary video. I'll talk to Kate later, Venmo some money to the kids because college students always need money, and then go to bed. All kinds of excitement, all before 10:30 PM.

CHAPTER 13
Professional Services – The Interview – excerpts

DT = Diamond Teams; **PC** = Potential Client

DT: First, let me welcome you to the Diamond Teams Interview portion of our application process. Getting to this point in our process is no small feat.

PC: Your process is quite arduous.

DT: We make the process arduous for several reasons: one being that we want to be sure that potential clients are serious about engaging our services. Are you serious about engaging our services?

PC: Well, yes. Serious.

DT: Tell me what do you hope to get out of engaging Diamond Teams?

PC: I came to my company and inherited an already longstanding team. They haven't been as welcoming as I had hoped. The person I replaced had not left voluntarily, and my team were extremely loyal to him.

DT: OK…

PC: I would love to tell you that I would like the team to plan a project to neutralize my predecessor, but that's not it at all. And I don't mean to make morbid jokes, but it has been incredibly difficult to build political capital with the team. I think what I would like to achieve is to have the team collaborate with me, clearly as their leader, on something high stakes but also closely guarded and proprietary. I feel what we would be engaging Diamond Teams to do with us would provide a foundation for bonding and loyalty.

DT: Our services, most certainly, can do that for you. How do you plan to broach the subject with your team, and what kind of timeline are you thinking? Do you have a target in mind that you would like to neutralize?

PC: How do your other clients typically manage informing their teams? Is it feasible for us to be able to complete our, uh, project in a week's time? Also, I don't have a particular target in mind. I would rather defer to Diamond Teams to assign a target to us. I have given this point a lot of thought. I'm afraid that if the target is someone we're familiar with, emotions would get involved, and I would be afraid that we might make mistakes. It's especially important to me that we make no mistakes, or that any mistakes are so small that they could be considered negligible. How do other clients do this?

DT: We can accommodate your request to have a random target assigned to your group. If you are approved and move into Implementation, then we would be able to work with your timeline, however, your team would need to be able to be out of office, say, for a conference for 1 week. They cannot bring spouses or significant others, and they cannot arrange to meet friends who may live in the city where the 'conference' is held. They would, in effect, be sequestered. Every waking moment of every day would be dedicated to your project. I will address mistakes, but for now, we're going to put that in our parking lot and revisit. It is important, though, to go through an exercise regarding how you plan to pitch this to your team. You are also going to need to predict, to an extent, how each person will react. After we finish the exercise, then our specialists will need to do a bit of fact finding about your team members to determine if each of them can successfully and confidentially complete your project. A part of this fact finding will involve social engineering to determine how much or how little your team respects you and in how high or low regard they hold you. Are you willing to allow this to occur? You may not like the results, or you may be surprised that your relationship is better than you currently think.

A brief pause.

DT: Are you ready to begin the exercise?

PC: I am.

DT: In front of you are photos of each member of your team.

PC: Wow. How did you know who everyone is?

DT: It's our job to know. Along with each photo is a blank sheet of paper, a pen, and a sheet of paper with a questionnaire. Every question has been selected based on several factors, one of those factors being what you have previously told us about your team. There are other factors like criminal background checks, human resource records…well…a lot of factors and sources that you would not expect to be used that are actually wildly valuable.

PC: Is everything legal?

DT: That is proprietary.

Buzzing sound from cell phone.

DT: I am so sorry to interrupt our interview. Can you give me just a moment to review this message?

Interviewer steps out of room, with only sound made being the quiet click of the door closing. PC remains seated, but there is the noise of writing utensil scratching on paper followed by sound of ripping paper.

DT: My apologies, but we have to cut our interview short. Before we adjourn for today, however, I need to retrieve the paper that you wrote on, tore, and put in your pocket. This is just a precaution, and it could have been your grocery list or a reminder to call your mother for her birthday, which is next Tuesday, isn't it? But we cannot allow any form of communication to leave or be removed from any part of the Diamond Teams Process at any time.

PC: How did you…

DT: We always know what happens when we have to leave the room. I don't think I need to remind you that you agreed to and signed the pre-application that you would not remove anything or provide any written documentation on any part of The Diamond Teams Process, and that doing so could be grounds for dismissal from The Process and that all further consideration would be terminated. You also signed a non-disclosure agreement, which is binding and enforceable.

PC: I'm sorry, and I understand, but I had a question that I wanted to remember to ask.

DT: But you did not write your question on the parking lot pad or on the whiteboard in the room. I do not wish to debate your motivations or your actions or any hypotheticals. Our process is strict, and we do not deviate from the accepted terms in any of our agreements. On behalf of Diamond Teams, I would like to thank you for your time.

CHAPTER 14
Kate, Sam, and Chris – *11 months and 3 weeks ago*

They decided to meet in Biloxi. They had never met there before, and it seemed like the weather was decent as long as there were no hurricanes or tropical storms in the offing. Sam flew in from a client meeting in Dallas. Chris drove from an onboarding meeting in Chattanooga, and Kate flew in from a teambuilding session outside of Boston. They tried never to travel together, but sometimes it couldn't be avoided, since Sam and Chris were married to each other. Kate, Sam, and Chris were equal partners in Diamond Teams, and even with two-thirds of ownership living under the same roof, their corporate membership and ownership seemed to work well. From time to time, of course, there were differences of opinion, but every dispute was teased apart, dissected, and then at its core, the three partners, without any typical emotional attachment to the issue at hand, would invariably come to the same conclusion.

Biloxi was full of casinos and pulled a decidedly geriatric demographic. Most restaurants had early bird seating and were slowing down for the night by around 6:30 pm. They stayed in a vacation rental, chosen purposely for being no-frills. No Wi-Fi? No problem. They had cellular and VPN, and anything else seemed risky.

Kate cooked poached salmon, serving it with an arugula salad with a lemon and olive oil dressing. As she set the food on the table, she said, "Could we please talk about last week's incident?" It wasn't really an incident. It was a debacle, in her opinion. The unthinkable had nearly happened, and they had a dangerous client who had slipped through all their carefully designed testing, analyses, and background investigations. The incident should never have happened, but because it had, there was an element overlooked or neglected in the Diamond Teams plan, and it had been exploited. "Let me backtrack. It wasn't an incident. It was a catastrophe. You can't call a pig a duck and expect it to quack. It was awful."

"He passed all pre-interview screens, the psych evaluation, the handwriting analysis, and he did very well in the interview. He opted for personal services, had a target in mind, and after completing a full criminal and professional background check on the target, everything seemed to be above board," Chris said while squeezing lemon on his salmon.

Sam said, "His financials came back clean, too. He's a dad, has a four-year-old he shares with his ex-wife, pays child support religiously, and appears to be a loving and hands-on father."

"Here's what I think," Kate said. "He fooled us and our experts. I don't care that he's a dad. Ted Bundy was a dad. I think he's a psychopath, and I think he feels much more intelligent than we are. I also think that he didn't care about losing the money in escrow. I think he really wanted to see if he could commit a murder and get away with it. We didn't question his fucking cochlear implant. What a dick. I wonder what he would have done if we had said something about it or wanded his head for a listening device." Kate laughed. "I mean, it IS a listening device."

Chris said, "I think he researched the hell out of us beforehand. I also think he knew everything about our screening, application, and interview, and I think he prepared thoroughly, and I agree with Sam, he banked on our not questioning his hearing appliance. He wanted to get away with a murder."

"And he almost did," Sam said with a mouth full of food. "Who rang the warning bell on this guy?"

"It was his liaison, Leeza, who felt something was off," Kate said. "She said she couldn't put her finger on it at first, but he became increasingly obsessed with the target."

"I did more digging on the client," Sam said. "Since he had signed the waiver for access to his medical records, I went ahead and requested everything." She reached under the table and pulled out an accordion file. "When he was sixteen, he had a head injury while playing football. He is completely deaf in one ear as a result of the head trauma, and before he started college, he opted for a cochlear implant. There was also a suspected traumatic brain injury, and it appears there were some documented personality changes following the injury."

"We are all over the implant, and I think we can all testify to something strange with Brown's personality," said Kate. "The cochlear implant that doubles as a bug. What a dick. Who does that? It's so nefarious and duplicitous. What was he hoping to do with it? He'd only implicate himself if he kept the recordings. Why?"

Sam said, "It makes sense. He had an insurance policy, definitely implicating himself, but he could also implicate Diamond Teams, especially with what he had documented on his laptop in his hotel room and what he had saved on the cloud. Parts of it weren't even true and were located nowhere in the recordings he saved."

"We confiscated all the tech in his hotel room," Chris said, "and our I/T guys sanitized everything they found. He was keeping a pretty detailed journal. I think Sam is right, though. The journal served as a record he could use as leverage. Or maybe he's just arrogant and wanted to memorialize the experience to go pull out of the closet and reflect in the future, 'I love to think back on that time that I killed that woman. Where are my detailed notes and recordings? What an excellent time it was.'"

They finished eating, cleaned up the kitchen, and decided to settle down to watch a movie on the old tube television. Sam and Kate stood around the stove with a package of Jiffy Pop, while Chris opened a bottle of beer for each of them.

"Kate, you were the one to lay down the hammer on this guy, right?" Chris asked, setting the bottle opener down.

She nodded. "His arrogance and expression of superiority were so far off the mark from any of the testing and screenings we had done on him. It was like he was a completely different person. He was incredibly angry and called me a fucking bitch. He yelled at the beginning but seemed to collect himself, which was scarier than the yelling. A **lot** of rage and fury."

"I saw the video, and I don't think he liked having his wrists bound," Sam said. "I spoke with Clark and Bruce afterward and asked them to do an incident report. Frankly, they are both worried about you, Kate."

"I think I'm going to be difficult for him to find, though. I took all the usual precautions."

"Kate," Chris chided. "You know the usual precautions aren't going to be effective if the client is a psychopath—because of the unpredictability; and the monied clients don't care about the money. They, not unlike you, like adventure. But they also relish the hunt. If you put psychopaths and seemingly endless supplies of money together and throw in a God complex or some kind of superhero/villain ideology, then you've got a recipe for disaster."

"I know that, and I know that you both know that," Kate said. "What gets me, though, was even as careful as we are in our screening, various analyses, and interview, we and our experts missed this one. I'm going to go back through every interaction that we had with that guy to find what we missed. We need to add that into our algorithm. This kind of person needs to be someone we can spot and eliminate within the very first stages of the process. He effectively partitioned his personality and character traits in a way that we did not and could not see."

"Agreed," Sam said. "I think we need to have the psychologists and Profile Man view all the videos and read all the transcripts and look at every scrap of paper the guy touched. We have to be able to eliminate these people much earlier in the process, especially if their emotions tend to run to extremes and the middle ground is the anomaly."

"I think, though," Chris said, "A long-time or lifelong psychopath is going to mirror us well enough that we aren't going to see past what we want to see unless there's some alarm bell or trip wire or trigger that wakes us up enough to think, 'Hey…this person is TROUBLE.' We can hope to get close, but getting past us is part of the psychopath's game."

Kate asked, "Have we initiated the protocols to monitor him? I want to be sure that he can't go after his liaison or anyone else from the team."

"I put Cleveland on it," Chris said. "He's incredibly good and will manage the project personally for the next six months. Real-time surveillance over the six months will alternate between Cleveland, Shannon, Angel, and Wesley. We can't afford for anyone from Diamond Teams who may have had even the most peripheral activity with this guy to be recognized."

"Agreed," Kate and Sam said in unison.

Chris asked the women, "Do we think that amped up surveillance and monitoring for six months is long enough? I worry that a highly organized psychopath may have no qualms playing a longer game."

Kate went blank for a moment then said, "I think he might get bored. If we don't see anything troubling in the next six months, we can adjust monitoring from daily to once a week."

Sam took a long drink of her beer, swallowing loudly. "I don't know. I worry about you and Kevin. If this guy manages to connect you to your real name and then track down your location, the situation could be really bad."

"Do you think that I need to have Kevin take some self-defense classes? I could probably spin it as something that I've always wanted to do as a couple, or something like that. He might go for it if he thinks it's for bonding purposes."

Chris was nodding while Sam said, "I think that's not a bad idea. I don't think you should be unprepared for even a moment."

Kate poured popcorn into individual bowls, giving them each a liberal dose of spray butter. "Who wants to talk to Profile Man? I did it last time, and I don't think I have the bandwidth to deal with him right now."

Chris said, "I don't mind. I'll get in touch and have a guys' weekend with him or something."

"Thank you," Sam and Kate said in unison.

CHAPTER 15
Kevin – *11 months ago*

With the kids in college, one in Chicago, and one in the Bay Area, Kate and I have had a lot of free time to spend together when I'm not traveling for work. She doesn't travel that much, but when she does, it may be for a week or two at a time.

About a month ago, we decided to take a ballroom dance class. We were terrible. It looked like we were fighting instead of dancing. We laughed so hard through the entire class, and our instructor tried ridiculously hard to keep a straight face, but in the end, he told us we should go home and practice what we learned, and then he could evaluate us for progress (or lack thereof) the following week. At that point, we would pass go or no-go. If we didn't improve at all, we would get our money back.

After class, Kate and I decided to go for cocktails. Very clearly, I recall looking in her eyes and seeing the sparkle from the candle on the table reflected there (and, yes, I am completely aware of how pussy-whipped I sound here). It felt like we were falling in love all over again, the intense gaze, tilted head, and smile that I knew she reserved just for me. Kids out of the house until summer, and the two of us experiencing life together, like we did in our twenties.

"Do you want to try Brazilian Jiu Jitsu or Krav Maga or something?" she asked. "If our dancing looks like fighting, maybe we should try a martial art or something. What do you think?"

"I'm game," I said. "Especially if it's followed by cocktails and deep-fried snacks."

"That could probably be arranged."

"Then, let's do it," I said. "I wonder if my hands could be registered as lethal weapons by the time we finish the class."

"Oh, honey," she said, leaning across the table. "You know what?" she whispered.

I shook my head.

"I don't think I could love you more," and she gripped my arms pulling me forward, meeting me across the middle of the table, gently kissing my lips. Who has two thumbs and thinks he's getting lucky tonight? This guy (I'm pointing my thumbs at myself).

The dance class was a failure. We did get our money back, and we registered for Brazilian Jiu Jitsu. We've been going to classes two nights a week for the past couple of weeks now. Kate took to it like a duck to water. She scared me with how naturally aggressive she was, and I was afraid to be her sparring partner after the first week. She was that good.

We're putting mats in our basement to practice at home. I'm going to speak to the instructor to get some tips for keeping up with my wife. She is a terrifying inspiration. If a mugger ever attacked us, I would sic her on the mugger.

CHAPTER 16
Guy – *10 months ago*

I went through the entire process with Diamond Teams. The process was long, somewhat precious, and incredibly invasive. Was it worth it? Yes, though it was a test of will and patience. They were giving me a blueprint to pull off the ultimate sin—murder. To drive home the point, God gave Moses his Top 10 List of Sins. If murder isn't the ultimate sin, it's definitely right up there. Diamond Teams was giving me an entire playbook for getting away with it. The downside was not being able to take anything with me from any of the prep sessions that we had. It was up to me to commit everything to memory and then document after our sessions. Of course, I signed a confidentiality agreement, a non-disclosure agreement, and a client agreement all of which stated that I would not document anything I learned during any phase of my relationship with Diamond Teams. Childish as it seemed, I crossed my fingers literally and figuratively. I had no intention of honoring my commitment.

The part of the process that worried me the most was the written sample that I had to provide. I knew that it was coming, and I knew the questions were fairly standard. What worried me, though, was if my handwriting provided any clues to my psyche. Even reading the literature on handwriting analysis and scrutinizing my writing for hours on end, there was a worry that in the heat of the moment, my thoughts might get away from me, and I might reveal something unfavorable about myself via a 't' crossed too low, or an 'l' with a loop too wide, something that would trigger a warning that I was not what I seemed.

Word circulated about Diamond Teams within one of the professional networking groups that I followed. It was hush-hush, and there was an air about it. Was it real or urban legend? Finding someone who had actually gone through the Diamond Teams process was fairly labor-intensive. What it did prove, though, was that Diamond Teams and the murder adventure concept were, indeed, not the stuff of fiction. My course then was set on finding someone who had made it all the way through the screening and applications processes. There was no web presence. It was like Diamond Teams existed only if you knew the magic word. It felt like real-life 'Fight Club.'

No one seemed to talk about it outright, just rumblings here and there, but there weren't that many people who had successfully been accepted. Eventually, though, I found a few people who had been referred or made referrals to Diamond Teams. These folks were my newest professional allies, and I would confabulate something during a cocktail hour while attending this professional meeting or that and talk about wanting to engage in some activity that would truly bond my executive team.

All I had to do was show up and walk the walk and talk the talk. These blowhards were like every other blowhard I had ever known. They liked to hear themselves talk, give the best advice and counsel, and know something that no one else could know because they were on a rung of the ladder that few reached. Their magnanimity knew no bounds.

I kept a mental tally of these people as possible targets when Diamond Teams would eventually approve my application. Ultimately, though, I decided that my target had to be someone completely random. I picked someone that I didn't know at all. I think I may have found my target on Facebook or Twitter-X or some other social media from a public library computer. There could never be a chance that I had ever interacted with my target in any capacity prior to my project assignment. However, when it came time to choose a target or to let Diamond Teams select a target for me, I supplied the name of the person from the library computer.

Eventually, Diamond Teams assigned a project liaison to me. She was very formal, very efficient in her communication, and explained the project in the most minute detail. My project and target were approximately 2,000 miles from where I currently lived, where I had ever lived for more than six months, where I had grown up, and where I had gone to college. Since I had named a target, Diamond Teams gave me an option to review a full dossier or to rely on what I already knew. Why wouldn't I want to view the prepared dossier? It would allow me to see just how comprehensive the Diamond Teams research compared to my own. Anything Diamond Teams created, though, could only be viewed electronically and in the presence of my liaison.

I had to learn about my target's likes, dislikes, routines, social and professional circles, which was more effort than I expected because it all had to happen without my target knowing that I was anywhere near the fringes of her life. She was a 40-ish attorney with some dubious clients, for whom she performed some dubious work. I followed her around, went to her gym, went to her country club, went to the bars she frequented. I watched her pick up men, sometimes women, and sometimes both. She had no pets, no plants, no friends I would consider intimates, no ex-husbands or ex-wives. I wondered who would miss her if she exited the planet. Her social media profiles were sparsely populated with few posts and even fewer friends. It seemed that she existed along a diaphanous tether to the world around her. Truly, who would miss her?

When I chose her, though, I had to provide my rationale for how I chose my target. I rehearsed this so much that it sounded impassioned, not rote, without sounding like an obsessive nut job.

My spiel: I've been following her cases because of the online publicity, and I don't agree with how she operates professionally. It seems that she observes the letter of the law, but not the intent, and she observes the letter very casually. By making her my target, I would be able to put to rest some of my objections by detecting her vulnerabilities, and, perhaps, reconciling and resolving, to an extent, some of my objections. I also stated that my connection to her was via six degrees of separation. She had done some work that negatively impacted a friend of a friend of a friend. Of course, this was fiction. I didn't know her. I didn't know anyone else who knew her. I really didn't care who she represented or what her clients did or didn't do. She was a means to an end.

Things did not go off as I had hoped, however, because my liaison subdued me with zip ties just before I pulled a loaded gun from an ankle holster. I had tipped her off in some mannerism or something that we had spoken about, and I had been incredibly careful and deliberate about what I had revealed about myself and my life. Some stray detail must have poked out like an errant spring from the stuffing in the mattress that I had built around myself.

And for the past two months, I have stewed on the indignity I suffered, and I have deployed significant financial resources, researched, and planned. Diamond Teams robbed me. They stole from me the one thing that I crave, complete dominion over another person. I don't even care about the money. It was always having the ability to swing the sword, or in my case, fire the gun, to be the one factor between life and death. How much closer to God could I be?

Ultimately, with complete certainty, I would have the chance again.

CHAPTER 17
Kevin - *a little less than 10 months ago*

"Hi, Dad. Remember how Mom told me to get my oil checked and all my fluids topped off and have my tires and brakes looked at before I drove anywhere more than 10 miles off campus?" Dean asked through a staticky cell phone connection.

Dean had been purging and packing to come home for the summer. Kate had been unusually Mother Hen-ish about Dean's driving home. She had been the same about Michelle's London internship. Initially, Kate had felt strongly that if the internship was something Michelle really wanted, then she needed to do the legwork and make all the arrangements. Michelle needed to take the initiative, and if she needed help, Kate and I would be standing by to assist. Michelle did a fantastic job. My girl had guts and gusto, and she wanted to make her mark in the world. About a month or two ago, though, Kate started to worry about everything. Going along with the Mother Hen theme, I don't know if she was freaking herself out about her baby bird leaving the nest or what.

There were nights when I could hear Kate on the phone, calling the airline, then the lodging people, and then she also did a deep dive on the company where Michelle was going to intern. She also ran background checks on the C-suite and the department managers and directors where Michelle would be working. If there was a stone to turn, Kate took it on as her personal mission.

"Sure, Dean, I remember. Why?" I asked. I did not remember. This was hypervigilance on Kate's part, bordering on cuckoo, but I wanted to go with the flow and see where the concern in Dean's voice originated.

"You're going to think this is some weird, truly star-crossed shit. I took the car in for an oil change. Every fluid was checked, and every single fluid was either super low or empty. They checked my tires, and two of the tires had nails in them and one of the tires had loose lug nuts. Last of all, they checked my brakes. I don't know how you lose a brake pad, but I had a brake pad missing, and one of my brake lines was in terrible shape. Have you ever heard of that much stuff being messed up on a car…at the same time?"

"Wow. Your mom's recent bout of paranoia may be for good reason. Did the mechanic give you any indication why all this stuff would go bad simultaneously? Dean, this is seriously disturbing."

"I asked him about the lug nuts. He said that I would probably feel some kind of weird vibration while driving the car at around 50 mph. He said that the vibrations could cause the wheel to come off. Then he asked me if I had pissed off a girl or something," Dean whispered because maybe whispering doesn't make it real. That's what Kate says anyway.

"Did you piss off someone?" I asked, echoing the mechanic's question.

"No, Dad. Geez." I could hear fear and frustration in his voice. I would have to tell Kate that her mother's intuition was spot on. I was now worried about our kids. Michelle would be so far away. Anything could happen.

"I'm relieved you did what your mom asked you to do," I said in a grave tone. I needed to get off the phone and speak to my wife. This young man, my boy, this person who occupied at least a third of my heart, could have been hurt or killed. He could have been stranded somewhere in a car that had everything wrong with it. Sure, we have AAA, and of course, he has a cell phone to call us, but there is always some dread when a car decides to go tits up.

Back in the days before cell phones, I was on my way to a wedding that was about a five-hour drive. My windows were rolled down, and I had the stereo turned up in my car, Motley Crue blasting from the CD player. I was in the flow of traffic, not the leader, not the tail. We were all going around 90 mph. I was a little too close to the car in front of me and did not have enough time to swerve out of the way of the 10-inch wooden block sitting in the middle of the passing lane. All I could do was drive over it and hope for the best. The car was momentarily airborne, followed by a not-so-gentle thud when it regained the ground. The airborne thing reminded me of 'The Dukes of Hazzard,' but I didn't feel cool, mostly shaken up. The next exit was a mile away. It seemed to be a good stop for a bio break and snacks and refueling.

Again, pre-cell phones, well, not really. The only cell phones that were around were still the bag phones, and anyone with a cell phone had to go to an electronics store to have an antenna installed on the car. That was NOT me. I was just a poor graduate student. While the gas tank was filling, I went into the gas station, which was little more than a shack. No cell phone. No navigation. No idea where the next decent-sized town was, and all of it, all of these circumstances were all right until I heard a loud bang. The station attendant and I dropped to the floor. After a minute or two, we looked out the window, and the only thing out there was my car, no crazy person with a shotgun—which was apparently where my mind and the mind of the gas station attendant had gone. Nope. My tire had blown. And it sounded like a gun.

I did have AAA, and they did have a toll-free number, and the gas station did have a pay phone. I had never changed a tire before, which meant I couldn't even put on the donut. The gas station attendant looked at me like I had three heads when I asked her if she could help me figure it out. She didn't know how to change a tire either. I waited 90 minutes for a wrecker to tow my car, and then I paid over $100 for a tire back in the mid- to late-1990s. During the wait, I kept picturing the hillbillies from 'Deliverance' lining up and asking me to squeal like a pig. The wrecker could not arrive soon enough. There was nothing my parents could do. They were several hours away. My mom told me to call her when I was all set and ready to get back on the road. She didn't seem worried, but she wasn't in the middle of Nowhere, USA. In my head, 'Dueling Banjos' followed me the rest of the way to the wedding.

And now, we're full circle. My son is possibly going to panic, and he's going to read my cues. I needed to nix the grave tone and reframe my reaction. "Dean, car trouble is one of life's great adventures. You hadn't even started your journey, so your adventure awaits you yet. Someday, you're going to be driving to another state to meet your dream girl and maybe have sex with her, and you will have a flat tire. Make sure you know how to change a tire. You'll get back on the road, and then you'll see the girl, fall in love, and bang the hell out of each other."

"Um, thanks, Dad," Dean said with the great ability to uptalk his discomfort.

"Kate, honey. Is there something you want to tell me?" I asked my wife. We sat in Adirondack chairs on our back patio, sipping gin and tonics enjoying a lazy Saturday afternoon.

"I don't think so," she said. "Is there something that you think I should want to tell you?"

"Dean called today from the oil change place. He said that you told him to get an oil change, have all of his fluids checked and topped off, have all the tires checked, and to have the breaks checked. Before you say anything, I know these are all part of the zillion point inspection in an oil change, and I know you know that. And we both know that the oil change people know that." I went through everything Dean said.

"What I can't figure out is why you went into all the detail and asked him to get an off cycle oil change. He still has another 5,000 miles before he needs to get the oil changed in his car. What's going on? Are you having some kind of anxiety or mid-life crisis? I've heard your phone calls to London double and triple checking everything is above board for Michelle's internship."

Kate looked intently at her glass, then she raised her eyes to me, making deliberate eye contact, "I'm going through something. I don't know if it's empty nest syndrome or what, but I feel strongly right now that I need to protect my babies." Her eyes began to fill, and her nose began the telltale red that signaled tears were on the way.

"Honey. I'm your partner. You don't have to go through this stuff alone. You can always lean on me." I reached over and put my hand on hers, gently squeezing, and hoping that I could give her some comfort, allay her fears in some way.

CHAPTER 18
Kate – *a little less than 10 months ago*

Who is Guy Brown? He's a fucking weasel, and I'm going to find that weasel. He doesn't understand a mother's wrath. That fucker went after my son. Obviously, I'm a grown-up, but I would like him to feel fortunate to be able to sip his meals through a straw. I want to duct tape him to a chair—again—and then I want to take a pair of rusty pliers and remove his teeth, one by one, without any anesthesia, and then I want to string them into a pair of bracelets. One for me, and one for him. And then, when he's asleep at night, with his dentures sanitizing on his bathroom sink, I want to sneak in and steal them. Then I want to follow him to work the next day and laugh at him when he goes to the boardroom for his first meeting of the day.

And when he goes to get implants or new dentures or whatever? I want to fuck with his dental insurance, causing him to have to pay completely out of pocket for new teeth. Then, when he gets his new teeth, I'm going to hire a thug to wait somewhere for him and punch him in the mouth. He can't fuck with my kids and not expect retaliation.

CHAPTER 19
Kate – *a little more than 9 months ago*

One of the best things about my credit card issuer is that they not only monitor my credit rating, but they also provide me with statistics about searches using my identity on the dark web. If someone is looking for me, I will eventually know something about it. This isn't a foolproof approach, but it does give me an inkling to be on the alert. However, I feel like I'm always on the alert. It could be a law enforcement agency, a dissatisfied client, or someone not even on our radar yet. Because of what Diamond Teams does, I live in a persistent state of hypervigilance. As the business has grown, my vigilance has grown proportionately. I worry for my family, my employees, and my closest friends. I worry that at some point, I am going to be called as a material witness, or I will be the defendant in a manslaughter case, or I may work my way into being situated in the crosshairs of someone who is so angry with me or Diamond Teams that they feel the only way to achieve retribution is by harming me or anyone within my orbit. I worry.

The last truly dissatisfied client was a couple months ago. Guy Brown. When I ended his project, his first reaction was cool anger, simmering just under the surface of the demeanor he chose to show us. As I went through more of the termination of services and reiterated the terms of the various agreements he had signed with Diamond Teams, his anger ratcheted up to barely controlled rage and then complete rage with spittle flying from the corners of his mouth, his hands balled into fists. His wrists were duct taped to his chair, and the perceived emasculation ratcheted up the fury. He would be a lesson to us because he didn't seem to have any of the hallmarks of someone we should've turned away.

I did want him to understand that we, too, had leverage. We could make his relationship with his son a bit prickly. In this case, I chose the wrong leverage. Instead of putting him in check, I turned up the heat to eleven.

I don't think it was the threat of violence that scared me. I am kid-sized. In my life, I have had Krav Maga training and Brazilian Jiu Jitsu and feel comfortable being able to take down a larger aggressor. It was the ball of white-hot rabid anger and the gleam of the promise of revenge that scared me the most. I felt it in my bones that this man would come after me. My mind went to crazy places after the encounter. What if he went to a sketch artist and then did a reverse Google image search? I know there wouldn't be any current photos of me on the internet because we routinely searched and scrubbed. But there was always the chance that something from childhood, high school, or college popped up, and then it wasn't that difficult. When I changed my last name all those years ago, I didn't think realistically how it might be the roadblock that bought me a little extra time in an emergency; and now, I considered, it was one of the smartest things that I had done.

Sam, Chris, and I agreed to daily monitoring Guy for 6 months, then paring things to weekly. I actually paid out of pocket to keep monitoring going on a daily basis. We watched comings and goings, internet traffic, financial transactions, and dark web activity. Because Kevin and I were terrible on the dance floor, it worked in my favor to get him enrolled in Brazilian Jiu Jitsu.

Kevin was a baseball player in high school, and he still had quick reflexes. He was comfortable in his body and limbs, and even though we were horrific dancers, he caught on quickly to the martial art. I thought it would be good to enroll the kids when they were home for the summer, but our daughter landed an international internship. Our son, Dean, was coming home and seemed pretty excited about learning a martial art. I had to temper his enthusiasm and let him know that advancing can be a slow process and that he would need to be patient and absorb everything in every class. Kevin was a better sounding board, though, since he was new to the discipline.

Dean went to the introductory classes, and I was proud. He took everything in, and I watched him as he watched everyone else. Then he watched Kevin and my class.

"Dad," he said, "you're doing all right holding your own when you spar with the other students; but, Mom, you are frightening. It's like you're everywhere, and I can see you taking in everything, calculating every possibility, and acting in kind. I can't believe that you and Dad were new to this at the same time."

"Oh, honey," I said. "I've taken so many self-defense classes, and I have dabbled a little in martial arts a number of times over the years." Did anyone in my family need to know my belt level? Nah.

"Dean," Kevin said, "This is not just a physical sport. It's extremely mental, too." He rubbed his hand across his brow, sitting on the chair next to Dean. "I was an athlete. I'm an avid runner. But this is something else, and I am loving it." He paused. "I feel very centered, and when I finish each class, I feel a deep contentment. I don't know if you'll feel that, but it works for me, and I'm really pleased that your mom and I can't dance. We can spar, and that's probably more useful for us in the long run."

Dean nodded. "My goal this summer is to spar with Mom and not have my ass handed to me."

Kevin said, a glint in his eye, "Ah, son. That's a great goal, a lofty goal, but a goal nonetheless."

Dean, too, was a high school athlete. He ran track, played club lacrosse, and wrestled. I felt confident Brazilian Jiu Jitsu would be a good fit for him, too, especially with his background. I was not wrong. He excelled.

If I were going to hire a family member at Diamond Teams, I would hire Dean. He has intelligence, physical fitness, and the ability to plan, observe, pivot, and find quick, effective alternatives. I'm his mom--of course I know how my children are wired up. However, I couldn't, in good conscience, give my son a job and tell him he couldn't tell his father what he did for a living. And to compound everything, it would be difficult to leave work at work, especially since so much of the work was remote. All that worry on my part, but this would be a non-issue. I could talk it over with Sam and Chris in the future since Dean was just finishing his sophomore year in college. But, for the record, he fit every criterion in our ideal liaison profile. One of Sam and Chris's kids also fit the profile, but we were all very hesitant, in no small part due to Guy Brown, to bring any of our children into the business. That asshole fired a warning shot (or was it a regular shot?) at my son, and it raised my hackles.

CHAPTER 20
Personal Services – The Interview

DT = Diamond Teams; **PC** = Potential Client

DT: I would like to take this opportunity, on behalf of Diamond Teams, to congratulate you on reaching this stage of our process. In a typical year, only about 5% of our book of business is Personal Services. I would like to manage your expectations, which is why I pointed this out. Do you have any questions for me so far?

PC: If you approve me, then when would we begin my project?

DT: Great question. This is something that varies from client to client and is dependent on a number of factors. Are we choosing the target, or are you? We do a lot of clearance on the targets, and sometimes it can take a lot of time, or it can be straightforward, and take the tiniest spot of time. We also do some monitoring to see how difficult or simple it would prove to perform all of the surveillance and approach development to see your project through successfully.

PC: Are you my assigned liaison? How is my liaison assigned?

DT: I may or may not be your liaison. While we continue to review all of the data that we have compiled, along with a detailed analysis of this interview, we will match you with the liaison who will best complement your executive function or thought and work style, along with various indicators that most closely align with our liaisons. All of our liaisons have undergone an even more extensive battery of tests than what you've already experienced, and without knowing every piece of their genomes, we do know them inside and out. That's a whole lot more than what you probably wanted to know. In essence, we're going to find you the best possible match as the liaison for your project should you advance beyond our interview.

DT: Do you have a target in mind?

PC: I thought it might be best if Diamond Teams selected a target for me. I don't want to know anything in advance and would like the whole experience to be something as novel as possible.

DT: Is the target's gender important to you? What about the line of work? Are there any deal breakers in your opinion for the target we select for you?

PC: No one under the age of 25. No pregnant women. I think I would do better, in my mind, if the target were someone whose morals were compromised. I would feel less creepy about invading their privacy.

DT: In prior materials in the process, we have asked you why you would like to be involved in a personal project through Diamond Teams. Could you talk that through for me?

PC: As a child, I was bullied. I have gotten past it, I think, through counseling, friends and family support. I have excelled professionally and personally. If I had not made the professional contacts that I have, I never would have learned about Diamond Teams and what you do. I think what resonated for me the most, though, was about being able to control a part of the narrative without hurting someone. So many of the bullies who were part of my early life liked to control the who they perceived as the weakest member of the herd, but they didn't care about hurting me physically or psychologically. What appeals to me about Diamond Teams is that the target never knows about me, and they never know they're being hunted, and they exit my project without being harmed.

DT: Would you have any regrets following the completion of your project?

PC: I suppose. If my target were a real dirt bag or doing something of a criminal nature, I would feel very gratified if they were brought to justice. It's not my place to mete out punishment, but it would feel amazingly vindicating if they could face a jury of their peers to answer for their crimes.

DT: Tell me about when you were bullied as a child.

CHAPTER 21
Kevin – *10 months ago*

I have been on lighter duty in our martial arts class. The last time Kate and I sparred, she dislocated my shoulder. The pain felt like what I imagined a hot knife would feel. She followed that by popping my shoulder back into the joint, which resulted in my field of vision going a blinding white for a moment. I may have passed out.

After all of the shoulder business, I stayed home for one class and watched a few TED Talks on my computer followed by research for professional development offerings. Staying home disrupted my routine, and, although new, the addition of our martial arts classes had become part of my routine. It just goes to show how quickly something can become routine or habit.

The world post-pandemic had changed, making it more critical than ever to stay on the cutting edge of attracting the best and brightest to our company, which meant that we had to have a richer corporate culture than our competitors. Competitors existed on two fronts: our space in the market, and then the talent pool. In my mind, the talent pool should be renamed the talent trickle. The shape of the average employee's wants and needs had changed following COVID-19, and what seemed like an amorphous blob of demands had taken on a shape that caused employers to bend, or, in some cases, break. It was always possible to find a conference that featured every buzz word floating around in corporate America, but teasing through everything to find the best of the best was the challenge. It would be so much easier if professional development conferences came with ratings from 'Consumer Reports.' When I landed on two or three options, I sent an email to some of my old friends from business school to see who would be up for hitting a conference. These guys were my core group of personal and professional networking contacts, but over time, the core group had peripheral groups who were usually add-ons to some of the conferences.

My email notification popped up, and even though I hadn't completed any information request forms my name was swept up in an artificial intelligence algorithm, there was an interest inquiry for an employee engagement conference that looked fascinating. I might see if Kate would want to attend as well. Once in a great while, she would come along to a conference, and it was nice to be able to debrief with her at the end of the day. When we both went to a conference, we made sure to hit different breakout sessions. It was like being in two places at one time, and we were generally good at relaying the high and low points of the breakout sessions. This conference, 'Engage in the Future by Engaging Your Employees,' wasn't happening for another six months. The conference center was located at the top of a waterfall in Snoqualmie Falls, Washington. I had a tough time turning down conferences in the Pacific Northwest.

I could picture how it would be at night. The window would be raised about 10 inches. A breeze easing its way into the room, the fresh scent of the pines, the sounds of the water rushing over the falls. I already knew how well I would be able to sleep. If we had a room with two beds, we could stretch across like starfish. The best sleep, and we would awaken completely fresh and refreshed. If Kate couldn't go to this conference, at the very least, I would go, if for no other reason than the promise of epic sleep.

I liked to brainstorm the names of seminars and conferences that seemed completely inane, keeping a list to see if somehow someone somewhere would put on a seminar with roughly the same theme. In some cases, my musings were 100% accurately predictive of the titles of what I would see on a brochure or website or email in the future. A few gems:

'To Be or Not to Be…Agile: Building Culture When Everyone is Out of Office;'

'Talking Heads: When All Your Co-Workers are Thumbnail Photos;'

'Put on Your Pants and Go Back to the Office: What Happens When None of Your Clothes Fit When the Edict Comes Down;'

'The Work-Life Balance Fallacy of Remote Work: Home is Work and Work is Home.'

I am eagerly anticipating seeing something like any of these advertised. One of my favorites, though, would have the members of 'N Sync as the keynote speakers, and the conference would be: "Tell me Why: Finding and Living Your Own 'Why'—Get in Sync."

CHAPTER 22
Kate, Sam, and Chris – *9 months ago*

"Kate," Sam began, her voice tinged with unease. "Bad news. There's been a ping on your original maiden name, your mom's maiden name, your dad's mom's maiden name, and your married name. I hate to say it, but it's probably safe to assume your professional name has been compromised, too."

"I *knew* it," Kate said. "It was at least a month ago, wasn't it? Do we know what other data was accessed?"

"I think it's probably prudent to venture that all of your personal data has been accessed," Chris replied, his voice heavy with regret. "Kate, I think we have to assume they accessed everything—your entire personal history. We're likely facing the worst-case scenario. I am so sorry to be the one to tell you this," Chris continued, his voice low, "we all know this is something that has always been a possibility, and we've made it in this business for 20 years without this threat level."

"Should we meet in person somewhere? We probably need to discuss closing out remaining projects, not taking on any new business, and exit strategy," Kate rattled off without taking a breath. She told them about Dean's car issues from a few weeks before. "I'm nervous."

Sam said, "Not a bad idea. We need to make sure that all of the employees are aware of the situation, too. They're going to have to be vigilant in case that guy approaches them with ill intent. I just hate having to do that to them. We're going to need to pay out the bonuses that we've invested, too."

"Right," Kate acknowledged. "It's not like this is going to be something that can go on a resume. I have to say, though, until now, it's been quite a ride, hasn't it?"

"Truly," said Chris. "We're lucky we have a top-notch CPA, aren't we?"

"Indeed," Sam laughed. "Do you have your calendars ready? Let's get something scheduled soon and get an implementation plan pulled together for folding Diamond Teams."

"Before I forget," Kate added, "Kevin is going to an employee engagement seminar in a few months. Do you two have any interest in joining us? If we're closing things, depending on the timing, this might be a good seminar."

Chris paused a moment, "You know. We may not have to fold up operations, but maybe just take a little break. We have plenty of resources at our disposal for dealing with this guy. I think we need to consider this option very carefully." After a couple beats of silence, Chris said, "Just think about it. We may not need to take extreme action. Just like we do with everything, we need to look at every angle. It's been a while since we've done a corporate threat assessment."

CHAPTER 23
Guy – *9 months ago*

A mere 90 days ago, when my murder adventure was in my sights, I imagined all the ways I could kill my target. So many different methods than the staid methods of Diamond Teams. I envisioned following her home after a late night in the office. Meeting her in the bar of her country club and offering her a ride home when she realized she'd had too much to drink and couldn't drive herself. I liked that one the best. She would think I was a nice guy. I could drive her home in my car—my DNA wouldn't be found in her car. I would help her into her house, get her a glass of water, put a couple Tylenol on her bedside table, maybe help her get into her pajamas. I could see her looking at me through alcohol-glazed eyes with fear, surprise, and shock in her gaze, as I put my hands around her neck and squeezed the life from her, and I could watch the life ebb from her, until there was no humanity left to wonder what was happening as her soul left her being.

The other fantasy I entertained was finding a way to date her without Diamond Teams picking up on the fact that she would actually know me.

I hadn't thought through the details beyond the fact that I would choke her to death while I was fucking her. Again, not the best option, though, because of the possibility of leaving behind DNA. She would have to be restrained to avoid getting my skin under her fingernails. I would have to wear gloves, remove all body hair, and definitely use a condom. All the preparation and precautions would require a high degree of planning, but was it equal to the reward of seeing the light go out of her eyes while I was pounding into her? Was *she* worth all the planning and precautions?

However, I planned. I planned to follow every little detail pulled together in my murder adventure engineered by Diamond Teams. The only thing that would deviate would be the final bit. The most important bit. The bit where I killed my target. I would use live ammunition and end her existence. Everything, though, went out the window when I was found out by my liaison, and it was entirely my own fault. In my soul, I *needed* to take notes and record my observations, feelings, and details—totally against the rules.

As a teenager, I had a head injury. No one wishes for a head injury, and, certainly, no one wishes for complete hearing loss in one ear. After my injury, there was so much hand-wringing about what to do, and I was so young, and what a tragedy, and looking for a silver lining, and Beethoven was deaf and look what he did, and on and on and on it went. I can tell you the whole thing was terrible. It was a loss, but I immediately went into problem-solving mode. People lose their hearing. It happens. What does the average person do? I can say that I made the most of a genuinely tragic situation. Not looking for a silver lining, but turning this tragedy into an advantage. I had to know what my options were, though— hearing aid and cochlear implant were immediate solutions.

I researched and made a decision. I opted for a solution that would have more adaptability to evolving technology. I became interested in applications that could be incorporated in the cochlear implant or could become stand-alone add-ons to the architecture of the device. At the time, spy gear was an interest, and I thought there were avenues to slip spy gear into my life under the guise of my cochlear implant. I would never fail another exam. Every lecture could be recorded, saved to the cloud, transcribed later. I could re-live some of the more poignant moments of my day. It seemed like an invisible solution or one of those 'hidden in plain sight' types of solutions.

Throughout the Diamond Teams vetting process, they had to have noticed my implant, but it was never questioned. They had my medical records, and there was no reason to think the thing on my skull was anything other than what it was. They had no reason to suspect that there had been extensive adaptation to the device, and I wasn't going to point it out either.

During the evening my project was terminated, the Diamond Teams risk managers went through my hotel room, found my phone, a remote receiver, and computer, erased all of them as well as everything stored on the cloud. I could have saved everything to a flash drive, but I knew it, too, would be destroyed. It could have been a nice piece of collateral to use for insurance, to leverage against Diamond Teams, in the event they turned me over to the police following the successful completion of my project with the dispatch of my target into the ever after.

That last night. The humiliation of that night. Oh, my god. It was complete embarrassment. The security team, the brutish hulks. Being ushered to an unknown location with a black canvas bag pulled over my head. When I see that kind of thing in the movies, it seems so very contrived. In real life, though, it is terrifying, and I may have lost my bladder. I didn't know if they would let me live or die or what because I knew my actions to break the rules were deliberate and intentional. Surely Diamond Teams had to know that, too.

However, the bust. GOD! This is what shames me the most. Always knowing this could be a possible outcome, I could have been cool, calm, and collected. I, on the other hand (and hindsight truly is 20/20), had been overconfident in everything going off without incident. My pride had never allowed for the possibility that I would fail. And herein lay my biggest error. I had been combative, violent, profane, levelling threats against everyone in Diamond Teams, making demands that had never been in scope in the client agreement. I was given a mild sedative, and, combined with the darkness from the bag on my head, the fatigue from all the hours of surveillance and late nights, I fell asleep.

After going wherever it was, I found my arms duct-taped to an office chair when I roused. Sitting on a couch across from me was a fiftyish woman, and I counted two or three security guards from this week's surveillance module. Large, quiet, intelligent-looking men. They could have been funeral directors, attorneys, or diplomats. They were dressed for a very important business meeting or something of the like. The woman wore her shoulder-length wavy hair down. Hair slightly obscuring her face, I realized, was by design.

"Mr. Brown," she said. "I'm Kathleen Diamond. I regret that we are having this meeting, and I regret that you flagrantly ignored the covenants carefully spelled out in all of the documents you signed, the commitments and promises you made. We provided our services in good faith, and you did not feel the need to honor your contractual obligations."

"*Ms. Diamond,* give me a fucking break," I seethed. "Do you think your contracts are enforceable? What would happen if the Department of Justice came through here? You would be shut down in a heartbeat. The public outcry would vilify you and everyone who works here."

"Mr. Brown," she paused. "You are certainly entitled to your opinion. However, what grieves me more than your failure, because you are a failure in the eyes of Diamond Teams, is how callously you're willing to treat human life."

"*Puh-lease,*" I said. "I chose someone who would not be missed if she left the earth. I searched for a long time to find someone morally corrupt. I found her. Diamond Teams gave me a vehicle to exert quick and final judgment. I couldn't possibly be the first client who has wanted to dole out punishment."

"I'm not here to talk about any of our other clients or targets, Mr. Brown. I'm here to talk about you."

"Kathleen, here's the problem. You are afraid of people like me. You take everyone to the brink, and then your fear paralyzes you and every one of your clients. You don't have the guts to do what needs to be done."

"If you say so, Mr. Brown. However, I don't believe you. I believe that you want complete control. You want to minimize your exposure. You want to be judge, jury, and executioner. I don't think whether the target is morally corrupt is important to you. I think it's the power and the game. I think it's you being smarter than everyone else, thinking you're going to get away with everything, not getting caught, and not having any culpability. It's you playing at being God or whoever your ultimate being is. Am I close?" She paused, looking at me intently. "I think you're a loser. I think people like you are a scourge, and I think you are the lowest life form."

"Kath-leen. Who do you think you are that you can talk to me like that?" I spat, my voice rising in volume. I could feel my salivary glands swelling, and I prayed I would spew spittle and gratify them with my anger. They wanted me to be angry. They were feeding on all of this, and they were enjoying my discomfort. I was bound to a chair, for Christ's sake.

I yelled at her and her security thugs, scanning the room and committing their faces to memory, "You came up with this construct. You are no better than I am. You get that, don't you? The only difference is that I have the drive and desire to do it all, while you sit in your little cubicle and press the stop button because you're too scared. You are pathetic, small, and unevolved."

"Again," she said calmly, "you are certainly entitled to your opinion."

She reached for a folder, and while she opened it, her eye contact never wavered as she stated, "You forfeit your escrow as a contract breakage fee. Your target became aware of you also. We have a bit of a mess to clean up because of you. She actually filed a police report today, and worked with the police sketch artist who rendered a fairly accurate representation of you." She held up the police sketch, and she was right. It was a remarkable likeness. "As part of our commitment to you, we are going to protect you, and the largest chunk of your contract breakage fee will be devoted to keeping you from being on anyone's radar. Maybe we could get a copy for you. You could frame it and hang it in Harris's room. Wouldn't that be nice?"

She was fucking changing gears and turning on the administrative mode, as she treated me like a bungling child, but she mentioned Harris, and he was never to be associated with this. She remained calm, and I think that wound me up while she told me I was stupid, selfish, and short-sighted, and I became more and more incensed, and the protection of Harris moved to the forefront of my thoughts. I needed to get out of this because the only answer was violence. I felt a hot churning in my brain, my pulse increasing, and I knew that I was completely out of control. Anything else that I did or said was going to escalate to a point that I couldn't dial back down. If I flipped out too much more, there was a chance they would be able to tell Virginia about my threats and my desire to get away with murder, hardly making me father of the year. I would say things that would put them all on alert. I had to restrain myself and allow myself to formulate a plan, which was so much easier said than done.

I tried to pull my wrists from the armrests, and with the duct tape, all I was successful at doing was shaking a fist with a pointed index finger. The humiliation. My rage. My fear of losing my little boy. It was total.

"Listen to me, *Mrs. Diamond,*" I said very softly, with each syllable carefully measured and uttered with a menace I would not mask. "I am coming for you. You do not say my son's name and get to walk away.

This," I nodded my head and again tried to raise my wrists. "You will get to experience humiliation, shame, and fear that makes THIS look like a visit to Disney World. You will experience loss, and you will not know when it's coming. You will be my ultimate target, and I will be looking for you. Until I come for you, you and everyone you love will need to sleep with one eye open, live your life always looking over your shoulder. Every time you go to your car, you'll look in the backseat or under the car. You'll have your brakes checked many more times than you ever dreamed appropriate. I will complete my project."

Her eyes never left mine. For a moment, I may have seen fear, quickly replaced by a quick, erudite stare. She was already planning her next move, and I knew how to end this encounter.

"Be very certain, Kathleen Diamond. You and your company are my end game. I will control you, your life, and your end, and I promise it won't be pretty or pleasant, and when I'm finished, when I have burned your life to the ground, there won't be anything left for paying respects. That is a promise, a 'covenant' I intend to 'honor.'"

"If you say so, Mr. Brown. I'm really sorry you feel that way, and I regret this is how we are going to end our association." She gave a very subtle nod, and was there a hint of a smile on her lips? Was she feeling pleasure from this interaction?

One of the security men approached me again with the black bag. God! Not this again. I felt a small pinch, and I knew that I'd be having another impromptu nap.

My first thought upon waking: Cunt. I would plan a demise so complete that by the time she saw it coming, it would be too late for her to unwind it.

It took me three months to find her, at no small cost. When she started her business right out of college, she buried her identity deep enough that it would be difficult to discover her actual name and location. However, facial recognition software and the internet have changed the game, and with all the game pieces now on the board, I just wasn't ready to play. I had already lined up how this was going to play out. I did learn some important lessons from Diamond Teams, and I would not fail to plan for every negative outcome without having a countermeasure to ensure success. Success for me, not for Katherine Navarro Banks Simpkins. Even better, too, she has children.

CHAPTER 24
Sam – *9 months ago*

Jesus and all the saints. I watched the video from the project termination with Guy Brown after Chris, Kate, and I met. I didn't like how things ended on the video. I also read through the incident reports that the security team wrote. I think all three of us knew this wasn't just going to go away. We would be seeing or hearing from Guy Brown again—sooner or later. He seemed like the kind of guy whose ire would fester like a canker.

I also thought about what Chris said. We didn't necessarily need to close up shop at Diamond Teams. We could lie low for a bit, and maybe start some prospective clients on the screening process. I wondered what that would look like. We would keep the daily monitoring going until Brown made his first offensive action. Hell, he may have already done it, and we just hadn't felt the impact yet.

Chris hates this guy (Guy!), and it seems to grow and take on a life of its own with each passing day. I see him staring into space, and I think he's either picturing Guy Brown and tearing him limb from limb, or he's picturing Kate and how worried she's been about this guy blowing up our entire business.

The thing about Guy…he doesn't know who some of our clients are or what they do or what they are capable of doing. He doesn't know that we do, indeed, have government clearance, and there are people who can make Guy Brown disappear with a simple phone call. We have the ability to cut him off at the knees, send his life into a bleak hole of woe.

When our kids were young, we read Greek mythology. Why not? There are a lot of life lessons in the stories. But there are death lessons, too. In the underworld, there are the Asphodel Meadows, which aren't terribly meadow-like, since the ground is covered in ash. There's Elysium, which paradoxically enough, is a utopia. There are rivers, and there are paths to Tartarus, a place of hopelessness so abject, so wholly consuming that death is preferable. I don't wish death on Guy Brown, but if he messes with us, we can arrange Tartarus on Earth for him.

CHAPTER 25
Sam and Kate – *8 months ago*

"Sam, I don't want to fold Diamond Teams. I think initially I jumped to conclusions too quickly, had a knee-jerk reaction, whatever." Kate paced around her kitchen, balancing her cell phone between her shoulder and ear, speaking softly.

"Chris thought you might have been reacting initially, and I think it's good that we are taking a step back and thinking through things," Sam said.

"What are you doing right now?" Kate asked.

"Besides talking on the phone to you, I'm putting together the month-end reports," Sam responded, continuing to key in data on her laptop.

"Dean goes back to school in a couple weeks. Michelle will come home from her internship for a week, and then head to school. Should I be worried about her? I'm not as worried about Dean because he did all the martial arts training this summer."

"I don't think you can be too prudent. She's at Stanford by herself, but there's some insulation because she's living in a sorority house. You know those houses are pretty locked down."

"Yeah, I guess," Kate said. "I think I would feel better if someone were keeping an eye on her for a little while, though."

"Totally understandable," Sam said.

"When are your kids heading back to school?"

"About the same time as yours. I think I'd be crazy worried if I had been the one to term Guy Brown's project."

A brief silence followed. Sam held her phone away from her head for a moment to make sure the call hadn't dropped.

"A weird thing happened," Kate said. "I don't know what to make of it. Everything makes me overreact right now. I mean after everything with Dean's car, I'm pretty jumpy these days."

"What happened?"

"The other night, I had to run to the library. I was in the building for maybe 15 minutes or so?"

"OK," Sam prompted.

"Well, while I was in there, someone keyed my car. None of the other cars parked near me had a scratch on them. Only my car. And it was like they really dug the key into the paint."

Sam took a breath, "Hmm. Did you let anyone at the library know? Do they have cameras in their parking area?"

"I did tell the library director, and they do have cameras in the parking garage and lot, but no camera pointed toward where I was parked—which is my fault, I guess," Kate mused. "But I don't know if this keying thing was random or if it was Guy. I think that every single thing that goes wrong is Guy's fault. I bought strawberries this week. I swear between the grocery store and home, they turned moldy. Then I immediately thought Guy had pumped my car full of ethylene gas, forcing them to over-ripen. It's completely irrational, and I know it."

"Don't let the paranoia get to you," Sam reassured Kate. "It'll make you crazy."

"I'm thinking about telling Kevin about Diamond Teams and what we do," Kate said, breathing audibly. "What do you think?"

"Well. You know what I think. I can't believe you haven't told him before now. I know that it was mainly to keep him safe and to provide him with plausible deniability for your kids' sakes, but they're both over 18 now. I think you should tell him, and I don't think it would be out of line to tell him about Guy. There's a very real threat to you and your family, and I kind of think he has a right to know."

"What does Chris think?"

"Chris and I are on the same page. We're in a different boat than you are because we both work for the same company. We aren't keeping anything from one another. But, like you, we haven't told our kids, and now that they're older…I just wonder if and when we should tell them what we do for a living. Heck. For all we know, they think we work for the mafia. Or maybe they think we're in witness protection. Maybe they think we're spies. Hard telling, and we're quickly approaching the point in time when we should tell them something. It will help them be on their guard if something like the Guy Brown situation ever comes up again."

Kate sighed. "OK. I'll tell Kevin tonight, and then he and I can discuss telling the kids. But I do agree that it's a safety issue now." Kate paused. "Please keep your fingers crossed that Kevin doesn't go ballistic. I don't think he will, but I do think he will be surprised. He might call you or Chris to decompress at some point. Would you let Chris know what's happening?"

"Of course. We'll both be thinking of you. I know this won't be an easy conversation."

CHAPTER 26
Chris – *8 months ago*

This morning promised today would be a banner day. Two separate incident reports. I know they were both linked to Guy Brown. The first report came from Leeza. She's a no-nonsense New Yorker living in Chicago in a brownstone with another Diamond Teams employee, Bruce. They are a dynamite couple, and we don't ever book them on the same jobs. Bruce has a 160 IQ, he's built like a sequoia, and he is loyal and dependable. Leeza, brilliant, wound up meeting Bruce in college. She scored 1550 on the SAT and was a gymnast. She couldn't decide between law school or business school after college, AND she could bench press her body weight. Unbeknownst to each of them, Diamond Teams scooped them both up. Leeza did wind up being able to juggle Diamond Teams and business school at the University of Chicago.

Leeza telephoned, and I could hear her breathing heavily. I could hear Bruce in the background, swearing a blue streak. Not good. "Leeza, what can I do for you?" I asked, because why beat around the bush with useless niceties?

"Jesus, Joseph, and Mary. I am so damn mad right now. Chris! I am spitting nails. I know this isn't your fault, and I know we take extreme precautions, but do you know what I found on my doorstep this morning when I went out to get the paper? And before you give me grief about getting an actual paper, I'm telling you I like having it in my hands. I like to hear the rustle of the paper while I turn the pages back and fold them. It's the New York Times, for fuck's sake. I *need* it to be on paper. Oh my god. I'm just so angry and flummoxed. I know this all came out in one breath. I need to sit down, or I might pass out."

The phone clattered to the floor or to a tabletop. Hard to say.

"Chris. Bruce here. Listen. Someone left a dead cat on our stoop this morning, and our newspaper was soaked in its blood."

Fuckity-fuck. And this is how my morning began. About an hour later came the second call. From Clark.

"Chris, I'm coming to you, not Kate because she would go bonkers and opt for a nuclear solution. She takes after our mom," Clark said, and I knew he was right. I'd known Kate for most of my life, and her first impulse was usually extreme, then she calmed down, processed everything, and almost always arrived at something optimal. Over the years, she could set aside her emotions, though, and see through the problem to clear the way to the finish line, but when it came to family—she was a lioness.

"I'm afraid to ask. What happened?" Maybe I wasn't afraid to ask, since I did put the question out there. I knew I wouldn't like the answer, whatever it was.

"My doorbell rang," Clark said. "My 12-year-old daughter answered and found a box on the porch, addressed to me. She wanted me to open it because she loves packages that come in the mail. There was no postmark on the box, and I was worried that there might be a snake in there or something. It had to be hand delivered, here, in Odessa, Texas.

"Imagine my surprise when I took it to my back patio, and I am glad I was wearing long sleeves, pants, safety goggles, gloves, and a hat. It was too light for a bomb, but not too light to be a snake, scorpion, or tarantula. But it was none of those, no. It was option D—wasp nest with a few live ones still living there and they weren't happy about having their house relocated to a box."

Clark paused. I remained silent. I had known Clark most of my life, and I knew he needed to say everything he was going to say before I would feel all right asking any clarifying questions.

"I've been stung, bitten, scratched. Whatever. But I will be god-damned if my kids are going to be on the losing end of some wacko's revenge scheme. Please talk to Kate and Sam. I'm assuming that Guy Brown has identified all of us who had a hand in shutting down his project."

After those two gems of phone calls, I thought my day would rate 2 ½ stars if I didn't get calls from Wesley, Angel, Shannon, or Cleveland. That afternoon, though, I got the cherry on top of the sundae. Sam tells me that she has spoken to Kate, and Kate's car was keyed the night before, and she's almost certain it was Guy Brown. That's three. My grandma always said bad things came in threes. Actually, she said celebrity deaths came in threes, but I'm paraphrasing, of course. Guy has shown us he could find us in the world and reach us.

What troubles me more are the three strikes in 24 hours—Chicago, Odessa, and Kate in Big Sky. Guy Brown has help, maybe not a team he trusts, but some paid help, for sure.

Growing up, our small town had a broom closet sized arcade. The arcade had a Whack-a-Mole game. Beating the plush rodents was fun. They poked their heads up, and you popped them a good one if you could catch them. All the laughter and joy from hitting those stupid little puppets, then the tickets streamed out of the machine, followed by redeeming the tickets for trinkets and trash. We worked so hard for a pencil or an eraser or a joy buzzer. We spent more playing the game to get the tickets than the prizes were worth. But it was fun. Eventually, childhood burned away like so much dew on an early spring morning, and we grew up, became homeowners, and we had real moles in our yard. Vexing varmints. I sat outside one morning with a spade across my lap, and a mug of hot coffee on the table next to me. I saw the ground displaced by the tunnel the mole was digging. My goal was to head it off at the pass by stopping its progress with the spade, and then I would trap and remove it from my yard. Great idea in theory. Instead, I decapitated it. Moles aren't just blind. They don't have eyes. One of the kids said that they do have cute 'hands.' Our buddy, Guy, is turning out to be the mole in my metaphorical yard. I only hope we trap him and don't wind up decapitating him, and I hope he doesn't destroy the yard or the house or the house's foundation in the process.

"Chris," Kate said later that night. Sam and I both sat in front of a computer, looking at the seriousness on Kate's face. "I think we need to let Virginia know about Guy stalking the target and share the police report with her. She can decide what is in the best interest of her son."

After the call, we unearthed the police report. We could have a bench warrant issued for Guy. It wouldn't amount to much because of being in another state, but the police report detailing the stalking would be damning, especially with the drawing from the sketch artist accompanying it. A letter or call to Virginia would likely be enough for her to put the brakes on Guy's visitation with their son. Kate continued, "I think we need to let Guy know we are serious, and we aren't going to allow harm to come to our employees and families."

CHAPTER 27
Guy – *8 months ago*

"Fucking fuck!" I shouted, slamming my cell phone down on my desk. Sitting in front of me was a copy of the police report for stalking my target, along with the police sketch, and a bench warrant for my arrest. It came certified mail this afternoon. What was worse was the phone call I received roughly an hour after the mail had been delivered. Virginia. She was talking about taking me to court. She, too, had received the packet.

"Guy, you weren't a good marriage partner, and eventually, neither was I. You have proven to be a good father to Harris, and I appreciate you. I really do." I heard the rustling of paper in the background, and I could imagine what Virginia was seeing—the goddamn damning packet. "But I cannot have a stalker spending time with Harris. In all the time I've known you, I know you to have a single-minded focus on certain things, but why this woman? You frightened her enough to call the police. Your actions were so overt the sketch artist was able to generate a very good likeness of you. Why are you stalking someone? What is going on with you?"

"Virginia, it's not what you think. I mean, it sort of is. I was stalking her, but…dammit! I did mean to stalk this woman, and I did not have pure intentions."

"Guy! Why are you telling me this? What is wrong with you?" I could hear her walking around on what sounded like hardwood floors. She was pacing, one of her self-soothing mechanisms. She huffed loudly. "Put yourself in my position. How would you feel about having your child spending time with a stalker? Are you going to take him on your…stalks? I don't want that for him. I don't want there to be even the most remote temptation you would do something like that." She took a deep breath, and I knew this was hard for her. "You want to see Harris. Fine. You can see him, but it's going to be supervised, and it's going to be here in my home. I'm really scared about you taking him and getting arrested while he's with you. We can go to court to hash this out, or we can see how everything goes with this stalking thing you've got going on. But I wouldn't be honest if I didn't tell you how much this bothers and worries me."

"Virginia, please, just don't forbid my seeing Harris," I begged. I was pissed for having lost control of too many things, and I should have seen this as a possible outcome of my actions.

Virginia said in a very quiet, trembling voice, "About five or six years ago, I had a student who was obsessed with me. He came to all my tutorials, office hours. He started showing up in classes he wasn't even taking just to see my lectures. He would stay after class and walk back to my office with me. One afternoon, late in the day, he followed me to my car and pinned me to it with his body." She stopped. "I have never told you this, but I was so scared. My body was shaking, and when he saw what he was doing to me, he backed away.

"He said he didn't mean to frighten me and thought I felt the same way about him. I told him I was in a committed relationship and did not reciprocate his feelings, but I truly did admire his devotion to astrophysics.

What could have been a dire situation de-escalated quickly, but only because he was really tuned in to what I was saying. He asked if I wanted him to drop my class, and I told him he could stay only as long as he respected my boundaries. If it was impossible, then he would need to drop the class.

"I cannot have my son EVER be a party to something remotely like what I experienced. If there's even the slightest chance this is a learned behavior, I need, deep in my bones, for him to be as far removed from something that would cause another woman the distress I felt as possible."

"Jesus, Virginia. I didn't know. Why didn't you ever say anything?" I asked. "Your professor or I could have intervened."

"I handled it. But you see how your situation distresses me? I know you, and I know how you get focused, and this really scares me, and I'm not doing my job as a mother if I expose my son to any of this. You're going to need to give me time, but I think you need to go to counseling. I think you need help. I don't know. Maybe we need to amend our custody agreement until you have yourself together."

My heart was breaking, and at the same time, all I saw was red, consumed by an intense storm of anger, fury, and rage. A pit was opening in my soul, it felt like, and it enlarged and gobbled more of my rational self. "I need to go," I croaked into the phone. "We aren't done talking about this. I would like to avoid going to court, though. If you want to draw up a contract with your stipulations, I'll agree to anything." I wanted to avoid court—too many outcomes out of my control. If a judge saw the stalking business, I might lose even supervised visitation, or I might have to answer the bench warrant, which would be a whole other can of worms. I would do whatever Virginia wanted.

And then, if my day couldn't get worse, my CEO called me. He, too, received the stalking information. As a matter of course, the company works to maintain a squeaky clean image. Everyone in the C-suite has routine checks done to monitor criminal activity, Google alerts, the whole nine yards.

"I hate to do this, Guy," says my CEO.

"What do you hate to do?" I asked, but I knew.

"In our regular criminal background checks, it looks like there's a bench warrant for your arrest for stalking. Please tell me I'm wrong about this," he said, but I knew he was looking at the legal documents, and we both knew he wasn't wrong about anything.

I sighed deeply. "You're not wrong. I'll deal with this and get everything straightened out." I promised, but I couldn't be certain everything could be straightened out. I did what I did, got caught, and would have to pay for what I did. What pissed me off was the $200,000 I paid Diamond Teams to bury all this shit. They were letting me blow in the wind.

"Guy, you're a valued member of our executive team, but I'm going to have to put you on a leave of absence while you're sorting this. We can't afford even a whiff of impropriety. I can't guarantee your job either, but if there's some way you can turn things around, I suggest you get on it right away," he said in a formal and detached manner, then said quietly, "please fix this. You need to fix this."

My son. And my job. God damned Diamond Teams.

CHAPTER 28
Kevin – *8 months ago*

I dropped my keys in the ceramic bowl on the hall table when I got home from work. The bowl was something we painted in a small shop in Mazatlán over spring break when the kids were small. The shop happened to be sandwiched between a grocery and travel agency just down the street from our hotel. I knew Kate spoke a little French and a little Spanish. She had mentioned it here and there over the years when we were watching a foreign film or if we were in a Mexican restaurant or something. On the trip with the kids, though, we were wandering around the town, and we got ourselves turned around. I speak a tiny bit of German—the bare minimum to meet the foreign language requirement in college—which was no help in Mexico. We stopped in a shoe store because…why not? Kate found an older woman working there and spoke to her in very fluent Spanish. They had a short conversation where it looked like Kate was introducing our children and me to the woman, who was nodding along and smiling, then wiping at her eyes. If I didn't know better, I would have thought the two women knew each other.

After a bit, the woman began gesturing. My guess was that these were the directions that would take us back to the hotel. Looking back on that episode now makes me wonder about the seeming randomness of the event. And I wonder about Kate's language proficiency. And I wonder what other languages are in her repertoire. And I wonder what else I don't know about my wife. I mean, how much do we truly know about any other person, even if the other person is someone with whom we've spent almost every day for the last twenty-some years?

The house smelled good, though. I sensed the lingering aroma of fresh-cut apples, caramelized onion, cinnamon, braised beef. It smelled like a special meal, like a special occasion. I pondered for a moment that I hadn't missed a birthday or anniversary or holiday, and I was sure that I was in the clear. Still, though, I was on high alert. It was a weeknight, and Kate didn't typically have time to throw together a showstopper of a dinner on a weeknight. Something was up.

I found my wife in the kitchen sprinkling cinnamon sugar on the top crust of a pie that looked like it had just come out of the oven. The table was set, and there were fresh flowers in a cut glass vase in the center, and it looked like it would be just the two of us for dinner. I didn't want to startle her, so I cleared my throat, and in my best radio announcer voice said, "Honey, I'm home."

She turned to me, her eyes bright, and smiled. "Hi. How was your day?"

"Good," I said. "How about yours?"

"Good, too. I talked to Sam for a while today and decided to take the afternoon off and make a decent dinner for us." She crossed the room, wrapping her arms around my waist, and gave me a lingering kiss.

"It smells wonderful in here, Kate. Is there a special occasion I'm missing?"

"No. Nothing like that. I just wanted to do something nice."

After changing clothes, I returned to the kitchen. Kate had plated everything and was pouring wine into rocks glasses, not wine glasses. OK. Now we were getting somewhere. She had something to tell me, and it required liquid courage for her to share, and it would require the same for me to hear.

"Kevin, you know I love you. You are the love of my life, my one great love."

"And you're mine, too," I said warily.

"This is about my work," she said. "I haven't ever been open about what I do, and now that the kids are older, I think," she swallowed back a great gulp of her drink. "No, I *need* to tell you everything about my business and, well," she trailed off. "Well, I need to tell you all of it."

For the next hour, she told me how she started her business and the premise of the murder adventure. She told me about how Chris and Sam fit in. She told me that she did have government clearance because they had actually trained agents from some of the acronym agencies. She told me her work was what made her paranoid for the kids and me. She told me about some of the large corporations that she had worked for in a team-building capacity and that all of her business came by word of mouth.

I told her that I had heard of a similar company called Diamond Teams from some of my professional contacts. She told me Diamond Teams was her company. I asked, "What would you have done if I had contacted your company to schedule a project?"

She gave me a Mona Lisa smile. "You never would have dealt with Chris, Sam, or me. If you passed our screening process, you would have been assigned a compatible project liaison. Either that, or I would have sat you down and told you everything and let you decide if you wanted to proceed." I hated the first scenario, being completely left in the dark. She would have been able to see everything about me through their screening process. I felt like I could have been so easily violated by my wife and her two closest friends. I never would have known, and I didn't like it. My mind was hung up on the violation, and I felt raw and exposed. Was it silly to feel like this about the person I loved and trusted most in the world? And I was incensed about the possibility of the tendrils of her work reaching into our family and causing harm or allowing the door to remain open for harm to enter our home.

At one time, I had entertained contacting Diamond Teams, but I didn't feel the need with the group of people who were on my team. I actually did a lot of team-building myself, and my team and I thought it was effective enough not to have to look beyond ourselves for planning. It seemed like it could be fun and meaningful, though, but, again, team-building was one of my fortés, and I wanted to prove to be a good steward of the corporate coffers.

"If I had come to Diamond Teams and gone through your screening, would you have reviewed all of my testing results?"

"I like to think that I know you well enough without needing to review anything Diamond Teams would have collected. I like to think that I respect you and our relationship and our life together not to look at your results. I would probably have only looked if you failed our process, and even then, someone else would have reviewed everything, and I would only be informed if there were something truly glaring or disturbing that would have been uncovered."

I turned that over a little bit. What would I have done if I had been in her situation? It's hard to speculate. It was like taking a pop quiz. No studying beforehand, but there was the expectation of knowing the material. After completing the quiz, the teacher would pass everything back randomly, and everyone would grade whichever quiz they received. Someone in the class would know how I did on my quiz before I did. Then after, we would return the quizzes to one another, and I would see how on the mark or off base I was. It wasn't private. Some other kid in class knew because they had graded my quiz. Not a big deal if I nailed it, but really embarrassing if I completely failed. Even more embarrassing if they had shared my score with everyone sitting around them. I like to think that we aren't terribly vindictive, but it's hard to tell unless there's some trust in the person grading the quiz.

Kate explained why she had never told me all of this before now and the need that I had to have plausible deniability. If she ever wound up in a situation where she couldn't come home because of the danger she could have put our family in, she had to know that our kids would always be able to remain in my custody. Um, holy shit, Batman.

She explained there had been a recent client who had gone overboard and his desire to seek retribution. He had plainly articulated intent.

"Ah," I said. "This is why we're doing Brazilian Jiu Jitsu, isn't it?"

She nodded.

"And this is why we need Dean to train as well. Am I correct in assuming that?"

Again, she nodded.

"And your paranoia for the kids, Dean's car issue?"

Again, she nodded.

"Jesus, Kate! Dean could have been hurt! What if he didn't go to the car place? What then?"

Tears slid down the apples of her cheeks, She had lied to me to my face about the paranoia, the reason for it, anyway. She couldn't have a free pass on this because it's our family affected by her and her work.

I leaned back in my chair, taking a long drink of my wine. "I am being honest here, Kate. I'm very hurt that you didn't feel comfortable sharing this with me at any time in the last 25 years that we've been together." She began to object. I raised a hand, signaling her to let me finish talking. "I understand why you kept this quiet. But, again, I'm hurt. How many times have we spent vacations, holidays, visits with Sam and Chris? Do you know how dumb I feel that everyone in the room was in on the secret except for me? Do you know—even though I understand why—I feel like you don't trust me? Do you know how that makes me feel?"

She reached for my hand, and I stood up from the table.

"Please," I said. "You're going to have to give me a little time to take all this in. I'm going to have questions. I want you to know a few things, though. I'm not angry. I'm hurt and embarrassed. Not embarrassed by you, but embarrassed to be on the outside. I do understand, and I know it couldn't have been an easy decision for you to make, but I don't like it even a little bit that you've kept this huge secret from me through the entirety of our relationship, and I do love you and will always love you, and we will get through this." I paused a moment, feeling a lump in my throat, "And I appreciate the fact you were thinking of the kids and the possibility of plausible deniability. But I don't know how any supposition would have held up in court. A couple together for upwards of 20 years, and one spouse doesn't know what the other does for a living? I don't think it would've played well in the court of public opinion. But, yeah, we can get through this. What does anger me, though, is how this is now impacting our family unit. I do understand the thoroughness of your process, and if this client is the first one who has gone off the rails, well…

"From one professional to another, when is the last time you all did a threat assessment, allowing for new technology being accessible to your clients and making an allowance to make it through all of your screenings by out-strategizing you? This very situation proves that you're overdue."

I looked at her sitting there, her eyes glistening with tears, and maybe the hint of a small, hopeful smile on her lips.

"What's your crazy client's name? I may have met him at some point in some of the conferences or professional networking groups over the years."

She whispered, "Guy Brown."

"I know him," I said softly. "He recently recommended a seminar to me in one of our networking groups. I think it was one of the conferences that I mentioned to you."

She visibly paled.

"Give me a little bit to get my thoughts together. I have known Guy for several years, and I could probably tell you about my experiences with him, my impressions. But it seems that we're going to need to deal with this in a couple of ways."

I excused myself and went to our home office. We have an overstuffed corduroy couch. I lay back on the throw pillows, then deciding to give my back and neck a rest, tossed the pillows to the floor. I fell asleep while thinking through everything Kate had shared. It was overwhelming, and I worried about the kids—Michelle more than Dean because I didn't think she'd had any kind of self-defense training, and she was far from home. And I thought about Guy Brown. He was brilliant but so strange. I had seen him at a conference about a month ago. We had all gone out for drinks, and he brought up the weirdest thing. I jolted awake.

"Kate, honey," I called out.

"Yes?" she called back to me in answer, walking swiftly into the room. Her eyes were red-rimmed, puffy, and her nose was red. I could see this was hard for her, and she made the best decision at the time with the information she had. I didn't have to like it, but her intentions were good. I would spend some time talking about all this with Chris.

"First of all," I said gently and patted the seat next to me. "We're going to be OK. It'll take me a little bit of time to digest everything and trust you aren't keeping anything else major from me." I paused. She sat quietly, pressed to my side, and I took her hand, and turned to face her, looking her in the eye, trying to convey my earnestness and love with the depth of my gaze, "Please don't keep anything from me. Do you understand?"

She nodded.

"Your being forthright with me is especially important. OK?" I asked in confirmation.

She nodded again. We were silent for a few beats. I leaned forward and kissed her lips gently. Actions being stronger than words and all that.

"OK," I said and breathing in deeply and pushing the air out of my lungs with a great sigh. "This is going to be weird. I had drinks with Guy Brown and a bunch of other people at the conference I attended about a month ago. I feel kind of stupid now, not knowing what it was that you do for a living, and I think he may have been testing me."

"What did he say?" Kate asked.

"There were around eight of us at the table," I said. "Guy leans in, sort of conspiratorially, and says, 'If you were going to plan a murder and totally get away with it, how would you do it?'"

Kate turned white and she started to shake a little bit. She was pale earlier, but this was something else altogether.

I went on, "Anyway, we're all brainstorming and coming up with movies and TV shows where the murderers didn't get away with their crimes because of some unforeseen circumstance or other. And we all began philosophizing about what went wrong. How could the situation have been avoided?"

Kate was nodding, and I continued.

"Do you remember one of the earliest episodes of 'Breaking Bad' where they put the dead body in the bathtub with lime, and it ate through the tub and came crashing through the ceiling of the floor below?"

"Yes," Kate said with a small smile.

"We all agreed that wasn't a good method for disposing of a body. We decided that people get caught because they don't know how to get rid of the body properly. We discussed that it wasn't necessarily the commission of the crime, the actual act, but more the series of events after the murder."

"OK," Kate said uncertainly, maybe uptalking a little.

"Hear me out," I said. "Let's say that you drug someone, or maybe poison them, and they're already dead. You can drag them about in an upright position and tell anyone gawking that they'd had too much to drink. Suddenly, not much explanation beyond what you've said and what they've observed is necessary. Right?" I was warming to the topic. "I mean, what the average person is seeing is somewhat ordinary, and with the explanation, it's not very important, and is easily forgotten."

"What else did you all talk about?" Kate asked.

"We talked about victim selection. You know that movie, 'Strangers on a Train?' Remember how the two guys didn't know each other and both had people they hated and wanted to murder? The whole bit with the 'crisscross?'"

"Sure," Kate said.

"Theoretically, if the one guy hadn't been crazy AND the other guy hadn't had his whole alibi being substantiated by someone drunk who didn't remember anything, they could have gotten away with their crimes. Well, the non-crazy guy didn't go through with his crisscross murder because he'd had a crisis of conscience, but you get what I mean."

I took a beat, squeezing Kate's hand, before continuing. "Guy Brown kept the conversation going for probably forty-five minutes to an hour. It was a very gory discussion but stimulating from the perspective that the crime had to be covered up. So," I gave a quick nervous laugh, "remember the woodchipper scene from the movie 'Fargo'? I hate to tell you how enthusiastically we warmed to the discussion because it was damn weird, and the eight of us were like a think tank. Anyway, Guy changed gears on the discussion about midway. He said, 'What would you do to exact revenge on someone who wronged you in the most grievous way?'"

Kate visibly bristled.

"I had no idea who Guy was to you because I had no idea what you actually did through your business."

"How did the discussion go, once you all started talking about revenge?" Kate asked quietly.

"Uh, well, you probably won't like this, but I suppose it will help us prepare for the worst," I said, looking at our joined hands. "We all kind of agreed that murdering the person you're trying to get revenge on isn't really the best solution. Once the person is dead, then you're done. They don't have to experience the prolonged anguish. No. What you do is go after something that the person loves more than anything, and you break it. You don't kill it. Then every single day that goes by, the person looks at their broken loved one, and the person KNOWS they're the reason for their loved one's daily experience. Can you imagine how horrible it would be if you KNEW you were the reason that Prometheus had his liver eaten by an eagle every day for eternity? That YOU were the sole reason for his torture?"

I stopped talking. Kate held my hand tightly, and I looked at her dear, dear face, marred only by the reddened eyes and tears sliding down her cheeks. I drew her to me and held her close, feeling her trembling against me. "I couldn't bear it," she said, her voice thick with grief. "I couldn't bear it."

CHAPTER 29
Guy – *the early years*

He was small for his age, and his teacher thought that would not bode well for him in kindergarten because he was SO much smaller than not just the boys in the class, but the girls, too. Mrs. Phipps could understand why his parents had gone to the school and requested an exception for him to begin kindergarten at age 4 because he was already reading, writing, and doing some basic math. He needed to be around other children for socialization, but he was so small and so young. Guy's parents were highly educated, and rightly or wrongly, thought themselves enlightened. They spoke to Guy as if he were a tiny adult, and as enlightened parents, realized that as Guy spoke to them as a tiny adult, that he needed to be around children his own age. Guy was the fourth child of four children, and he was younger than his next sibling by 6 years. Everyone in the home spoke like tiny adults, except the adults—because they were average adult-sized people.

Tiny Guy began kindergarten. His brothers and sister dressed him for the first day of school. "You need to look cool to the other kids," his sister Jane said. "You have to fit in, and you have to look average. Think like a chameleon."

Guy's siblings had average names, Jane, John, and Mike. Guy was unusual because he should have been named something like Jim, Bob, or Joe, but his parents were thinking their fourth child would be a girl, and her name would be Sue. They had been pressed, and Jim, Joe, and Bob had been far from their minds. "He's a guy," Guy's father had said, and his mother wrote that on the slip the registrar from the hospital presented to her.

Maybe there had been a communication error between Guy's parents, but Guy always felt that he rather liked the name Guy better than Jim, Bob, or Sue. He knew there was a song called "A Boy Named Sue," and he didn't want his parents to think that Sue could be a viable option for him.

Mrs. Phipps, though, always watched out for Guy. He was so small. What she didn't count on, though, was his big personality and his charisma. Every child in the class seemed to fall under the spell of tiny Guy. By the end of the first week, Mrs. Phipps had no worries that Guy Brown would fare well in kindergarten and be the one to set the tone for the rest of the class. Mrs. Phipps' challenge would be to keep Guy engaged and interested and to balance that with the needs of the rest of the class. While Mrs. Phipps taught the rest of the class their ABCs and how to write them, Guy sat quietly and read the Harry Potter books. Each day, Mrs. Phipps had a sharing session for the children with Guy relating what he had learned in his Harry Potter reading for that day. Mrs. Phipps was quite pleased that Guy was reading with comprehension, and his recall for detail was excellent.

Mrs. Phipps continued conducting her class in this manner through almost the end of the semester. She realized the kindergarteners weren't going to catch up to Guy. He could probably move to first grade. This posed a lot of concerns because he would be a four-year-old in a class with 6 and 7 year olds, again, the youngest and smallest—but probably even smaller since the kids were a full year older than the kindergarteners.

At the beginning of December, Mrs. Phipps held a meeting with Guy's parents.

"Thank you for taking time out of both your days to come meet with me," said Mrs. Phipps.

"Of course," said Mrs. Brown. "Is Guy doing all right in your class?"

"He certainly is," said Mrs. Phipps. "The other kids love Guy. They look out for him because he's so much smaller, but they also seem to look up to him, too. He is a natural leader and very quickly became probably the most popular student in the class."

"That's good, isn't it?" Mrs. Brown asked, glancing at Mr. Brown and Mrs. Phipps in turn to ensure that this situation was better than they had hoped. Mr. Brown nodded, not adding anything to the discussion.

"Mr. and Mrs. Brown, I would like to see Guy be able to take this time and flourish academically." Mrs. Phipps opened the manila folder that she had brought with her, showcasing some of Guy's work.

"In art, his work seems similar to the other kids because, as a four year old, his fine motor skills have yet to develop further and mature. But in math and reading, he's relegated to doing what amounts to independent study because he's so much more advanced than the rest of the class, and I think a four-year-old needs more handholding because he's only 4 and shouldn't be left to independent study."

Mr. and Mrs. Brown nodded in agreement.

"It's for this reason," Mrs. Phipps said, while taking in a deep breath, "Because I don't want to hinder Guy's learning and mental stimulation, that I have a couple recommendations for you to consider."

Mr. and Mrs. Brown leaned toward the center of the table where they were sitting.

"Please," said Mr. Brown softly, his voice surprisingly deep. "Please share your recommendations with us. We want the best for Guy."

And so it happened that Guy was in kindergarten for socialization purposes, but he attended math and reading classes with the third and fourth graders. The older children immediately took to Guy because he was average in looks and dress, though quite small, but his big personality and charisma immediately won them all.

The summer after kindergarten, Guy had a growth spurt, which made him almost the average size of the average 5-year-old, but still he remained small for his class in first grade, since his classmates were still a full year older. However, Guy remained popular and well thought of by his teachers, his fellow first graders, and the students in the fourth and fifth grades, where he went for math and reading.

Guy's first-grade teacher recommended testing for Guy, to get a pulse on where he was from a learning standpoint, because everyone who had met Guy wanted to do right by him. Everyone wanted to see how much and how quickly Guy's brain could take in and interpret information and learn.

Guy's parents were brought in again during December of first grade, but they didn't meet with Guy's teacher. This time, they met with Mr. Owen, the principal.

"Mr. and Mrs. Brown, I think that we aren't going to be able to accommodate Guy's learning needs here in the elementary grades in a traditional sense. I know there are considerations and concerns about having Guy become socialized with kids his own age, and I genuinely appreciate how important it is. But there's a balancing act," said Mr. Owen, raising both hands and mimicking a scale. "On the one hand, we have socialization and development," tipping one scale down. "And on the other hand, we have academic learning." Mr. Owen tipped the other scale down, then demonstrated trying to balance both.

"It is our desire that Guy finds a place to fit in the world," said Mrs. Brown. "He fits perfectly in our family, and we love that, but we are just a small player in what will be his worldview."

"I have personally observed Guy in his first-grade homeroom, math, and reading classes, and he is a unique child in that he is liked by everyone he meets. I have noticed that he does a lot of maybe not behavior mirroring, but social engineering, which is unusual in children that young, but he appears to have mastered it. And when I say social engineering, I mean in a positive sense."

Mr. Brown quietly cleared his throat before saying, "Mr. Owen. You aren't telling us anything that we haven't been able to discover in the last year from our conversations with the school counselor, although social engineering is new. What would you recommend?"

"I think that we should move him to middle school AFTER he completes second grade. He will be fine here for the rest of this academic year and next. We'll keep him with his cohort but put him in the fifth grade advanced math and reading. My other recommendation would be to get him signed up for an online foreign language class. That will stimulate another part of his brain and should enable him to sleep better."

In January, Guy began taking a Spanish class online through the local commuter college. The following January, Guy asked to take French, another romance language, and to continue on with Spanish. His parents were pleased with his progress. They became nervous as second grade came to a close. He was newly 7 years old and would begin middle school in the fall, which put him in a building with classmates who would be 10-14 years old, but Jane and John were in middle school and would be able to look out for Guy. There was such a substantial difference in maturity between a 7-year-old and a 10-year-old. Some of the 6th graders would be kids from his advanced math and reading classes. Would that be enough to justify plunging their boy into an environment full of kids on the cusp of puberty and adolescence?

What no one counted on, though, was Guy's ability to function deftly as a social engineer. He was a chameleon, and his growth would eventually catch up, but he fit in with any group he encountered. In retrospect, if Guy hadn't been so gifted socially, he would have been better off interacting only with children his own age, but he would have been so bored academically, and that could have played out as his developing into a mischief maker. Eventually, Guy would make mischief, and he would be the architect of many schemes that would end badly for some of the people he chose to involve, but he always foresaw the unfortunate ends.

One day, school was closed due to a snowstorm that had hit during the night. Mr. Brown took the day off to be with his children. At the time, the children were 6, 12, 13, and 14 years old. Mr. Brown thought it would be fun to have a chess tournament. Everyone knew how to play but Guy. Mr. Brown spent time in the morning explaining the chess pieces and how they moved. He also explained that there were different strategies that could be employed that could help in winning the game but since they were going to have a tournament, they would skip the strategies for now. Since the family only had the one chess board, Guy decided to find the rule book, giving it a read while the tournament commenced. He was surprised that a game that looked so simple could take such a long time to play, but the rule book made completely logical sense to Guy. Guy liked when things made sense.

Around mid-morning, Guy had finished the rule book and ventured into Mr. Brown's study to find a book he had noticed on the bookshelf that talked about strategies in chess. Guy initially skimmed the strategy book, and he smiled. The strategies made complete sense, too. Chess was a game of strategy and seemed to be steeped in logic. If Guy could harness the logic, which was a tall ask for a 6-year-old, he could control the game. He could win the game; and, in the bigger game, if he needed to lose, he could engineer that as well. All that logic--it lit up something in his brain, and he liked the feeling.

He took the book with him and sat next to the game that was in progress and watched the haphazard way the game was progressing. There was no strategy or finesse. They weren't playing to win. They were playing to save playing pieces. Guy noted that in the best strategies, the players had to be willing to give up some of their pieces to ensure the success of the other pieces on the board. Guy didn't win his father's chess tournament that day, but he did learn something else that would serve him well for the rest of his life. People were nothing more than playing pieces on a board, and people were predictable. He could win if he set the correct strategy in motion.

After the snow day, Guy would challenge his father, brothers, and sister to chess games. Sometimes he won, and sometimes he didn't. What his family didn't realize, though, was Guy's losses were orchestrated. He wanted to observe the behavior of someone who thought or knew they were going to win. Most everyone who played chess with Guy and won felt badly for taking advantage of a little boy. They didn't know that they were simply data points, and, yes, there was a bigger game afoot.

CHAPTER 30
Guy – *the teen years*

By the time Guy was 14, he had, in essence, been an only child for two years. He was no longer the smallest boy in his grade. He had experienced a few growth spurts that put him on the growth curve, and being the youngest in his grade had no longer correlated with his being the smallest. Guy, however, had made peace with being smaller than the others in his cohort. When he realized that he had become average, he expressed compassion to the kids in the younger grades who were struggling with being small for their age or grade. Guy was beloved.

During Homecoming when Guy was 14, and again, when Guy was 15, he was named Homecoming King. He was allowed to go to the Prom when he was 15, and he and his date were named Prom King and Queen, respectively. Guy enjoyed what he was able to enjoy throughout his high school years. He played on the tennis and golf teams, and he was the president of the chess club. He had a high school transcript and resume that any student or parent would be proud of having. He had made his mark.

Guy attended high school, graduating at the age of 15. By the time he had graduated, he had near native fluency in Spanish, French, Italian, Portuguese, and Romanian. He had also earned a bachelor's degree in history. He felt that if he didn't understand the past and didn't learn from it, and that if others didn't understand or learn, our society would be doomed to make the same mistakes over and over again.

He knew his theory to be true in all his observations of life around him, life in the media, and life portrayed in the arts. He loved "Groundhog Day" for its depiction, though comical, of the simple illustration of his theory. Guy also wasn't conceited enough to think that his theory was his alone, but it was easier than researching to see who had first come up with the premise. But the movie (and all the other movies that were similar to it) made sense; was logical; and supported Guy's theory of history being a repetitive state if we don't see the patterns that emerge and course correct to affect a different outcome.

Having the opportunity to course correct was where Guy felt that he could be of service to his friends and family. He found, however, that his people like to plod along, and maybe they would happen unintentionally into a course correction, and then there were all the occasions that ended in exactly the most predictable outcome because of the pattern that the outcome always followed—which frustrated Guy to no end because things didn't HAVE to end that way.

Mrs. Brown was the parent chosen to explain reproduction and sex to Guy. She was very clinical about it but explained everything very thoroughly.

"Honey, once a penis is inserted into a female, or even once there is semen on the head of the penis, there are live sperm on the scene. Once there are live sperm in the vicinity of a vagina, you open the door to pregnancy."

"Like without penetration?" Guy asked. "What if the man pulls out before he ejaculates? Can the woman still get pregnant?"

"Ah," Mrs. Brown said. "A woman can become pregnant without penetration, but it's much more difficult. And the second part of your question is a good description of the 'pull and pray' method." Mrs. Brown thought for a moment, clicking her tongue on the roof of her mouth a few times. "You know your cousin Sally? Uncle Frank and Aunt Jen were using the pull and pray method, and BAM! There's Sally 9 months later. It doesn't matter how unlikely you think the chances are. And guess what? You're not special. Things like this happen to everyone, even my sister."

Guy's mind spun from the revelation. He asked Mrs. Brown timidly, "Uh, so, uh, condoms?"

Mrs. Brown smiled wearily, patting Guy's hand, "Condoms aren't 100%--only abstinence is 100% as long as no semen gets anywhere close to a vagina—but condoms are fairly reliable."

"And knowing all of this, people still do the pull and pray method?"

"Yes, Honey, they do," Mrs. Brown stated plainly.

That afternoon, Mrs. Brown received a baby shower invitation honoring her niece, Sally. Mrs. Brown knew on good authority from her sister Jen that Sally, too, relied on the pull and pray method. Mrs. Brown had no idea why Sally would think that she would be special enough to have a different outcome, knowing that she was conceived in the same way.

Guy had a happy childhood and adolescence, and he managed to graduate from high school unscathed by the angst of youth. During graduation summer, Guy turned 16, and he and his friends were playing touch football in the yard. Even though touch football isn't supposed to have tackling, people do manage to fall down, and then other people manage to fall on one another. Guy fell after a fairly clumsy touch or shove, and he hit the ground hard. He saw stars after hitting the ground.

He knew his head had hit something or maybe just the earth itself. He was pondering this right before everything went black.

When Guy awoke, he was in a hospital bed, and there were bandages affixed to the side of his head that had borne the brunt of his fall. His parents were sitting in the chairs in his room: his father reading a magazine, and his mother knitting. She looked up as Guy began to stir.

"Honey. You're in the hospital. I'm so happy you're awake. Your father is going to get the doctor. She will be able to discuss the injuries you've sustained."

Guy tried to nod, but his head throbbed, and he couldn't hear much of anything through all the bandages on his head. He closed his eyes again, then felt a nudge after what seemed like a few seconds. When he opened his eyes, the doctor stood in front of him, and she had a spiral bound notebook-type thing with her.

"Oh, good. You're awake," she said. "I'm Dr. Lake. Don't worry about talking or nodding. I'm going to show you some pictures to explain what has happened to you. I'm also going to stay on your good side."

Guy was confused about the "good side." He knew that one side was better than the other because of all the bandages. There had to be several inches of bandages covering his bad side because he couldn't hear anything through all the padding.

Dr. Lake set down her display on the tray table, and placed Guy's hand on the side of his head where he felt like his head was covered. All he felt was a bit of gauze under and surrounding the ear. He had been mistaken. The covering was thin, not a thing like what he expected. He knew that whatever Dr. Lake had to say, he wasn't going to like it.

Dr. Lake began, "You were playing football with friends. You fell and hit your head pretty hard, quickly losing consciousness. One of your friends ran into the house to tell your mom what had happened, and your mom contacted emergency services. The ambulance brought you here.

While you were unconscious, we ran plenty of tests and performed imaging, and then we waited for you to wake up."

Dr. Lake took her spiral display that was some kind of flip chart of the ear. "You have sustained a brain injury. There has been substantial damage to your inner ear. Luckily, your hearing is fine on one side. Unfortunately, you aren't going to be able to hear anything on your left side. The damage there is permanent." She pointed to the different structures in his ear, and described the damage that was found in the imaging studies that had been performed. "You may think you hear buzzing or ringing, and you may think that your hearing is coming back, but it's not. Your brain is attempting to make sense of the change in the inputs and creates static or noise, but you're not hearing actual noise, and you're not going to be able to hear actual noise on your left side."

Dr. Lake paused, allowing Guy and his parents to absorb everything she had said, and the room remained silent for the better part of a minute.

"I'm sorry," Dr. Lake said when she noticed that tears were rolling down Guy's cheeks. "You have some options to consider, though. You can choose to do nothing; you can choose to try out a hearing aid; you can opt for a cochlear implant…"

Dr. Lake spent the next 30 minutes explaining the pros and cons of each alternative. "There's no rush for you to decide on what you want to do going forward. This is a big decision, and you need to consider what will be best for you, not to mention that this injury itself is going to take some time to get over. You might want to talk to a counselor while you deal with the grief of losing part of your hearing, because there will be grief."

Ultimately, Guy chose to see a counselor, and he chose to have a cochlear implant. He also chose to defer school by one semester to allow himself time to get used to living with the cochlear implant. But processing his grief was where the bulk of his time was spent.

He knew that he could overcome losing his hearing, just as he had overcome being the youngest and smallest child in school. He had excellent coping skills, but it still seemed unfair. He developed some bitterness at the unfairness of his injury and plight, and the bitterness festered after some time. In retrospect, not only was there grief, but there was also significant depression that went untreated, which exacerbated the festering bitterness. Mr. and Mrs. Brown noted the change in the disposition of their once sunny Guy, their Guy who faced obstacles and conquered them.

Life went on, though. Guy slowly came back to himself, although more negative and jaded about the world around him. He knew that he was fortunate not to have sustained an even worse injury. His academic plans were postponed by only four months, and then he would be right back on track.

He would leave home and attend an Ivy League school in January, at the age of 16. He might be slightly unusual, given his age, but he wouldn't be the only 16-year-old matriculating. He would be more noticeably different, though, with the cochlear implant wires sticking out of his head. Guy resolved not to make a big deal about it and to have a 15-second explanation, and maybe a joke about Frankenstein to put people more at ease. Deep down, though, he resented having to put a spin on this shitty thing that had happened to him.

By the one-year anniversary of the accident, Guy had made a list of platitudes and questions he didn't want to hear:

1. I am so sorry that happened to you.
2. You are so lucky that it only affected the hearing in one ear.
3. What does that thing feel like on your head?
4. Can you shower with that thing on your head?
5. Do you know who knocked you down? Are you going to go after him/her?
6. Do you know ASL? Can you read lips?

7. Is that a hearing aid?
8. My grandparents have hearing aids, too.
9. How did you know anything was wrong?
10. How long have you been deaf?
11. You're lucky to be alive.
12. You should be grateful that your injury wasn't worse.
13. My (insert friend or family member) had the same thing. Do you want the name of his/her doctor?

The list wasn't that long, but there were variations on the themes, and if he added those to his list, it would be seemingly never-ending.

Guy liked being average, and the implant stirred interest and made him less average. One of his buddies, though, loved all things science fiction, and said to Guy one day, "Wouldn't it be cool if we could tinker with the wiring on your implant and turn it into a long-range listening device or even a transmitter to a recording device? Think of what you could achieve just by getting lectures recorded. We hire a transcriptionist, and then we sell the lecture transcripts. People who don't feel like going to class can just buy the transcripts or even the recordings from us. We could make so much money!"

Turning the lemon into lemonade improved Guy's outlook and seemed to buoy him from his depression, but it couldn't dislodge the festering seed that had been planted the day of the touch football game that had changed his life.

CHAPTER 31
Guy – *the college years*

The day of the football game jarred something loose in Guy's brain. He was likely concussed, but there may have also been a traumatic brain injury of some kind. He was never truly the same after that day. He was mostly affable to his family, sometimes irritable, and on occasion full of rage and some rare violence. The violence was shocking because he had been a very peaceful and non-aggressive child, adolescent, and teen.

Guy resented starting college a semester late. He felt that he had missed out on critical bonding with the other students in his class and that it would be impossible to forge the relationships that had already been carefully laid down like train tracks and railroad ties. He worried he wouldn't find a way to fit. His roommate was a sophomore whose previous roommate had either withdrawn from school or requested a new roommate assignment. The kid, Siggy, kept to himself, smelled of feet as did most of his belongings and his side of the room. Siggy was into sci-fi, fantasy, D & D, and was a future prepper. He was worried about nuclear holocaust, zombie apocalypse, global pandemic, a military or dictatorial state. He had begun drafting a design for a bunker or biome or some crazy farm where he could flee and remain perfectly self-sustained and under the radar of the government, military, the infirm, or the undead.

Because of his sheer terror, Siggy was focused on finding a like-minded female that he could tolerate for extended periods of time who would also tolerate Siggy and, in turn, be a suitable partner for continuing the existence of humankind in the event of a global extinction event or something. Guy was more concerned that Siggy would need to find a girl who didn't mind the smell of feet.

As strange as Siggy was, he was surprisingly good-looking and didn't seem to hurt for female company. However, because of his extremist leanings, he had very few second dates, and after three semesters struggling to find a companion, he had withdrawn and had become more introspective, and his mind had turned into something resembling the inside of a laundry dryer, tumbling thoughts and ideologies like garments, endlessly. Siggy's parents pulled him out of school in the middle of the semester, leaving Guy alone for the remainder of the school year.

Guy then occupied the whole room, and on some of the quieter, lonelier nights, there was a ghost of the aroma of Siggy's feet. Guy, however, determined that he would be notable and memorable not only to his professors, but to the other students who lived in his dorm. Under Siggy's old bed, Guy installed a UV light and cultivated cannabis. He was quickly known, liked, and regularly included in the best social activities on campus. Guy could have grown oregano or basil for all the other students knew. The main cachet came from the UV light. Guy knew something wasn't right with his brain, perhaps a late effect of the concussion, and for that reason, he decided not to drink alcohol or take drugs.

At the end of the term, Guy had to decide if he would go home for the summer or stay on campus and take classes through the summer. Guy had a unique opportunity. He could split part of the summer working on a master's degree in history, and part of the summer pursuing a business degree. Guy didn't feel like subjecting his family to his terrible mood swings and his fits of anger and felt it best for everyone if he stayed at school. He knew his mother would be relieved, recalling the look of true fear on her face after he had punched a hole in the wall. He had seemed unprovoked, maybe slightly miffed that his preferred breakfast cereal wasn't even going to fill his cereal bowl one morning. She had been taken so off-guard that she couldn't react. Guy seemed to collect himself, looked at the hole with a quizzical look on his face.

Guy decided not to go home for any of the summers he was in college. He focused on finishing his master's in history at the end of his freshman year, completing his business degree in the middle of his sophomore year, and earning an MBA by the end of the second semester of his junior year. He could graduate from his Ivy League college at 19 but thought it might not be terribly difficult to stay an extra year to pursue a degree in psychology, graduating at 20. He felt psychology would help him better understand himself but would also help him unlock the psyches of the people around him. When Guy sat down with his advisor, a mousy and elderly little woman who eyed Guy with the gaze of a hawk, he felt she could see right through him, and that's why he chose her as his advisor. The people who actually *saw* Guy were so rare that when he found one, he clutched them to himself incredibly tightly.

Guy's advisor informed him that because there was a good amount of overlap between his history classes, high school AP classes, and business classes that he only needed two or three classes to finish a degree in psychology between summer school and the first semester of his senior year. If he focused during the second semester of his senior year and appealed to the psychology department, his courseload could be concentrated on psychology and be approved for one or two additional classes, complete the qualifying exams, and work on a dissertation through the spring. He would graduate, and then finish his PhD during the summer or fall afterward, with the worst-case scenario being completion in the spring. The official tally after Guy stayed four and a half to five years, was the previously earned bachelor's in history, a master's in history, BBA and MBA, and a PhD in psychology. Guy pushed the limits to obtain the PhD. He approached his psychology studies with a feverish intensity that his professors had not seen before. He worked exhaustively on his dissertation, and his friends, family, and faculty were impressed and shocked by his productivity, and the deep thoughtfulness that had gone into Guy's doctoral dissertation. It wasn't just hurried, it was good work, and some of his readers and his doctoral advisor thought there were groundbreaking theories being tested and validated. Some of the readers of Guy's book said his thoughts, theories, tests, and conclusions gave them chills.

Upon graduation, Guy had received numerous offers from various employers, and he wrote them on slips of paper, taping them to chess pieces that he felt corresponded to the jobs or the employers. He put everything on his chess board, working through chess-playing strategies to determine which company and job would springboard his career, which he could leverage into a checkmate. He knew that he wanted to be the best at whatever he did vocationally, and he felt strongly that the world owed him respect for all he had done in his incredibly young life. One of the shortcomings throughout the period following Guy's injury was in his not having some kind of therapy to help him process his feelings and his anger and further assessment of the possibility of a traumatic brain injury.

During Guy's final year in his Ivy League college, he met a girl, a nice girl. She came from the Midwest, was brilliant, unassuming, and pretty in an understated way. Virginia was her name. She studied astrophysics. In the warm months, she and Guy would lie side by side on the roof of her dorm, and they would hold hands, make plans for the future—their future—and look for signs and meaning in the cosmos. Guy brought Virginia home to meet Mr. and Mrs. Brown, Jane, John, and Mike. Virginia brought Guy home to meet her family, and he found them to be suitable replacements for any sitcom family, but he loved Virginia—he thought he did anyway. He would do anything for Virginia.

Guy and Virginia had sex for the first time on Virginia's twenty-first birthday; Guy would turn twenty-one the following year. They used the 'pull and pray' method, and Virginia became pregnant. Guy and Virginia did not want to be parents at twenty and twenty-one, but they stayed the course and were married. Guy's job paid enough for Virginia to get her doctorate in astrophysics or stay home with the baby or whatever it was she wanted to do with her life. At sixteen weeks, there was no fetal heartbeat. Labor was induced and a baby girl was delivered to her young, distraught, and devastated parents, while their own parents waited just outside the room, mired in thick and twisted grief.

Guy took a week off work to stay by Virginia's side. They saw a grief counselor, a couple's counselor, and individual counselors. They spoke with their parents multiple times daily, because if there was one thing that Guy knew as someone with a PhD in psychology, it was imperative to give voice to and process their feelings. Virginia suffered grief and postpartum depression. Each morning, she awoke, and lifting her head from the pillow was almost too much effort for her to muster. Eventually, with the help of the pharmaceutical industry (and counseling), the tethers between Virginia's head and her pillow began to wear away.

After coming through the mental fog of loss during the better part of the following year, what Guy and Virginia discovered was the fact they were ready to start a family. They knew they were young parents, but they could provide a loving, if not woefully over-educated, home. Virginia began working toward her doctorate. Guy worked in strategy in the Fortune 100 company, his top choice from his chess exercise. He wanted to be Chief Strategy Officer by the time he turned thirty. Virginia and Guy decided to let the chips fall where they may as it related to family planning, but they would try in earnest for a baby again when Virginia finished her PhD.

CHAPTER 32
Guy's twenties

Guy and Virginia Brown settled into their twenties: he, putting in 75-80 hours per week as he climbed the ladder toward his goal of Chief Strategy Officer; and she, putting in 75-80 hours per week immersed in astrophysics. In the early years of their marriage, several things happened. Guy had a final growth spurt, topping out at an even six feet. He also filled out, and as his height and weight crept up, he began working out. He had always been a cute, adorable fellow, but he became handsome. The charisma that carried him through childhood had never deserted him, and people were drawn to him. Likewise, the subtly pretty Midwestern Virginia grew into her looks. Guy and Virginia were a beautiful and striking couple. The attention they received in response to their exceeding good looks was new. They saw each other little because of their goal-driven ambition.

Virginia kept a change of clothes in her lab. She kept a blanket and pillow in her car. Guy kept several changes of clothes in an apartment he rented close to his office. He also kept a mistress or two there from time to time. After a bit, Virginia kept clothes in a spare bedroom in the home of one of the physics professors' homes. The professor, young, good-looking, not overly charismatic or personable, drew Virginia to him like a tractor beam. They had met in the faculty dining room and began an ongoing dialogue about Russian literature and music. And still, Virginia and Guy felt the magnetism that had drawn them together initially when their paths converged, but the times of convergence grew farther and farther apart.

One weekend when they were both home at the same time, they came to the realization that more of their clothes were stored in other locations than in their own closets. Virginia didn't have underwear to change into. Guy had no gym socks. They ran the dishwasher once every two weeks or so. Their refrigerator, at one time stocked with fresh fruits, vegetables, meats, and cheeses, housed a half-drunk bottle of Riesling, some condiments, and some moldy Havarti.

They decided to have sex one last time, being sure to use a condom, and then came to the conclusion that their marriage was over.

Guy and Virginia sold their house. Their parting was simple and amicable, and they continued to hold one another in highest esteem. The timing of their union was unfortunate, and maybe in a different timeline, things could have worked out for them. They left the door to their relationship open. From time to time, Virginia and Guy would meet for dinner, ending the evening by falling into bed together, not even pretending to bother themselves with birth control.

Guy's apartment had become his only residence, and with its proximity to work, and without the need to lay pretense to his marriage, his focus on work was of laser precision. At work, Guy was often called Dr. Brown by those junior to him in rank—everyone of his rank was older, and most in the several rungs below him were older, too. Guy continued to enjoy his easy charisma, and he could often be heard in the boardroom saying, "Please. Just call me Guy." But secretly, he loved the doctor title.

His climb to Chief Strategy Officer wasn't a completely smooth climb. Guy wasn't the only one who wanted the role. The others vying for a chance at the job had much more experience under their belts. They had lived life longer and been smarted from life's lessons, which could have been viewed as advantageous. Guy refused to be ground down by his youth, though. He felt that given any set of circumstances, he could accurately predict outcomes based on the behaviors of the players. Because of this ability, he was a very keen strategist. He understood people and had always understood people. He was an invaluable ally and asset to his company. Guy's CEO and COO felt that losing Guy would be a tragic loss to the company. He held nearly Rasputin-like status in the C-suite.

Guy kept a mental list of the people and other associated nouns having thrown obstacles in his path. Once he reached his goal, he had no intention of loosening his grip on his position, unless there was something bigger and better he wanted, and besides his goal, he didn't have enough interests to tape onto his chess pieces to gauge how each would fare in his daily life.

There had been a peer at a conference who had attempted to make Guy look ignorant of some tax law or other. Guy set the man right, but he also noted the man's name. When the man checked out of the hotel at the end of the conference, he was astonished to find an additional $450 charged to his corporate credit card for adult movies on demand. This man would have to do cleanup with the hotel to get the bill straightened out, then at work with HR or his boss to explain that someone was out to get him or there was some computer glitch or something crazy, who knows, because why would he ever watch porn and pay for it with his corporate credit card?

There had been a woman Guy had met in a bar who worked for a rival, but she, too, was in strategy. Guy knew her by reputation prior to meeting her. He was jealous, and his plan was to wine and dine her, then hate fuck her, and leave her wondering what she had done wrong. His plan was completely de-railed, though, when, upon meeting in person, she was lovely and admired him and his mind. She invited him to play Settlers of Catan with a group of her friends. He obliged. Another time, she invited him to play Risk with a group of her friends. Again, he obliged. Before long, they were dating, sleeping together, playing games of strategy, and, it turned out, she held a grudge just like Guy did. They would fantasize orchestrating corporate takeovers, besmirching reputations, acting as puppeteers of the destruction of careers and elevating themselves to the highest echelons of their respective companies.

They agreed they would put to rest any rivalry between their two companies. It was pointless since they were so completely compatible and so like-minded.

They decided to go to Australia for vacation. It was a long flight, and they did their best to assimilate to the local time upon arrival. They did some shopping and sightseeing, and then went to bed, completely exhausted. In the morning, Guy was the only one of the pair who woke. His darling, his scheming paramour had died in the night from a blood clot that had lodged in her heart.

Guy was devastated. There would be no one who could replace her. He and his grief returned to the States, and Guy threw himself into work with a fervor that could not go unnoticed.

His strategy sessions, large, small, and individual were legendary around the office. Everyone from Senior Manager and higher wanted to have an opportunity to participate in or observe one of Guy's meetings or workshops. The company was leaping past competitors at breakneck speed, and people in the industry took notice. Recruiters and CEOs from other companies routinely contacted Guy for lunch here, drinks there, golf, tennis, conferences, concerts, etc. Everyone wanted Guy. He was the most popular girl at the school dance, so to speak.

By the time Guy was 25, he was named Chief Strategy Officer. He was given a choice between Chief Innovation Officer and Chief Strategy Officer. He had a homing beacon set on strategy, and there was no way he was going to pass up strategy for innovation. After accepting the promotion, Guy was in a small funk. What was his next role? He decided to hold his own strategy session to plot a course for his career. His methods hadn't failed him yet, and he knew the only counsel he could trust implicitly was his own.

Guy made the decision that he would master the psychology of business, strategy, and business strategy. He also decided that he would document the archetypes of the characters with whom he worked in his company, vendors, and in rival companies. He wanted to pick off the contenders who crossed him or might cross him, or he wanted to learn to build leverage against these people. He created his own mental system of lockboxes. Each lockbox held a profile, then a listing of how the individual would react in any given situation, and how Guy and his charisma could win or tank the person, and what would the outcome be based on the various situations. He lined up all the archetypes like little soldiers and subbed them in and out in the chess game he played in his mind.

There was one deterrent to Guy's plans, however. It originated from a phone call from Virginia. When Virginia and Guy saw each other, it was a comfort of sorts, like the corduroy slippers he wore as a child.

She and Guy had met for dinner and sex around six weeks previously, for Guy's twenty-sixth birthday. Guy, always happy to hear from his ex-wife, was surprised by the call. This call was premature, off-cycle for them; they would typically get together every three or four months, and it was like corduroy slippers every time. She, Guy surmised, was calling for a reason.

"Guy," Virginia began. "I have some news for you. I think you will probably be pleased to know this, too. Think of it as a belated birthday present." She took a deep breath and blew it out. He could hear her clearly over the phone, which meant she had something big to share. Not much rattled Virginia, and Guy prickled with the excitement of what Virginia was about to tell him. "I am expecting, and it is your baby. It is early days, and you know what we went through before, but I am already seeing a high-risk obstetric specialist. I am not taking any chances this time around."

Guy, already surprised by the call, was now completely beside himself with this news. "Uh, wow, Virginia. Congratulations! What does the professor think? Is he going to be the baby's father? How do you see me fitting into all of this?"

"He knows it's your baby. He had a vasectomy after he received tenure. The two of you are the only men I see; thus it has to be your baby. He is happy to be a father figure, since we do live together, but he also wants to provide as much space as you would want to be a father to our child. He understands and respects whatever role you want to have. You can be as hands on or off as you wish." Guy could hear Virginia chewing on something, and he would bet his last paycheck that it was carrot sticks dipped in French onion dip. Besides Virginia's snacking, there was momentary silence between them.

"I would like to go to your doctor appointments with you. I would like to be there for the baby's birth. You get to choose what last name the baby has. I would like to be involved and be a true, hands on father to this child. It would mean the world to me." Guy wiped away a tear.

"It's crazy, isn't it?" Virginia asked. "We tried and tried after the first time, and nothing happened. Then when we weren't trying but were just sloppy, here we are." She paused a moment. "I don't want to get married again. Do you?"

Guy hadn't given any thought to the prospect, but he felt his relationship with Virginia worked well the way it was currently, and her relationship with the physics professor seemed to be a good fit for her, and he didn't see the point of turning her life upside down any more than necessary, especially because a baby would create an entirely new apple cart in just eight or nine months. He felt an all-pervasive, complete love for this child, and he told Virginia he would be a father to their child that she could trust and feel proud of for their little one.

When the baby was born, it was a boy, and Guy and Virginia named him Harris. He was average in his height and weight. He arrived on his due date. Throughout the first year of life, he hit each milestone at the time the average baby did (as described in all the parenting books). Guy put together a beautiful nursery in his apartment, purchased books, toys, all the things a baby could possibly want or need. Right around his first birthday, Harris began walking, and his babbling had been sounding a lot like words. Virginia called Guy to tell him Harris's first words were 'bye-bye.' Until Virginia finished nursing Harris, Guy would keep the baby on the weekends, and he loved every single thing about being a father, and it didn't hamper his work life or his pursuit of female company.

Harris filled a void in Guy's life, a void Guy didn't realize even existed. Guy wondered about love and how it could be defined or quantified. At one time, he thought he loved Virginia, but this feeling he had for Harris eclipsed everything he ever felt for his former wife. Each time he swung his son up onto his hip, or grabbed his hand, or attended a program at the Montessori school Harris attended a few days each week, he felt something all-consuming he had never experienced in his life. Guy chalked up the feeling and emotions to love, the truest, purest form of love there could be, the love parents have for their children. With certainty, Guy knew that he would throw himself in front of any threat to his child and would focus lethal force on anything that threatened his relationship with his son.

As his twenties came to a close, Guy, the committed father of a four year-old and self-avowed ambition-obsessed workaholic learned about Diamond Teams. He had strategized the hell out of his work and personal lives. He had even helped create another human, He had reached a potential in nearly all the corners of his life that he had not imagined possible. He wondered if he could out-strategize Diamond Teams. Seeing as how he had created a life, he wondered if he could actually accomplish an undetectable murder. Probably not, but he wondered if he could engineer a situation where he could totally get away with it and be an undetectable perpetrator. That could be interesting. Guy began lining up the playing pieces for a new game.

CHAPTER 33
The Diamond Teams Staff Meeting:
Post-GBrown Incident – excerpts
7 months and 3 ½ weeks ago

Chris: It looks like everyone has logged on to a secure line, and we are all accounted for companywide.

Sam: Thanks, Chris. I'm going to take it from here. I trust everyone has had an opportunity to view the whiteboard to see today's agenda. Also, I trust that no one will be taking notes from today's meeting and that no one will be recording the meeting independently. Remember, you are all very valued and trusted employees of Diamond Teams, and we have all signed a whole bunch of legal documents that promise we won't do anything like that.

Brief pause, some low chuckling

Sam: We're not going to beat around the bush here. We had a client who went off the deep end and had planned to terminate his target himself. To give you some background, he sustained a head injury as a teenager that rendered him deaf in his left ear. He has had a cochlear implant since shortly thereafter. At some point, he has had the opportunity to engineer the implant to work as a device that not only restores his hearing but also acts as a bug that transmits to a receiver for recording and transcription with storage to the cloud or other terminal devices.

Diamond Teams female employee (unidentified): I was the client's project liaison. Something felt off to me, and while we were surveilling the target, I requested that his hotel room be swept for recording equipment, laptops, and so on. While all this was going on, we were nearing the final stages of his project, and I noticed that he had become increasingly focused on his target—but not in the way that we usually see our clients focus on their end objectives. What I also observed was that the target had started to notice the client. He had become sloppy in his surveillance. It seemed like he wanted to be seen, like he wanted her to be frightened.

Chris: The target did alert the police, who very quietly sent a sketch artist to her place of work, and a sketch was rendered—a very good and accurate depiction of our client. We interrupted and terminated the project. We have had to assume the escrow fees to work with the authorities to clear up any misunderstandings and to request their intervention with the target to allay any and all fears.

Multiple voices rumbling in the background.

Chris: We brought the client in, and he became angry and threatened violence and revenge against Kate, primarily, since she was the person to confront the client about his behavior. Bruce and Clark subdued the client and were witnesses to the termination proceedings, and they can corroborate and provide any color to what I'm reporting.

Bruce: Hey, everyone. This is Bruce. We did have to administer a light sedative to incapacitate the client to bring him to the meeting site. We also duct-taped his hands to his chair because we really couldn't gauge the level of anger or violence he would display. In our training, we are all very good at assessing our clients' emotional and mental states throughout their projects, but we had not encountered anything like Guy Brown. Clark and I wrote incident reports following what we had thought would be the closeout of the project, and we both recommended ongoing monitoring of Kate, Mr. Brown's liaison, Kate's family, and Bruce, and me, and our families. We have also monitored Sam and Chris' family, too—to cover our bases. Wesley, Cleveland, Angel, and Shannon have alternated coverage, and we have been monitoring credit reports on both the internet and the dark web.

Cleveland: We finally had a hit about a month ago on the dark web that Kate's identity, though buried for the past 20-some years, had been accessed. At that point, we notified Chris, Sam, and Kate. We are going to open up the floor to discuss some of your thoughts about proceeding. Before we do that, though, we're going to need about an hour of your time. You are going to be able to view the video of the termination meeting with Guy Brown. After you have finished the video, we are going to put everyone into moderated chat rooms to discuss the video, your thoughts, feelings, insights, and ideas for how we move forward. We have some ideas already, however, we wouldn't be Diamond Teams if we weren't tapping into the best and brightest minds in strategy.

Throat clearing.

Shannon: I would like everyone to bear in mind that Guy Brown is a chess player. He plays to win, and he plays to lose. When he plays to lose, he watches his opponents and their methods for success. We have not found Guy Brown to be a player of Go. We have also observed that he does not use a Go-based strategy method, which we found interesting since he is the Chief Strategy Officer for his employer, and they are known for their aggressive and innovative strategies in the marketplace and in their operations.

CHAPTER 34
The Diamond Teams Staff Meeting 2:
Post-GBrown Incident – excerpts
7 months and 3 weeks ago

Sam: Thank you everyone for taking the time to meet again. One of the things that we pride ourselves on at Diamond Teams is our ability to observe, plan, plan for any pivoting that needs to occur, and take action or non-action. We pride ourselves on having the best of the best minds in our employ, and you do not disappoint.

Kate: Selfishly, I am so grateful for all of your ideas, and we have held a number of smaller meetings with chat room groups because you each followed the Guy Brown thread in many of the same ways, but you all came back with different ways of addressing and resolving the situation. Each group addressed a different potential reaction and pathway that Guy Brown might pursue based on his threats and based on what we have from all of his screening materials and personality analyses. I think we have all assumed that he never planned to abide by any of the covenants in any of our client agreements. You have all also had the benefit of reviewing his psychological assessments, which may be invalid. Guy Brown is a PhD in psychology, and he would be skilled in invalidating any of our testing. All that said, I am adding an outside guest to this meeting. This is something we have NEVER done before, but I am personally vouching for this person and have vetted him thoroughly over the last twenty-plus years. I'd like to introduce you to my husband, Kevin.

Kevin: Hi, all. I'm sure this is weird for you to be speaking with a co-worker's family member. I'm only here to provide you with some color and to talk about Guy Brown as I know him. As you already know, Guy is the Chief Strategy Officer for his employer. He and I and a handful of people you probably already know as Diamond Teams' clients have been running in the same professional circles for a number of years. We wind up at the same conferences and professional development retreats and other meetings. At a meeting a few months ago, Guy brought up the idea of revenge and exacting the perfect revenge. It is for this reason that Kate and I have serious concern for each other and our families. We are also concerned for any of you who had face-to-face interaction with Guy Brown as well as your families. Guy has resources to uncover everyone's names, addresses, and family members. If you haven't brushed up on self-defense lately, it might be a good idea to hit your dojo, gym, or whatever self-defense you espouse. It would be good to equip your loved ones accordingly, too.

Kevin takes a long drink of water and clears his throat.

Kevin: I will tell you what Kate has been telling our family for years, and it seems to have sufficed up until this point. She has projects that require government clearance, and some of the projects have some inherent risk. At this time, there is an increased threat level that may require you and your families to exercise enhanced vigilance. This is what we are sharing with our children who are in college. We have advised them to be aware of anyone new who enters their lives, and we have cautioned them from being alone with these people or allowing themselves to be under the influence of drugs or alcohol while we are currently addressing this risk/threat. If something seems too good to be true, it is. Mistrust everything until told otherwise by us, and only us. Also, come up with a pass phrase and a non-sequitur answer for your pass phrase that only you and your family know. Do NOT share it outside your family unit or whatever your primary circle of trust looks like. On another note, Guy is charismatic, good looking, likeable, and incredibly broken on the inside. If you ran into him on the street, he is someone you want to grab a beer with or go with to a ballgame. But he might cut your throat on the way to your car.

Kate: Based on the discussions from the breakout chat rooms from the previous staff meeting, we are going to embark on three separate exercises. Each of you will be assigned accordingly to one. The sessions have already been planned to the most minuscule detail, and they will be happening over the next two weeks. Clear your calendars. We will handle everything related to Diamond Teams' business and scheduling.

CHAPTER 35
Work Group 1 – Moderated by Wesley
7 ½ months ago

Wesley and his work group met in person in Billings, Montana for a long weekend. They were staying in a small farmhouse, and everyone brought sleeping bags. They had no internet, no technology, not even a television. They were, for all intents and purposes, off the grid. Wesley brought steno pads and pens for everyone. He joked that it was like 1986. They would cap off the weekend with a bonfire to destroy all of their pads and enjoy some s'mores and work stories. Until this blip, they had no worries related to their work. If there was one thing about this situation, though, it was looking at their work from an opposing lens. Diamond Teams had become the target.

Unlike Kate and Sam's Assassin game from high school, the target and assassin knew who one another were and could prepare. They could anticipate the strikes, and because the stakes were different, vanity for one and self, family, or vocational-preservation for others, there were layers and options for prepping.

Wesley began the weekend with teaching everyone to play Go. Wesley had played since middle school and had become a skilled player. Eventually everyone would play Wesley. They all started with small boards, playing against one another, and then worked to the 13 x 13 boards. Whoever played Wesley first would also play Wesley last, for the sake of fairness. They played chess, Risk, Settlers of Catan, Oregon Trail, Ravine, Root, and Mafia.

On day 2, over breakfast, Wesley asked the question, "When we chatted during our online meetings, we said that Guy Brown's revenge would be destroying Diamond Teams—the company itself--and Kate's professional reputation." Wesley looked around the room, making eye contact with everyone. "Are we still on board with that? Our group was the only group that wanted to tackle the company and rep angle."

The group eyed one taking ginger hits off their mugs of coffee, and their heads bobbed in agreement. One of the men in the group said, "At the first hint of him issuing a press release or recommending someone to Diamond Teams, or even anyone coming to Diamond Teams who would even know Guy Brown peripherally, we systematically unhinge him from his workplace, which seems to be the love of his life."

Shannon, who had monitored Guy over the previous several months, said, "We know everyone he has slept with, had breakfast, lunch, or dinner with, taken a meeting with, sent a Valentine to in 4th grade. We have a database of all the major and minor players in his universe. If he gets any hits from anyone like that we will see them coming. What we won't see," Shannon thought out loud, "are the people that he meets illicitly in a club, people he can pay off. We don't know if he's going into a back room at his dry cleaner's to hire a hitter or some kind of mob lawyer or corporate spy or whatever. We know when he gets his car washed, but we don't know who he talks to in the tiny office inside while he waits on his car. We don't know if he's leaving something on the front seat of his car, or if he's picking up something in his car when he retrieves it." Shannon paused before adding, "We are going to have to tighten up screening new clients to ensure that they haven't been in any city where Guy has been since the incident."

Wesley asked the group, "So, how do we fuck Guy Brown? Do we make an offensive strike or wait for him to engage?"

Someone asked, "Can we launch a series of baby offensives that don't point to Diamond Teams? We've done enough research into his professional life to know all the heads he has stomped on in his path to Chief Strategy Officer. There are bound to be stories, truths, and proof to pull back the figurative curtain. It would take maybe 5-7 blows to knock him back a bit, maybe give him some kind of humility. It would force him to take his focus off his revenge and pay attention to getting his own house in order."

Wesley responded, "Great start. Let's make sure that we provide that as one of our solutions and come back to it for consideration when we have more. My question would be, though, since you all saw the video, and we all saw his threats and his explosive anger: after Guy gets his house in order from the smaller, more non-Diamond Teams-oriented offensives, would he return his focus to Diamond Teams? Would he connect the dots on these smaller offensives and tie it all back to Diamond Teams? Would he suspect Diamond Teams after the first offensive? If any of those possibilities entered his mind, then what would be our next move, and was the first move our best move? I like the anonymity angle, but I can't bank on the level of his paranoia or lack of paranoia."

Wesley produced a canvas tote bag. He lined up index cards in seven colors, set out markers, dice, spinners, several boards with grids, some white boards, and Candy Land and Chutes and Ladders boards. "Build the game. There's a character. Let's call him 'Guy.' He's like the minotaur. He's moving around trying to get to his reward. There's a mountain or something, and at the top or at the end of the trail or whatever, there's Diamond Teams, or Kate, or all of us, and she's tied to railroad tracks, or maybe there's lava coursing down a mountain, or dynamite about to set off an avalanche that will kill us all…whatever. At any rate, the minotaur's reward is Diamond Teams or Kate or all of our demise. We've spent the better part of the last twenty-four hours playing games of logic and strategic thinking. We've been calculating risk as we went along to try to beat our opponents. Devise the game to keep Guy, the minotaur, from reaching his reward."

Like a game show host, Wesley swept his arm toward all the supplies he had laid out. "Pair up, or grab whoever you think you need to pull together a game that shuts that weaselly little shit down." Wesley rubbed his hand down his face. "I'm sorry, everyone. Guy Brown gets my dander up, and I love my job and this company too much to let him turn my world, all of our worlds, upside down."

And so it went. Games were devised, played, and everyone rotated through everyone else's games. By nightfall on day two, every game had been played enough that everyone in the room could shut down Guy Brown. After dinner, they celebrated with champagne, then made their way to their sleeping bags, exhausted.

On the final day of the work group meeting, a truck blazed up the drive and Profile Man emerged. Wesley and the group led Profile Man through their games and solutions over lunch. Profile Man shared some insights, nodded, asked questions for clarification, finished a glass of iced tea, shook hands with each member of the team, made prolonged eye contact with Wesley, returned to his truck, and departed as unexpectedly as he had arrived. Wesley turned back to the assembled group, saying, "I think our work here is done. Do whatever you want for the rest of the day, and we'll burn our notebooks tonight. I'll image the games and add them to the fire, too."

CHAPTER 36
Work Group 2 – Moderated by Bruce and Clark
7 ½ months ago

Bruce, Clark, and their work group flew to Berlin, Germany. It was difficult to find somewhere that was a technology-free zone, but they took a van to a campsite just outside the city, offering privacy and a primitive vibe. Everyone in the group was instructed to pack for the weather, along with very severe black clothing. After setting up camp, they cooked on the camp grills. They were under strict orders not to speak to one another until after they returned to camp late that evening. They would be taking the van into Berlin to a warehouse club that featured death metal, industrial metal and rock, and goth rock. They would drink. They would not interact with one another. They would blend with the rest of the clientele. They would feel the anger, the angst, the dissatisfaction with society, the unfairness of life, and the disadvantage to those who had so little to begin with, or those who had plenty to begin with but lacked boundaries, love, and/or a moral compass. They would feel the creeping feeling of preying on weaker souls, leveraging their advantage and spawning it into control and subjugation. At 1:00 a.m., they would make their way back to the van and depart for the campsite. They would shed their black clothes, don sweats, and burn everything they had worn that night.

Once seated around the bonfire, Bruce and Clark opened up the discussion. "How does everyone feel?"

One of the women, a twenty-something redhead said, "I feel a lot of pent up something. I feel cheated that I wasn't there long enough to get something out of my system. I feel like I was short-changed."

One of the men said, "That's funny. I fucked some girl in a bathroom while her boyfriend licked my balls."

One of the other women said, "I knocked a guy out with a beer bottle because he kept bumping into me."

Another person said, "I saw a guy put Rohypnol in someone's drink. I grabbed it and swapped it back with his drink. When I knew he was out of it, I took him to the alley and violated him with a beer bottle. He didn't resist, and from the smile on his face, I could swear he was enjoying himself. Then I stomped on his shirt, hard enough to leave a boot print."

Clark said, "OK. Are these things you would have done at home with your friends if you were going out? What played into your actions? Was it the fact you could get away with what you were doing? Was it anonymity? Was it the venue? The music? The clientele? Being far away? Did you recall a time when you were at someone else's mercy? Was this a form of revenge for you? At the end of the night, what you did…was this satisfying? At the beginning of the night, how did you feel? Did you go in thinking you were at an advantage?"

Bruce passed out steno pads and pens. "We're going to burn everything before we leave. Nothing comes with us. None of your stories come with us. We are looking for solutions, but we need you to be in a certain headspace."

Clark asked, "How many of you were drinking tonight?"

All hands went up.

"Good. How many of you would say that you probably shouldn't operate a motor vehicle at this moment?"

Again, all hands went up.

"Very good. How many of you feel that you could go back out and have a second wind?"

And again, all hands went up.

"Great," Clark said, the cadence of his voice changing, slowing down. "I would like you each to look into the fire and concentrate on the color and heat of the flame. Feel how it's a comfort to you. It feels like home. It feels like snuggling up in a soft down comforter. You are beginning to settle in, and the more you nestle, the hotter you become. You are trying to get out of the comforter, and it has become a binding rope. You are in your kitchen, and there's a man with a knife. He's holding it over an open flame, and you see it turning red, then bright yellow-orange. Your wife, mother, girlfriend, father, husband, boyfriend, son, daughter, dog, are in the room with you. They are all bound and gagged. The man with the knife turns away from the stove. He walks over to you, calmly, with a serene look on his face. He touches the knife to your thumb. It doesn't hurt right away because the metal is so extremely hot and cauterizes right away. After around 30 seconds, a stinging discomfort sets in, and it is little more than an annoyance, and you notice a greyish welt erupting. The man says, 'I'm Guy, Guy Brown. Just testing the knife on you. It doesn't really hurt until it cools just a bit. I'm going to try it next on your mom. Does that sound good? I'm going to make my way around the room and do some sculpting. It's fun for me. Not so fun for all of you.' He turns, facing each person in the room and holding the knife out. 'OK. So…where's mom?'

"Guy approaches your mother, and he removes her gag. She is shaking under her binds, and she is crying, her grimace almost an angry smile. 'Oh, Mother,' says Guy. 'You have a lovely smile, but I think I could make it even prettier.' He closes the distance between your mother's face and the knife, plunging the knife in the lateral edges of her mouth, just a centimeter or two deep. Your mother screams in pain, and behind your gag, you scream in anguish, staring at the elongated smile running from your mother's lips to the apples of her cheeks. The blood drips, and the heat of the blade creates third-degree burns, boiling blisters, and immediate swelling. Guy next approaches your father, suddenly turning his back to face you directly. 'Do you want to know why this is happening?' he asks. You nod your head vigorously.

"'You and your company deceived me. You robbed me. You stripped me of my agency. I don't plan to hurt you. On the contrary. I'm not going to kill you or any of these loved ones. I am going to maim every one of them—but not you. You will watch. You will see the pain in their faces. You will see the boils, blisters, welts, and scars on their skins, arms, legs, faces, backs. I will strip them of their clothing in front of you. They will be humiliated, and I will flog them. I will violate them in the worst way you can imagine. Their suffering will be significant and lasting, and they will never be the same. And you will know this is all your fault. And you will know, that I, Guy Brown, am the architect of all this. Because of what you did to me, I am doing this to you in return, ten-fold.' Guy paces back and forth. 'What I just did to your mom? It's only the beginning of what's going to happen to her.'

"He returns to your father. 'Hi, Dad!' he says with a smile on his face. 'I can help with those worry lines on your forehead. What do you think?'

"Guy sets to work on your father's forehead, and your father passes out from the pain. 'You know what I have always heard about balance? If you amputate the big toe, there's a ton of physical therapy involved, including re-learning to walk. That big toe is really important to your gait.' Guy removes your father's shoes, and he looks like he can't decide which big toe to take. 'I kind of want to take them both. Simple solution.' He bends over your dad's feet, and after a couple of good blows and some swearing when the toes don't come off right away, Guy proudly holds up his work, tossing the severed toes into the kitchen sink.

"'You know, when a man reaches a certain age, he gets up in the night to go to the bathroom several times. They call this benign prostatic hyperplasia, or an enlarged prostate. My former girlfriend liked to stimulate my prostate when we were having sexy time. Do you know how to stimulate the prostate? Usually it's a gloved finger entering the anal opening and pushing in until the prostate is reached. Invasive, yes, but, eventually, it's pleasurable. At least a finger is pleasurable. I didn't bring any surgical gloves, though.' Guy raises his hand in front of his face to hide false embarrassment. 'I brought this bottle brush to see if I could reach dear, old, Dad's prostate. Maybe I can fix it or stimulate it or something. I might even be able to remove it for him. That would be a public service. If he doesn't have a prostate, I reckon he can't get prostate cancer. Or can he?' He nods his head back and forth a bit before saying, 'Ah, who cares. We can just see how things play out.' He loosens the binds on your father's legs and bends your father over. You close your eyes but can't stop hearing the sound of your dad's zipper being pulled.

"Guy stops momentarily and asks, 'Would anyone like to hear the soundtrack?' He removes your dad's gag. Guy proceeds to move in with the bottle brush, and you hear your father's screams. After a bit, there is silence. You moan and writhe in agony. You find yourself crying, sobbing, trying to turn your head away.

"He moves to your significant other, and as he begins to brandish the knife again, I arrive," says Clark. "Everything behind me freezes in place. I am going to unbind everyone's hands and feet and remove your gags. It turns out that everything you just experienced was a movie. You have the ability to re-wind the movie and prevent anything from happening to your loved ones. Find the pad of paper and pen resting on your lap. You can re-write the movie and prevent any harm coming to your loved ones, leaving you with no memory of the old movie. I am going to count back from five. When I reach zero, you may begin writing. The words will flow out of you from a creative place, freely, without any impediment, and everything you write will be your perfect story. Five, four, three, two, one, zero." They picked up their pens and pads and began to write. Clark continued, "When you are finished writing, place your pen and pad back on your lap. I will gently touch your shoulder and lead you to your next destination."

Clark stood to the side of the group while they wrote. The first person finished in twenty-five minutes. Clark gently touched the woman's shoulder and stated, "Close your eyes and take a deep breath. When you open them again, you find yourself nestled in a fluffy white comforter. You are lying across a king-sized bed in a beach resort. The screen door is open, and a gentle breeze blows the sheer white curtains into the room, where they kiss the side of the bed. When you hear a knock at the door and the words, 'Room service,' you will be totally awake and present here at our bonfire refreshed and alert."

When the last person finished writing two hours later, Clark rapped quickly on the back of a notebook and said, "Room service."

Each person would awaken fresh and clear-headed with no memory of the 'movie' and what they had just experienced. Clark and Bruce collected all the steno pads and pens and described the itinerary for the next day.

The group retreated to their tents, and though refreshed, they were ready to call it a day. Bruce and Clark stayed up later, reading through the movie script revisions.

In the redhead's story, Guy Brown couldn't do anything to the knife because there was no gas stove or open flame. The redhead had sat alone in her apartment waiting for Guy, and when he arrived, she took him down, removing the knife from his hand. She then cut his Achilles tendon. Guy couldn't get off the floor. So, she called 9-1-1, saying someone entered her home, and she disarmed her would-be attacker. She also stated that she had subdued the attacker, who would now need an ambulance. The story continued with Guy being sentenced to 35 years in prison.

In one of the other stories, Guy entered the kitchen where the floors had recently been mopped and polished. He slipped and fell, hitting his head on the way down to the floor, never regaining consciousness.

In one of the longer stories, Guy goes skiing the weekend before his planned home invasion. He finds himself cut off by a stronger, faster skier. Guy overcompensates, gains more speed than he can handle, and panics, losing his balance. He finds the easiest thing to do is to fall. The high speed combined with the fall ends with Guy landing wrong and fracturing his femur. The fracture turns out to be a compound break. The Ski Patrol arrives and transports Guy to an ambulance, and then to a small mountain hospital. After two hours of surgery, placement of several screws and a rod, and another hour in recovery, Guy awakens in his hospital room. The doctor tells him that he will experience quite a bit of pain, but the trick is to stay ahead of the pain. Guy is on a morphine drip for today, but he will be switching to oral oxycontin and will be discharged from the hospital with a prescription for oxycontin, however, the oxycontin post-discharge is for use on an as-needed basis. It turns out that Guy needs a lot of oxycontin. His physical therapy is excruciating, and his bones aren't mending as he had been told they would. Guy begs his doctor for an additional month of oxycontin. The doctor relents but tells Guy he's only going to write the prescription for one month, and Guy needs to transition to ibuprofen or something similar to help with pain and inflammation. In a week, Guy has taken all the prescribed oxycontin, which was meant to last a month. He finds a drug dealer who can supply his oxycontin. Guy is sweaty all the time, has dark circles under his eyes, and has become unreliable at work, arriving late, missing days altogether. He has conversations with the CEO, CFO, and COO. They express their worry. After these meetings, Guy feels angry, like he's being ganged up on. One night, Guy goes to a club to find a girl and some oxycontin. He finds a girl, and she has heroin. She also has oxy, and she has Fentanyl. She tells Guy any one of the drugs or a combo will take away all the pain. Guy takes the girl back to his apartment, and the girl asks him if he wants some heroin. Guy says it's not his thing. He's strictly a pill guy and sometimes a powder guy. No injections. The girl gives him the Fentanyl. Guy swallows it and waits five minutes. He waits ten minutes, and he's still in pain. He thinks the pill must have been a placebo or a dud or something because it isn't working at all. The girl offers him heroin again, telling him he can snort it just like cocaine. Guy decides after twelve minutes the Fentanyl is a waste and decides to try the heroin. He is in so much pain. The girl takes a razor from her handbag, cutting the drugs into neat little lines, then tightens a dollar bill into a small cylinder, small enough to fit into an average nostril. She goes first, taking in four lines. There are five left, which she indicates are all for Guy. He dives in. They both lean back against the sofa, closing their eyes. The girl's head topples onto Guy's shoulder. His neck stretches backward, and in this pose, he appears to be staring at something in the ceiling. Guy and the girl don't wake up. They aren't discovered for three days, when the CEO, CFO, and COO contact the police to conduct a welfare check at Guy's apartment. The autopsy reveals the girl and Guy both overdosed on Fentanyl and heroin. Apparently, even if the pill had been a placebo, there was plenty of Fentanyl in the heroin the two had snorted. The medical examiner would state that a bull moose could have been subdued by the amount of Fentanyl found in Guy.

There were variations in the other stories, but permanently removing Guy Brown from entering the kitchen was the prevailing theme.

Clark and Bruce knew that eventually Guy would set his sights on everyone involved in halting his project, which included Bruce and Clark and the project liaison, Leeza. Bruce and Leeza were college sweethearts and joined Diamond Teams unbeknownst to each other. They worked for the same company for two years before Kate, Chris, and Sam sat them both down to explain everything to them. Their commitment to Diamond Teams was nearly unparalleled with the two of them living together and keeping their professional lives completely partitioned from their relationship.

In the evening, Clark asked Bruce, "How would you want to do it, you know, go after him? Do we need to put him down? Do we enlist a friend from an acronym agency? Do we create a legend that is indisputable and lands him in the penal system for the rest of his days? What's your pleasure?"

Bruce thought for a moment then said, "Physical violence won't solve anything. It would amp him up and point him directly at us. Substance abuse might be a viable option."

Bruce said, "I think a complete accident would have him so obsessed with dealing with pain control, it could take precedence over his desire for revenge against Diamond Teams. While he's going down an oxycontin rabbit hole, I could see him losing his job after failing a drug screen and losing custody of his son, which is a point in our favor. But how do we handle the possibility of erratic behavior? There's always the possibility he gets to drug rehab and doesn't overdose."

Bruce and Clark decided that tomorrow would be a new day, and they and the group might have some fresh insights they didn't think of while they were around the bonfire.

In the morning, they all piled into the van. They drove to a farm where they learned to milk cows and churn butter. While they toiled over the butter churns, Profile Man arrived on a motorcycle. He shucked the helmet, hanging it over the bike's handlebars, and put the kickstand down. He ambled over to the cows, settling on a stool and began milking in earnest. Bruce and Clark spoke with Profile Man for a bit. They flipped through some of the steno pads, reading some of the entries. When he finished filling the pail, the profiler introduced himself to each person in the group, shook their hands, and returned to the bike, placing the helmet on his head and cinching the strap before leaving the farm.

Over soda crackers and freshly churned butter, Bruce said to the group, "Tonight, we pack up camp, and we move to a hotel. We'll have a nice meal, feel like the civilized, educated professionals we are, and then tomorrow we go back home."

CHAPTER 37
Work Group 3 – Moderated by Angel
7 ½ months ago

"Hi, everyone," Angel exclaimed, waving her hands to catch everyone's attention. Angel was the only person working for Diamond Teams who was shorter than Kate. She babysat Chris and Sam's kids when she was in high school. Sam didn't trust easily, and when Angel was in college, she contracted with Angel to nanny her kids during the summers. She and Chris brought Angel along on family vacations, and as they spent more time together, it became apparent that Angel fit the Diamond Teams profile. Sam and Chris shared their observations with Kate, and it was arranged that Kate would come for a visit, and while there, she could make the acquaintance of the nanny. Eventually, the timing was right, and Diamond Teams made an offer to Angel, which she accepted.

"I hope you love the Catskills as much as I do. We were lucky enough to be able to take advantage of this fabulous camp during the off season. Some of you may recognize the camp or you may recognize the names of the owners, who are past Diamond Teams clients." Angel continued,

"The other two work groups are meeting this week, too. I would like to share with you what the other two groups' focuses are. One: Guy Brown will go after Diamond Teams and destroy Kate's professional reputation and destroy the company. Two: Guy Brown will go after the family members and loved ones of each person who had a role in ending his project, with the intent of catastrophic injury that lasts a lifetime." Angel visibly shuddered after describing the second focus. She continued, "The third focus is on Guy going after everyone who worked on his project, starting with Kate, and eliminating them. This may be the simplest solution for him, but we don't think it the highest probable solution either. There are too many variables and the payback period for Guy would take too long. However, you all know that if you fail to plan, you plan to fail.

"During the next few days, we are going to play Commando. We are all staying in the camp's cabins. You all should have brought a backpack with you. We're going to hit the mess hall where you will receive a paint ball gun, paint balls, night vision goggles, a flashlight, batteries, a black beanie, and a space blanket. It gets cold up here at night. There are rations for everyone for freeze-dried foodstuffs and jerky and canteens with water and also water purification tablets.

"For *possibly* the next two days, we are going to play 1 round of Commando every 4 hours. You're going to have to figure out how to fit in sleep or rest yourselves. If you think you can sneak away and grab a nap between rounds or after you've been eliminated in a round, great. The rounds are going to be fast paced, and we are going to take advantage of the woods and all the camp structures. You may not leave the camp's boundaries, which are clearly marked throughout the woods with barbed-wire fences. Our group is the largest of the work groups, and every round is played to the last man or woman standing. Each person's goal is to maximize the number of kills. You get 1 point for every kill, negative 5 points for being the first person eliminated in a round and bonus 5 points for being the last person standing in a round. I will always have the point totals. You can ask me at any time what the point situation looks like, and I will provide the information to you. In the final round, the person with the highest number of points will be the target of everyone else here. That person will have a 10-minute lead on the rest of the group. When we get to that point, I will provide additional instructions to everyone.

Angel clapped her hands, exclaiming, "This will be fun, everyone. But more importantly, after you get your feet wet in the first round or two, you might want to start thinking strategically about who you want with you in the final round and who you might want to go after. Or you might be thinking about being the last person standing and how that might look. As soon as we finish the final round, we will debrief.

"One last thing. I'm not telling you how many rounds we may be playing. It could be 4, or 10, or something different. Formulate your strategies accordingly."

Angel looked around the group, making eye contact with each person. "Go get your packs, and meet me in the mess hall in five minutes. Everything is laid out there for you. The rations are exact. If anyone is shorted, then someone is cheating, and cheating may be part of your strategy—hamstringing your peers. It makes you an asshole, but it doesn't make you wrong. Knowing that little tidbit, do not dally. See you in five."

Everyone dispersed to their cabins to grab backpacks, essentials, and contraband then gathered in the mess hall, with the first person arriving in four minutes. After appropriating the Diamond Teams' official provisions, one person was short a flashlight, and a few people skimped on jerky to spread the wealth amongst their co-workers.

Round one lasted three hours and forty-eight minutes. The last person standing was Sam. She, Kate, and Chris had each taken part in one of the work group breakouts. Round two lasted two hours and twenty-two minutes. The last person standing was Sam. Rounds three through six were won by a variety of individuals. By round seven, some participants were tired, but others had taken advantage of the down time between rounds, and some were somewhere in between, but maybe a little hyped from the ADHD medication making its way amongst the group along with some strategy that had begun to develop. One of the subsets of participants, a group of four, had decided that it would be best if Sam could be recruited to their group. She already had a sizable number of points, which might put her in position to be the prey in the final round. She may have been lying low in subsequent rounds to remove the target from her back, but she was still formidable and had shown the strength of her hand early. The informal leader of the group of four was a former physician named Chun, who had quietly led a discussion by stating, "Sam would only be strategic, never sloppy. She took us easily in the first two rounds to show us that she could run circles around us if she wanted. She's been letting herself get taken out quietly and easily since. I think we could talk to some of the other groups to see what would happen if we all avoided her. We could observe if she's trying to play to win or be taken out. Also, she may know how many rounds are being played. She may jump back in for a win at any time. If she's aggressive, then we know she's playing to win and going for the final round which could be soon. If she's not aggressive, then she may be playing to hunt. If that's the case, then we need to identify who is the stealthiest person here. I will be upfront with you all. I'm playing to hunt and to evade as necessary to hunt."

Chun met on behalf of his group with Leeza, Guy Brown's former project liaison, to review what he and his group were thinking. Chun and Leeza agreed that at least two groups would need to coordinate and gain enough critical mass. They first had to align on their goal. They opted to hunt in the final round, which meant they and their groups had to be careful not to amass too many points in the lead up rounds. Leeza agreed to get point totals from Angel. They would also need to determine who would be the most challenging participant to hunt, thinking it would be ideal preparation for hunting and potentially eliminating Guy Brown. Out of the remaining participants, they had gleaned that there were two other splinter groups, and they would need to convene with the de facto leaders of each. The coordinated effort would shine a light on their goal: They needed to find someone to be in the final round who would operate most like Guy Brown, and that person may already be the cream floating to the top. Chun and Leeza both thought that they were nearing the end game, though, and point totals should be fairly revealing.

When Leeza and Chun reconvened, it was clear, even though she was lying low and not winning subsequent rounds, Sam had enough kills to be the leader for the final round. Chun and Leeza deduced Sam was sussing out the rest of the participants to determine strengths and weaknesses, strategies, coordination between groups, and general cohesiveness.

Between rounds, Sam kept a log on each participant rating leadership, strategy, communication, demeanor, disposition, aggressiveness, kills, and rank on the leaderboard. She categorized each participant as leaders, rogues, team players. She also had navigators, innovators, hunters, and prey. She laid them out on a grid. She didn't need to label herself, but thought herself a game maker.

Leeza and Chun sent word out to their groups to meet in the woods. They took the approach that Sam would latch onto one person from each splinter group to infiltrate and bring strategy back to her. In the final round, she would only have to last four hours without being pegged with a paintball. Having a game plan and signal set would lead her to victory confounding all of the Diamond Teams' operatives. Leeza and Chun had to seed the infiltrators with plausible misinformation that could be fed to Sam. During their meeting in the woods, they confirmed their theory: Sam had eyes and ears in each splinter group.

The other group leaders followed the same plan. To move the game along faster, they had to keep their kills active but low to get enough disparity between first and second place to force a final round. In rounds seven and eight, the groups achieved their mission, noting that Sam did not win either round. Leeza received updated totals from Angel.

At the conclusion of round eight, Angel brought everyone together. "Round nine will be the final round. At this time, I am not going to be sharing point totals with you. I am also not going to share with you who you are going to be hunting. The person who has the highest point totals will have a ten-minute advantage. If you are observant, you should be able to determine who you are hunting. Remember this: You are Diamond Teams. The prey is Guy Brown. He is out to get you, and you are out to get him. I know that you all have worked together and have been discussing your attack plans and strategies, and I applaud you. All you have to do is neutralize your target in less than four hours.

"Some of you may be collaborating with the target, and I want to be clear that if the target manages to evade being neutralized, collaborators will be identified in the debrief. You all get a special walk of shame," Angel smiled and fanned her fingertips on one hand against the opposite. "I don't think you will like it much, but do what you think you need to do. You all have free time, and the next round begins in twenty-five minutes."

Sam went into the game forming her own splinter group. She led the group, and she told each member of her group individually who she thought was going after the Guy Brown role for the final round. She also placed these people in the corresponding splinter groups. She then told them that they all needed to scatter to pre-determined spots as soon as the final round began. They also needed to be unseen for fifteen minutes prior to the beginning of the round. "Go wherever you need to go to be invisible and able to get to your initial position as soon as the round begins," she advised. Sam had all the plans, and she had all the people. She would be surprised if the round lasted more than ninety minutes. She would systematically take out every splinter group.

Fifteen minutes before the final round began, Sam's group disappeared. Ten minutes before the final round, Sam quietly slipped into the woods. When the round began, Sam waited. She didn't think it wise to sit and wait for four hours to elapse, just to say, "Ha! I found a great hiding place." It wasn't the object of the game. She kept her own group in play for the first twenty minutes, looking for the signs they had placed throughout the woods—stacks of sticks or rocks here and there, indicating where teams were localizing throughout the woods. She quickly and quietly worked through half of the splinter groups, then went back to her own team. At the thirty-minute mark in five-minute intervals, there were touchpoints with each team member at previously appointed landmarks. In each meeting, Sam eliminated everyone on her team, which left her less than half of the remaining participants, and she knew where they were supposed to be.

What Sam did not count on was the one point of the plan that was kept solely between Chun and Leeza. They found an abandoned hunting blind about twenty feet up in a tree that had been hidden by the dense branches and darkened tree leaves of the woods. The two of them were the one sub-splinter group that Sam could not infiltrate. They stayed in the blind, and when there were only the three of them left, they deftly returned to the ground and followed Sam, eventually flanking her. She had not known why they were nowhere near their respective groups or why they were bucking the strategy of the entire hunting contingent. As she was piecing things together, she realized she was in trouble. She had lost control of the game and was being hunted, and she didn't know if she could pivot quickly and get to a safe space. She had eliminated all of her allies. Thirteen minutes after leaving the hunting blind, Chun and Leeza each aimed and fired their paint guns at Sam. Game over.

In front of the mess hall was a nice flat grassy area that would normally be occupied by picnic tables during summer camp season and a flagpole that would ordinarily fly both the American and camp flags. Today the tables were in storage until next year, and the flagpole stood empty. A faint whirring braced the trees, followed by a helicopter making a soft landing just out of reach of the flagpole. Profile Man descended and strode into the mess hall.

He spoke with Sam and Angel, and then he spoke with Chun and Leeza. He made his way around the tables in the mess hall, shaking hands with each participant and introducing himself. He circled back to Sam and Angel and found a place at one of the empty tables and stayed through the debrief.

Angel began, "First, I would like to congratulate all of you for identifying the highest point getter in advance of the final round. Not everyone checked in on the point totals. However, if I'm right, I think there may have been five or six splinter groups, and I did receive inquiries from almost all of the splinter groups, and I think there may have been a couple that combined, and then there was one tiny secret splinter group. Am I right? That's what I gathered from my vantage point anyway. If you were the leader of a splinter group, please raise your hand."

Six hands went up. "Very nice!" Angel paused, looking around the room to see who the leaders were. Sam consulted her notebook to see how this jived with her notes. Angel continued, "Leaders raise your hands again to indicate in what round you formed your groups." Some hands went up indicating twos and threes, and there was even a group that didn't form until round five. "Interesting," Angel said.

Sam stood up, joining Angel at the front of the room. "I positioned myself as the Guy Brown analogue. Did anyone else want to follow that path, too? And if you did, why did you change direction? At what point in the game did you make the decision?" A couple people indicated they had intentions of getting to the final round, but as they watched the game's action, they wanted to hunt more than to evade.

"Does anyone want to know my game plan? I didn't mean to win the first two rounds, but the competitor in me really loves playing paintball. It's a guilty pleasure in my off time. Angel, Chris, and my kids can attest.

"I figured on alliances or splinter groups. Then I figured on the groups' consolidation to bring everyone's resources into a laser focus. My goal was to get my own group and to share the point totals with them individually and shaving a few points off my total to convince them I was a hunter, too. Each person in my group was also in another group and alerted that the prey for the final round was someone in one of the other groups. We developed some various signals (which came from my Girl Scout days) of rock, stick, and leaf formations, where I could pick off the hunters from the other groups. What ultimately got me, though, was the tiny group of two. It was a secret. I couldn't infiltrate it and failed to plan for it, which resulted in my ultimate failure and demise.

"However, I am thrilled to have been bested! The game was so much fun for me, and I learned a lot about all of you and your own strengths and weaknesses. Every one of you is with Diamond Teams because you bring something special to the table, and we work to play on matching you with the work that plays best to your strengths." Sam went back to her seat knowing that her loss was a win.

Angel resumed the debrief, eliciting discussion about the game and thwarting Sam, and then the eventual plan for Guy Brown, and what a plan would look like. There was some terror if Guy would somehow have eyes and ears in Diamond Teams because, at the end of the day, they all had each other's backs, and trusted one another implicitly— fear generated by the thought of Guy Brown breaching the trust that was a cornerstone amongst the staff of Diamond Teams.

Profile Man took in everything, nodding as appropriate, but revealing nothing he may have been thinking. As the debrief ended, he thanked everyone for allowing him to visit, and returned to the helicopter.

CHAPTER 38
The Company Picnic – Profile Man's ranch
Morning Session
7 months and 1 week ago

Buses, vans, and trucks rambled down the gravel, but mostly dirt, drive to Profile Man's ranch. Kate, Kevin, Chris, and Sam greeted everyone from the wraparound porch. Profile Man directed everyone to the barn to the side of the house. It was a large structure; rusty red painted wood gave way to thick sliding steel doors. Bales of hay rested below what looked like the second-floor openings of haylofts at either end of the barn. Inside the barn was a completely different environment. The floor wasn't dirt or hay or wood planks or beams. It was polished concrete, and the walls were bright white. Recessed lighting kept the space from being a complete assault on anyone's vision. The air was cool, dry, pure, dust-free. Along the back wall were barrister's shelves that ran from floor to ceiling, and they were filled with books, protected by tempered glass. As modern as the rest of the room seemed, the shelves were strangely anachronistic, adorned by a ladder that rolled along a track the width of the barn.

For the company picnic, the room was set with tables to accommodate Diamond Teams. The tables featured electrical outlets, and there were tablets distributed for every employee of Diamond Teams. Projected on the wall from Kate's laptop was the Diamond Teams logo. It was a simple diamond or vertically oriented parallelogram. If anyone noticed the similarly oriented 'N' sandwiched inside a diamond when they came through the security fence to the ranch, no one said anything.

After everyone had arrived and found their assigned seats, Kate entered the barn with Kevin, Sam, Chris, and Profile Man. She addressed the group, "Thank you all for coming to this company picnic. I know that each and every one of you has met this gentleman." Kate gestured to the older man. "I call him Profile Man, and I'm sure many of you refer to him as such, too. Before I started Diamond Teams, though, I called him 'Dad.' This is James Navarro, my father."

There were murmurs around the room and some looks of surprise, but once everyone took a closer look at Kate and James, there was no question of the resemblance they shared. Sam continued, "James Navarro, or Dr. James Navarro, is a forensic psychiatrist who worked for an alphabet agency as a career, retiring from one of these places a number of years ago. I am purposely being vague about this, so don't try to do math, and don't try to guess which organization. When we were teenagers, I called him Dr. J, and now I just call him PM—get it? Short for Profile Man, not Prime Minister? He was one of the first five investors in Diamond Teams and has served as a consultant since the inception of the company. He has a multi-pronged interest in our situation with Guy Brown."

James finally spoke. "I would like to welcome you all to my wife and my ranch. We came out here after Kate finished college. You understand that we wanted to create a new legend for ourselves and allow Kate to create something that would insulate her based on where she was going professionally as well. Everything that she has done since she hung up the

Diamond Teams shingle has been intentional and deliberate. Her hires of Sam and Chris couldn't have been more spot on.

"When the three of them pulled together the three work group strategy operations that you all completed, we debated how best to handle each experience. We also debated what kind of involvement they would each have in the operations. Kate and Chris opted to remain participants and not leaders, and Sam took a more significant role in the game, but not as a facilitator. Every facilitator was chosen, and as a group, we rehearsed the framework of every operation. We did what you do before planning a murder. We went through all the fishbone diagrams. We assigned probabilities to every outcome that might occur during the operations—with the exception of the splinter group of two in the Commando experience. Some of the hijinks in the Berlin club were anticipated, though, not as specifically, but we knew what to expect."

James took a moment to think. "We toyed with micro-dosing LSD, but we decided not to go that route, and we had a fantastic resource in Clark, who was one of my residents at some time in my past." Clark gave a little salute from where he was seated. And now, many pairs of eyes shifted in his direction, and the air buzzed with a hive mind trying to see if there was a resemblance between Kate, James, and Clark. No one voiced the question, though.

Chris joined Kate and James, holding one of the tablets in an outstretched hand. "Everyone, could you please use your credentials to log on to the tablet in front of you? We are on a very secure VPN here. You would not believe the encryption we have been able to achieve. I know I'm geeking out, but this is stuff that matters to all of us. You will all see a schematic of a building. This is the convention center in Indianapolis, Indiana, and the site of an upcoming conference. The thing you need to know about this conference is the size—it's not a big one, but there should be around 150-300 attendees. The breakout sessions do not occupy a bunch of rooms, and the space for the conference is concentrated to one area." Chris stopped for a moment and zoomed out of the schematic to show more of the convention center space.

"The convention center, however, is large, and Indianapolis, has proven to be a city that can accommodate a lot of convention and conference business. The weekend of the conference that interests us is the same weekend as a large national cheer competition. There will be people from all over. There is also going to be a hardware store supply convention for the 'Do It Best' stores." Chris zoomed out more, and he tapped on his tablet lighting up the areas occupied by the cheer competition in bright orange, and then the areas for the hardware convention in bright green. The other, much smaller conference was highlighted in lavender, and eclipsed by the other two events.

"We have resources, not just within Diamond Teams, but friends in high and low places. We know Guy has resources. He dangled a carrot in front of Kevin a few months ago, and we think Guy is expecting us in Indianapolis. Kevin will go to the conference, and he may make mention in a group email to his professional acquaintances that he's bringing his wife and does anyone have any insight into the breakout sessions because nothing is posted yet on the conference registration website, and she might enjoy the breakout sessions, since she's an entrepreneur herself.

"We have already been in touch with the conference organizers, and the breakout sessions had not been solidified when we spoke to them and have not been posted on the conference website. We are requesting that they not be posted until after Kevin's email goes out to his conference friends. Everything should check out in the event Guy is trying to confirm Kevin's story. Guy may even call the conference organizers to see when the breakout sessions are going to be posted. At any rate, we're covered. There's no reason to suspect Kevin knows anything."

Sam raised her hand, and Chris called on her. She said, "We have games that we developed, movies that have been written, and an operation of hunting prey. It will be key to take all of what we have created and experienced and what we can feasibly predict to devise a plan. I have some ideas, and I'm sure you all have some ideas

"We have created a video that does not feature any of you; however, it does feature ideas, proposed solutions, scenarios, and various outcomes based on the strategies employed. We are approximately 90 days out from the Indianapolis conference. We think it highly probable that Guy will start to focus his energies on doing something in Indianapolis. We are going to increase our focus on Guy and everything he does because at this point, we know he can't act alone, and we are going to need to know who and what else we're up against to arrange countermeasures or to design counter-offensives."

"I think we're forgetting to tell you one of the bigger details. We live in a time of hyper-surveillance, and we are completely surrounded by technology and methods of communication. None of us has social media, but it doesn't matter if you happen to be accidentally in the background of someone's family photo that winds up on Instagram or TikTok. Facial recognition software takes a short time to identify you. We can talk to outer space so fast these days. All of this to say that Leeza, Clark, Bruce, Cleveland, Angel, Wesley, Shannon, and I cannot be anywhere near the convention center in Indianapolis. We can't take a single chance that we get picked up by security cameras, drones, cell phones, whatever. This lunatic figured out where I live and keyed my car when I was at the library. We have to assume that he has every resource at his disposal the same as we have. He might not, but if we assume he does, then we're ahead. We're safer and have an advantage." Kate giggled a bit. "You all are going to love where we're going to be. We'll be in an RV that is labeled 'IMPD—Indianapolis Metro Police Department.' We won't leave the RV, but we will be watching all the action from everywhere we can, and then some gratuitously placed cameras in eyeglasses, hearing aids, earrings, nose rings, lip rings. You get the picture. You will all have jammed comms units. They are configured specifically for your DNA. You drop one, lose one, or someone removes it forcibly, it goes dead, and it doesn't work again until reunited with your ear. The signal can't be split, and it can't be cloned or pirated or anything like that. One final thing. In ninety days, the weather in Indianapolis will be quite different than it is today. If you look at your tablets or the projection screen, you will see the temperatures on the dates of the conference for the past ten years. There's no pattern, and we already have a meteorologist who will do forecasts for 72 hours ahead of the conference's official start and then provide regular updates. I would love to see a slip and fall. There is some beauty in a random accident."

James clapped his hands together, and he smiled a large and genuine smile. "You are all going to choose an icon. 'C' equals conference attendee. The megaphone is the cheer competition. The hammer is the hardware convention. The coveralls are convention center maintenance. The martini glass is the convention center food and beverage service. The question mark is the convention center concierge desk. The 'H' is the hotel staff. The feather duster is hotel housekeeping. Please see your tablets for the key to each icon. If we wind up top-heavy in one area, you will be reassigned based on your particular skillsets for the roles needed. Within each icon grouping, there are various roles, which are outlined for you. Take your time to review all the roles to choose which you think will suit you best."

Chris chimed in, "What's fascinating is having worked with all of you for such a long time in some cases," which was followed by quiet laughter, "and having all the testing data required to work with Diamond Teams, we are almost certain we know what each of you will choose. I'm hedging my bets that I will see maybe two or three surprises. We know you know your strengths, though. Have I mentioned how much I love my job and where I work?" The volume of the laughter increased just a bit.

As the morning progressed, roles were chosen without much surprise, and plans were hatched. Kevin registered for the conference, and he followed up with an email to his professional networking group, asking about the breakout sessions and if anyone had any inkling of what they might be since he'd like to bring his wife along and she might register, too, if the breakout sessions would be of benefit to her and her business.

Lunch, ironically called a Hobo Dinner, was a welcome departure from the morning's information dump. Each person, equipped with an aluminum foil pouch, made their way through a line of meats, vegetables, seasonings, and sauces, filling the pouches, sealing them, and marking them with their names. The pouches were thrown into a large fire pit outside the barn. Participants of each work group gathered to catch up, talk about work, life, and the world in general. Kate, James, Kevin, Sam, Chris, and the workgroup moderators circulated to uncover if anyone had had any strange or out-of-the-ordinary occurrences lately. New neighbors, new teachers in kids' schools, new significant others, anyone new who might have insight or access to the lives of anyone within Diamond Teams. There were a few, and digging into the backgrounds would begin as soon as the lunch break ended.

CHAPTER 39
The Company Picnic – James Navarro's ranch
Afternoon Session
7 months and 1 week ago

The first slide projected after lunch was a timeline of events, which illustrated that there had been a few minor offensives launched by Guy, but nothing too horrible, mostly scare tactics. But it did prove his ingenuity and shine a light on the resources at his disposal in being able to locate everyone involved in his project termination.

- Day 0 = Project Termination – threats and promises of revenge
- Month 2 = Sabotage of Dean's car
- Month 3 = Murder, body disposal, revenge conversation
- Month 4 = Kate's car gets keyed; Bruce and Leeza receive dead cat; Clark receives wasps and wasp nest
- Month 5 = DT Staff Meetings 1 & 2; Work groups 1, 2, & 3 meet; Company picnic

- Months 6 & 7 = Prep for Indianapolis conference
- Month 8 = Conference

Guy was unaware that the C-suite and board of directors of his company had been Diamond Teams' clients while Guy was busy earning the education of a lifetime at his Ivy League college. It could be extremely easy to make a call to the CEO to pull Guy aside to highlight some small error, poor judgment, badly made comment or oversight. With work and his son being the dual-focus of his life, anything negative would be internalized quickly, and it was unlikely for Guy to show anger to the people who had given him his dream job, and unlikely he would make a connection to Diamond Teams, but it would put him into a defensive mode. It would be the start of putting him into the role of prey. They would wait to see if Guy had any other offensives waiting in the wings.

There were two primary areas of focus for Diamond Teams. The first was to develop a strategy for dealing with Guy at the conference. The second was to complete a risk assessment of their whole operation and plug any holes. The first piece of the prep strategy would be to see if Guy continued to remain fired up about his project termination or not. The remainder of the day saw the Diamond Teams employees gathering in their icon groups and receiving their official role assignments for the conference. Always one point in developing a plan was: Do nothing. Not a solitary group neglected the age-old tenet.

The groups each huddled over their tablets and the schematics of the convention center. They hunted down the local hotels, apartments, and rentals. They began cobbling together legends and working on social media for the personae they would adopt, and then they worked through getting familiar with the city hosting the conference, Indianapolis.

Chris, Kevin, Clark, James, and Sam began working through the risk assessment, knowing they would have people coming in and out of the assessment process based on their skillsets: human resources, information security and backup, technology, disaster recovery and business continuity. James and Clark, both psychiatrists, tapped out once they had been exhausted as resources and worked on their own as they poured over all the intake forms for potential clients and for potential employees of Diamond Teams. The next people up were the information security people who shoved off to a separate area to comb through every protocol they had in place for keeping all parts of Diamond Teams' data behind a wall the people at Fort Knox would envy. The tech crew, though, were the dreamers. They were the spy gear gadget folks who thought about things like hearing aids (but missed the mark on the cochlear implants). They were makers. In a former client's project, while she was surveilling her target, they put a wig on her with fiberoptic capability to receive and transmit sound and video. They developed tools and then looked at how to break them. If they thought it up, certainly, someone else had, too. And if they could break a tool, how quickly could it be put back online? How quickly could a new tool or piece of tech or programming or comms be detected? They spent enormous amounts of time testing the toys they created. The tech crew were the one group in Diamond Teams who lived in the same vicinity and worked in a secure lab, which also appeared, from all outward appearances, to be a garage which worked on only Rolls Royce vehicles. Ironically, their lab-garage was in a town where no one drove a Rolls Royce. To provide legitimacy, Diamond Teams rented a Rolls every few months to have something parked outside the lab-garage. In twenty years, not a soul had ever wandered in to have a look or inquire about repairs.

The last part of the assessment was disaster recovery and business continuity. How would Diamond Teams keep going in the face of fire, hurricane, tornado, military or terrorist action? When the core group reached this part, they started calling names of individual employees to come take a gander at what had been created thus far and asked for additional input. Each employee then hit the human resource, information security, and tech tables, where they were asked to repeat what they had just done with the disaster recovery and business continuity team. At any point, they could go back to any group to add something they thought they had missed.

They worked until late in the evening. Kate was tired, but energized, and she felt good about the direction they were taking and how they were all going through a genesis of ideas. She and Clark took a moment to discuss their thoughts on how the day had gone.

Clark started. "Dad did a great job with removing the veil, don't you think?"

"Yeah, but I'm going to call him James while I'm working. He's 'Dad' when he's calling to check on the kids and stuff. You know, if you hadn't been in med school when I started Diamond Teams, you would have been my first hire."

"Kate, that stinks of nepotism," Clark said.

"But no one but us would know, since I changed my name," Kate rejoined. "But you were smart to change yours, too, before you finished your medical degree."

"If you knew this was what you were going to do before I went to med school, I never would have gone. I would have maybe done something different and waited for you to finish college."

"Clark. No. I am so glad you went to medical school. Psychiatry and neuroscience are what put us into a position that we've been able to run a company for over twenty years and only have one person like Guy Brown get past us." Kate paused a moment, glancing at the lighting in the barn. "What's your gut on Guy? If you had to predict what he's going to do…"

Clark rubbed his chin, also glanced to the ceiling, before stating, "This is going to be a word dump, I think. Are you ready for it?"

"Lay it on me, wise one." She winked. "I can take it."

"OK. Guy only takes calculated risks because that's his job. He computes the probabilities of things happening, and then he makes his decisions from a mathematical vantage point. I have gone through the images of every scrap of paper he filled out, every test he completed, and every interview and face-to-face interaction we have had with him, including the project termination video. He displayed all signs of anger, rage, and fury. But going through everything, he clearly lied to us multiple times, and none of the videos showed any sign of duplicity. When I watched everything again, however, I finally did see his tell. I re-reviewed all the videos, and sure enough, I can now tell when he's lying. It's so tiny, though, you would miss it. His intent with Diamond Teams was never pure from the outset. He planned on success, and had he not thought himself superior to everyone else in the room, he would have had contingency plans; but, of course, he didn't. My prediction: He might fire off a few more warning shots, and then nothing. He would want to lull all of us into a false sense of calm. I predict nothing big will happen in Indianapolis. I think he'll be a good little soldier because he thinks or knows Kevin is aware of your business. He isn't going to want the professional networking groups to think he's a psycho and can't afford for rumors to circulate. AFTER the Indianapolis conference, though, I think he's only going to focus on hurting you. My prediction: He'll go after Michelle since she's in California. Guy sometimes lectures at Stanford. Their paths may cross. He's young, good looking, charismatic, and smart as hell. He is Michelle's type. He will go after her in some way, and he will hurt her in a way that will scar you all for the rest of your lives. Hurting your children is a thousand times worse than hurting you or Kevin, and I do think he has taken Dean's measure and has calculated it isn't the best outcome for him. Unpleasant, but there you go. My official prediction."

"Do you think I should tell Kevin?" Kate asked, drawing her shaking had over her mouth.

"Dad and I discussed this already, and we both think you should have the conversation with him immediately. We also think you need to prep Michelle. Guy has eyes on all of us, but he doesn't have ears, which is ironic since he has the cochlear implant and is deaf in one ear. You are going to need to speak to both of the kids and tell them what you do for a living. You can choose to let them know about Dad and me, but you, at a bare minimum, need to self-disclose. You then need to talk through Guy Brown. Show them photos. They need to know what he looks like. You can do all of this via video calls. Since you can't just jet off to California because of Guy's surveillance, I would send a female employee and arrange for her to live in Michelle's sorority. She would need to train Michelle in self-defense, for sure, and she would probably do well to take her through some of the basic psychological games Guy may play on her when they invariably meet. Didn't Chun graduate from Stanford undergrad?"

"He did. Double-major in biology and business," said Kate.

"It might make sense for him to contact the head of the department to see if they have Guy on the schedule to guest lecture in the Spring. Once you have a date, you have an event horizon of sorts. At least you'll know when they would first lay eyes on each other in person."

"Do you think he'll do anything at all in Indianapolis?" Kate asked.

"It's possible he could have a slip and fall that results in Kevin being pushed into traffic, or maybe Kevin gets some mysterious food poisoning, or, heck, bed bugs? I don't think Kevin is going to sustain any severe damage if Guy does decide to do something. But everyone who had anything to do with the project termination AND their families should do routine checks of vehicles, avoid any ride share services, and come to the company if anyone new shows up on the fringes of their lives. We can check them out and clear them quickly."

"When I retire, and you can be sure I will retire," Kate smiled. "I want you and Chris to run the company. Sam and I will probably retire within six months of each other to ensure smooth transitions. I hate to say this, but I'm going to say it anyway. Dean would be an amazing addition to Diamond Teams, and Sam and Chris have a daughter who fits our profile perfectly. As long as we can be assured not to have more Guy Browns as clients, I would be pleased for those two to join the company."

"What about Michelle?" Clark asked. "I have casually done some testing on her, and she's a high tech-business type. She could do quite well with the tech crew and work her way into the admin structure."

"I never thought of her that way. It does make sense, though," Kate said. "I can pitch it to them both separately to see what they think."

"Make sure to convey to them their communication after you have told them about Diamond Teams must be done over a secure channel. Everyone should operate as though they're aware they're being watched."

"Yep," Kate said. "I guess I'm going to have an uncomfortable conversation with Kevin now. Thank you for the chat," she said and hugged her brother.

CHAPTER 40
Sam and Kate – *1 day after the Company Picnic*

Sam called Kate to check in. "Hey, what's new? I didn't have a chance to catch you after the 'picnic.'"

Kate shared everything Clark predicted, and she told her about the conversation she had with Kevin about talking to Dean and Michelle.

"How does he feel about telling them?" Sam asked.

"He doesn't like it, but he understands, and he knows the only way you be prepared is to know what might be coming for you. He also thinks since they're both over eighteen, it makes sense for them to know. I'm also telling them about you, Chris, Dad, and Clark. You all are my family. They need to know how deep our roots go, and maybe they might be interested in joining the company in some capacity when they're finished with school."

"Chris and I were talking about telling our kids, too," Sam said. "Alexis would be a dynamite addition to Diamond Teams."

"She would, I agree. Are you going to tell them about the Guy Brown situation?" Kate asked.

"Chris and I haven't come to consensus on disclosing anything about Guy yet."

"So, I'm going to tell you this, because when Kevin and I were talking about the situation with our kids and Clark's prediction, Kevin said something about Guy going after one of your kids. It would wreck both you and Chris in one fell swoop, and it would destroy our relationship, and Diamond Teams would implode. I mean, you would be blaming yourselves, and you'd be blaming me."

"Fu-u-u-c-k," Sam said on an exceptionally long exhale. "Oh, my god. And Kevin…he just came up with this?"

"Yeah. I said the same thing. I wanted to tell you because it may be something you and Chris want to address in your own conversations. It's so icky, I didn't want to tell you, but I knew I'd hate myself if something bad happened to your kids and I didn't warn you first. If there's an upside, with Alexis at Berkeley and Michelle at Stanford, it would make sense for the two of them to meet for dinner from time to time. Or do you think it's better they remain physically separated? Also, do we know if Guy does any guest lecturing at Berkeley? I don't have my notes handy, and since this was a new bent on the situation, I haven't stopped to look. And I think I need to tell Clark, Bruce, and Leeza, too, even though Bruce and Leeza don't have kids yet."

Sam breathed deeply, sighing, then said, "OK. Here's how we're going to handle this. You are spiraling, which does no one any good. Have Kevin call Clark. I will have Chris contact Bruce and Leeza. I will follow up on all things related to Guy and Berkeley. I will discuss everything with Chris later this morning. I will call you this afternoon or tonight and fill you in on the details. Sound good?"

Kate agreed, and the two ended the call.

CHAPTER 41

Chris, *one day after the Company Picnic*

These two women are two of the strongest, smartest women I know. Sometimes I think they're too smart for their own good. When I get to the end of the day, when I put my head down on my pillow and pull my wife in close to me, the cares of the day leave me. I have peace and a little spoon to my big spoon, and if this were all I could have in life, I would be a happy man.

Sam and my life has been wonderful. We found each other again after college. We run a company together and work together daily. We have three grown children, with our youngest, Alexis, starting her junior year at Berkeley. Our oldest, Pat, went to the Naval Academy, and he's set on joining the JAG Corps after he finishes law school. Our middle, Temple, graduated from college this Spring and wants to take a gap year to figure out what she wants to do with her life. She moved back home after graduation, and she's been planning a trip through Asia with some of her friends from college, which would put her far away from the Guy Brown business—I think.

We're going to tell the kids everything tonight. They need to be prepared. All of them. Tonight is the night our kids grow up and face the realities what exists in the world around them, and they learn Mom and Dad can't protect them from everything. It breaks my heart, and I am livid Guy forced this kind of eye opener on our kids when they could have remained a little sheltered for just a bit longer. Granted, Pat has probably had his eyes opened to plenty simply due to his attending the Naval Academy, military service, and now law school. I can't imagine anything like this will shock him much, but I do anticipate his instinct to protect his sisters and family to rear its head.

These three were precious little white-blonde babies and toddlers just yesterday, it seems. Sam and I did a good job spacing them out, I think. Sam was a champ through each pregnancy. Her poor ankles looked like Mason jars by the end of the eighth month, and these babies were large babies. They all entered the world at around nine pounds apiece, all vaginal births. When Temple was born, I wasn't sure we were going to make it to the hospital in time. She was born fifteen minutes after we arrived. She couldn't wait to join the world, and she approached everything with fierce enthusiasm. She would be an amazing adventure travel guide. She has this zest for life and the unexpected. She is our Amazon Princess. She's tall, like me, and gregarious, and has no fear, but she wants to find her place in the world.

I know Clark has done some testing on all of the kids, and I know he has ideas on who would be a good fit for the company and in what kind of role. I'm going to make it a point to get his thoughts. But I love the idea of Temple being out there in the world, white water rafting one day, and hiking through Death Valley another, and scuba-diving in the Caribbean another. I can see her on a camel in the desert. But she may not want to do any of these things. Maybe she wants to be a fashion designer or an astronaut or whatever. It's her choice, but I cannot wait to know what she decides her life path will look like and where it will lead her.

Alexis is a carbon copy of Sam. She's got this crazy smart brain and may wind up going the CPA route, but Clark has told us she is absolutely the profile we would want to bring in to the company at some point. I don't want any of the kids to change their plans based on what Sam and I do. I want it to be an option for them. And Sam and I have agreed not to mention anything about joining the company during the call we're going to have shortly.

It's not like we're in the mob or anything, and they all know we're in consulting. We just haven't told them exactly what we do—which we will share tonight. Then we'll hit them with the double-whammy, "We have a client who went completely bananas, and he might come after any one of you."

CHAPTER 42
Guy – *7 months ago*

Leave of absence. I'm bored. I'm lonely. I read emails all day long, hoping to receive something saying all the stalker stuff was a joke. Hardy-har-har. Come back to work. We miss you. But, no. Nothing resembling a welcoming missive from anyone. I've read quite a bit and have been thinking about authoring some journal articles. I had been thinking about writing a book addressing power dynamics and exercising interpersonal strategy effectively to leverage relationships in the workplace. It could be a very useful tool to anyone in business, which is built on relationships. I would get caught up in a project, engage my mental muscles, and focus until the job was done in a very machine-like manner.

What would ordinarily make me a regular human, though, is my time with Harris. Virginia called to inform me she has the opportunity to spend the next two months in Florida doing something with NASA. If this stalking stuff hadn't come up, I know she would have asked if I could take Harris for the time she's away. She did me the courtesy of telling me Harris would be with her parents while she's gone, and I'm sure he will enjoy his time in the Midwest, but it's upsetting, and I ruminate all the time. I am a parent, and someone once told me as soon as you have a child, your heart and hopes are pinned to your tiny person forever. Your heart grows legs and starts walking around outside your body, and you have to be able to sit there and watch. Act when necessary; hold your tongue when all you want to do is advocate for your child; offer advice that will fall on deaf ears and not say, "I told you so." I would have to ask my parents if this was how they felt about us.

I did manage to attend a conference and asked a bunch of colleagues, Diamond-Teams-Kate's husband Kevin was part of the group, about getting away with murder and revenge. I was dumbstruck to pick up the fact Kevin didn't know what his wife did for a living. While we were at the table going through all the what-ifs and how-tos, Kevin was throwing in great suggestions, which I noted in my journal. I like to think I'm strategic in all things, but I didn't go as far out of the box as Kevin and the others at the table had. They were like a contingency of chaos, terror, and harrowing experience. These people were in the wrong line of work. They should be churning out screenplays. They could be the eight horsemen and women of the apocalypse. But my takeaway was Kevin not knowing anything about my connection to his wife.

I went back to my room and rethought my plans. I could do nothing. I could fire a warning shot because I had found out who all the people in the room were when my project was terminated. I also liked the idea of the long game. They were now on alert and would remain on alert for so long that they would become complacent eventually. I could wait, but I didn't think the long game was the best option. There was a conference coming up in Indianapolis. Our group was all planning on attending. I could do something during the conference, but the better solution was the kid angle. Kate and Kevin had a daughter at Stanford, and I was due to guest lecture there in the Spring. I could do something to her and really ruin her life, which in turn would be fantastic retribution to Kate. It wasn't enough, though.

I had done enough research on Kate and the other owners of Diamond Teams to know Christopher Kono and Samantha Kelley were married to each other and had three children. If I went after one of their kids, it would probably destroy their marriage, their relationship with Kate, and cause such severe disruption in the management and ownership structure of Diamond Teams they would fold. I mean, this was turmoil of a scale I could only imagine. Christopher and Samantha had a gloriously beautiful waif of a daughter at Berkeley. She would be easy to overpower, and I was confident in my charm with women. I could make some calls to offer my services as a guest lecturer while I was out in the area. I had to surmise none of the children knew exactly what their parents did for a living since Kate's own husband didn't even know.

I think the Indianapolis conference could be interesting, though, to gauge how much Kevin knew. Kate may or may not have disclosed what her consulting company did by the time the conference rolled around.

If I let the Indianapolis conference transpire without any overt activity against Kevin or anyone in the Diamond Teams family, they might think I had simmered down. However, they kept my money, fucked with my job, and took my kid away from me. They ended my project. They bound me, drugged me, humiliated and insulted me, and invaded my privacy. Granted, I lied to them from square one. Granted, I was going to kill someone. But come on. Were my job and son equal in measure to what I had done to them?

I still wanted to complete my project with my intended target and now wouldn't get to because everything would point directly to me. At present, it seemed, I had all the time in the world to channel my anger and go into a period of planning. I would look for the silver lining with respect to my project, figure out my Harris situation with Virginia, and see if I could get the stalking thing expunged or sealed in order to get back to work. When I was banished from the office, I took my special coffee mug home. It was a good, sturdy stoneware piece with a bright yellow sun peeking over the horizon on the front and said, "I am a ray of fucking sunshine." Definitely not politically correct, but it would be my mantra while I tried to reassemble my life.

First and foremost would be addressing Diamond Teams. My plan for destruction pointed me at the waif. There was so much to learn about her, her environment, her temperament, her own skillset. I would need to weigh out every possibility of accident or purposeful harm.

When I was little, my siblings talked about urban legend. There was the story of the girl who went to a party, guzzled a doped-up drink, and awoke in a bathtub filled with ice and a note telling her to call 911 immediately because one of her kidneys had been harvested. It was false, but if it had been true, what would the girl's life have been? I know people only need one kidney, but if it were harvested in a non-sterile setting—like a hotel room--by someone who wasn't a renal specialist or an organ transplant surgeon…There was merit in the urban legend route. It was so wacky, but the outcome could be completely awful, possibly causing death. Did I have the stomach to find and cut out a kidney without causing the patient to bleed out? I'm sure there's got to be something on YouTube. There were videos of procedures in surgical suites, operating rooms, and medical school lectures all over the web.

In the meantime, I could work on ratcheting up dread as the day drew nearer for the conference in Indianapolis. Screwing with Kate's son's car was a whim, which I should have avoided. I showed my cards too soon, and she came back tit for tat—plus my job. Diamond Teams knew something was coming but not knowing what, when, where, and to whom it would happen.

CHAPTER 43
Kevin – *6 months ago*

Michelle was home for a week between her internship and going back to Stanford. This was a couple weeks ago. Kate and I decided to do everything in person, face to face, no electronics. Kate, Dean, and I piled into the car, making our way to the airport to pick up Michelle. Our next stop would be lunch. Kate and I woke up early and worked together efficiently assembling sandwiches, salads, sides, drinks, and cookies. We pulled into the cell phone lot at the airport and awaited Michelle's call to alert us she was through customs and baggage claim and ready to rejoin our family. Kate would drive to the pickup zone, Dean and I would jump out of the car and grab Michelle's suitcases. If she wasn't already standing on the curb, Kate would make a loop, and Dean and I would go into baggage claim to locate our girl.

We were lucky, though. Michelle was standing on the curb, her suitcases wedged next to her. She looked like she was having a lively conversation with someone. We could see her wide smile and gesticulating arms. As we got closer, we could see she was speaking with a man. My heart jumped into my throat. It could NOT be Guy. AB-solutely not. It would be too weird, and it wouldn't be a coincidence either. When we pulled up, Dean hopped out of the car and grabbed the man Michelle had been speaking to. Dean did the bro-hug and dragged the stranger to the car.

"Mom, Dad. You remember Todd? He went to junior high with us? He moved away before high school. He was in London, too, also doing an internship," Dean said.

Another car pulled up and Todd waved to us as he wove a path through us to his family's car. "Great seeing you all!" he called.

The security guards ambled toward us, prompting us to load up and leave the airport. We were running around the car, opening and closing doors, along with the trunk. If the airport security footage were in black and white, we would look like the Keystone Cops.

"I can't believe Todd was there the whole time I was. It would've been so cool to see him. His internship was with an investment house. He said he discovered what he doesn't want to do after graduation," Michelle effused. "Where are we going for lunch? I'm hungry. Plane food doesn't cut it. And I want to hug and squeeze all of you, and of course I want everyone's love directed my way!"

Dean jumped in, "Mom and Dad are taking us to a state park for a picnic. They woke up early and put everything together."

"Don't worry, honey. We're not going hiking. We know you're probably tired. We wanted to do something special to welcome you back," Kate said, while glancing up toward the rearview mirror to see the kids sitting in the backseat.

Michelle and Dean were showing each other photos on their phones and talking to each other for the rest of the route to the park. Once we arrived at the park, we drove leisurely through, looking for a hill overlooking the reservoir below. After two wrong turns we found the hill, parked, carried blankets, plastic grocery bags, and our exquisitely decorated picnic basket (decorated by the kids when they were little), to a beautiful spot under a tree. We worked together to lay the blanket on the ground, used the basket as a weight on one corner and everyone's shoes as weights on the others, while Michelle regaled us with some of her fonder moments from her trip. Dean took his phone out of his pocket to play some mood music, and Michelle wanted to grab some family photos. Kate was quick to shut them both down for the moment.

"While we're eating, we want you to leave the phones in the car. We have some big things to discuss, and we don't want the phones to be a distraction."

The kids looked at each other, worry making an appearance in the furrows of their foreheads. I chimed in, "It doesn't have anything to do with the two of us, per se, but it is extremely important we have your 100% focus."

They both went back to the car and returned phone-free. Once everyone had full plates and drinks, Kate began the story of how she began her business after graduating from college. When she said, 'murder adventure,' both kids' eyes grew wide as saucers. I don't think I have seen the kind of wonder they displayed since they were little. It was sweet to see there were still tricks we could pull out of a metaphorical hat to mesmerize them. For me, this was the second time I had heard the full history of Diamond Teams and how the operation had grown and how it had come to have a sort of clandestine presence on the corporate landscape. Dean raised his hand to ask a question.

Kate said, "Hold your questions until I finish, ok? You're going to have many more and some of the questions may be answered throughout the rest of what I'm going to tell you."

Eventually, Kate reached the point in the story concerning Guy Brown, his project, his true aims, the project termination, and the promise of retribution. Then came the bit about Dean's car being sabotaged, Kate's car being keyed, the wasp nest and wasps going to Clark, and the dead cat going to Bruce and Leeza. She told them about why she hadn't ever gone into detail with me about her business, and I held her hand through this part. She also dropped the bombshell: Grandpa James, Uncle Clark, Sam, and Chris also worked for Diamond Teams.

"Holy shit, Mom," Michelle exclaimed. "This is some pretty heavy stuff for my first day back on US soil."

"I know, honey," Kate said in a reassuring voice only a mother could master. "The whole company has been meeting to develop strategies and plans for dealing with Guy. He isn't going to go away." And then she shared Clark's prediction. Michelle began to look alarmed, then angry, then finally cooling somewhat when Kate shared my prediction and rationale.

She said, "I know he guest lectures at Stanford almost every Spring. He may try to add Berkeley to his itinerary this coming Spring. If he does, then he could have a backup target in case he's unsuccessful with one of the two of you. My gut is saying Alexis will be his prime target, but you need to be aware and prepared for every eventuality."

Kate grabbed a tote bag lying to her side and took out a variety of photos of Guy, and we spread them out on the blanket for the kids to peruse.

Michelle said, "Can I say I think he's kind of hot?"

Kate responded, "This is exactly why we're showing you photos. He's young, attractive, highly intelligent, charming, and charismatic, but there's something broken up here." Kate pointed to her temple.

"Mom, Dad," Dean interjected. "Should I take a semester off or try to do an exchange semester at Stanford in the Spring to be near Michelle?"

"Your mom and I thought about the idea briefly, and we don't want to give Guy three targets. Diamond Teams can more easily monitor things and devote more resources to two targets than three."

"I know it's your company and all," Dean said. "And I know it would probably be all 'nepo baby' and stuff, but I think this could be something right up my alley, at least for a while, after I finish school. Would you keep me on your back burner?"

"And maybe," added Michelle. "Could you keep me on your back burner for your tech crew in the Rolls Royce garage-lab? I have so many ideas, and some of what I did during my internship would dovetail nicely with your geek squad, though, I'm sure they're nice people."

"They're the best," Kate said, trying to hide a smile. "I will back burner both of you unless you tell me otherwise, and just because I started the company, I can't promise anything. Everyone who works for us goes through extensive testing."

We spent the rest of the afternoon enjoying the park, the food, the sounds and smells of nature, and the hint of oncoming fall. There was nary a moment of silence while we discussed how best to prepare Michelle for Guy's visit to Stanford. She would have first semester to prep, learn, and practice, and we assured her it wouldn't take away from her schoolwork. We wanted her to be savvy and safe and never to find herself painted into a corner.

Dean said he would get her going on some basic Brazilian Jiu Jitsu before she returned to California. Kate said her preference for the discipline had been the fact a smaller person could have an advantage over a taller person due to a lower center of gravity. "Mom has sparred with me, and she regularly takes me down. I haven't been able to best her even once this summer, and I practice all the time. Also, I think she's had a lot more training than she lets on to Dad and me." Kate looked at Michelle intently, watching for any signs of fear, worry, or apprehension, but I think it was information overload, and Michelle needed to have time to absorb everything. Dean seemed to take everything in stride, but Guy Brown was probably not lining him up in his sights either. Dean was intuitive, and on some level, he knew Michelle and, more likely, Alexis would be Guy's top choices.

We packed up everything before the crickets struck up their orchestra and the frogs would begin to sing. Kate took her phone from the glove box in the car. I put my arms around everyone, and we all looked up toward the phone for my favorite family photo. I see life, light, and love in everyone's eyes and smiles. And, God willing, we would be prepared. Our Michelle would be a bad-ass, ready to take on what looked like, to all outward appearances, a handsome, intelligent man with a penchant for putting himself into a higher order than everyone around him.

CHAPTER 44
Chris – *6 months ago*

When we told our kids what was going on, we did a webinar. Both Temple and Alexis were home, but Pat had to be included via video. Our house is incredibly secure, but ensuring wherever Pat is located would have the same safeguards is impossible. We had to give him access to Diamond Teams' secure and encrypted VPN. I hoped we weren't opening things up to a bunch of red ants in our efforts to keep out a solitary hornet. The risk assessment opened my eyes wide, and I decided we would update and review the risk assessment annually going forward and create a threat assessment team that would meet monthly to ensure security firm-wide.

Sam and I gave the kids the rundown on everything, from soup to nuts. "People, strangely enough, pay us for this service. They pay us a lot, actually, and until Guy Brown, we never had a single problem. Not one."

"Now, you guys," I said very seriously. "You're not going to like this next bit." I told them about Guy, and showed them the photos. The girls fanned themselves as they looked at the handsome nut job. Pat looked non-plussed, but I could see him sizing up the threat. He could easily take Guy Brown. Pat was tall, like me, and played tight end in high school and college football. Pat was a beast. He could have been on one of those Viking television shows and fit right in.

Sam went through Clark's prediction then followed with Kevin's prediction and why Kevin's prediction would actually yield a better result for Guy. "We think he's going to come after you, Alexis. We know he's going to guest lecture at Stanford in the Spring, and he will probably add Berkeley, since he has time on his hands right now. If he fails his task with you, then Michelle would be the backup, but you're in the starting block, honey." Sam ran her hand through Alexis's hair.

"He's got to know I would be a terrible target, though. Right?" Alexis asked.

Alexis had been an interesting child. We knew she had ADHD by the time she was three or so, and we knew she would have to be medicated. To help her focus, we enrolled her in activities like tennis and gymnastics, where losing focus could end in being hit by a tennis ball or not nailing a landing or falling from an apparatus. We put a ping pong table in our basement, and we all became terrific ping pong players thanks to Alexis. We put her in swimming, and she loved the water. Build-wise, she took after Sam, and we knew Alexis would be swimming for joy and fitness, not for competition. She wasn't going to be tall enough to be competitive, which is fine. Not every kid is an elite athlete, and our having an elite athlete might be problematic with our line of work. We put in an in-ground lap pool, though, and Alexis would swim laps for two hours every morning to burn off some of 'the excess' she liked to call it. The exercise would bring her down just enough to focus on getting ready for the day and reviewing all her homework for accuracy and completeness.

When Alexis started kindergarten, she would watch Power Rangers with her two older siblings after school. She told everyone in the family it was her goal to be the next Pink Power Ranger. She dropped tennis and picked up karate. When she received her first uniform, Sam and I saw the light in her eyes. Gymnastics helped her, sure; but she was instantly committed to karate because of Power Rangers, and as she learned there was more to karate than breaking boards, we watched her bloom. It sounds crazy, but karate took our baby girl from a tender rosebud to a fully-double rose. We had to slow her down because she began to progress too quickly. However, her sensei was very quick to inform us to support her in any direction she chose and at any pace keeping her focused on learning and advancing.

She kept up with gymnastics and karate all through high school and into college. She broke boards and bricks, but she could also do a damned impressive floor routine. Alexis could tear up anyone. When she entered a room, she scanned the landscape and quickly assessed the best escape route, and she found the biggest human threats to her. She was very popular in her sorority. During her freshman year, she gave everyone rape whistles and pepper spray. She also showed her sorority sisters how to stay safe, and she gave everyone her phone number. She wanted no one to be in a jam with a lunatic, criminal, or college-aged ass hat and not have any options.

A large part of Alexis's ongoing dedication to martial arts had to do with a horrible event rocking our family when Alexis was fourteen and Temple was sixteen. Temple had come home late one Saturday evening. Alexis was in her room, her bedroom door mostly closed, watching videos on YouTube. She heard Temple sprinting up the stairs, followed by Temple's door closing. What alarmed Alexis was the sound of Temple crying and her attempt to stifle the keening. Alexis texted Sam to say something was wrong with Temple, and, not to worry, she would check on her older sister.

Alexis didn't knock before entering Temple's room. She was shattered by the look on Temple's face. Her eyes were swollen from crying, and her face was drawn. Her normally styled -without-looking-styled hair was disheveled, looking pulled all out of place from running her hands through her locks. Her mascara had run far enough down her face not to render her like a panda, but more like she'd been working in a coal mine and wiped her face with her sleeve. And she was holding herself as tightly as she could, maybe to stop from shaking. Alexis approached Temple, knowing she would need to keep as even a tone as possible and not to make the situation look or feel scarier or more severe than it already was. But it was very, very bad, and Alexis knew it.

"Hey, Temple," she said casually. "How was the party tonight? Anyone there I would know?"

She sat on the bed, and the two sisters leaned back against the pillows, staring straight ahead at Temple's closet door. Alexis waited patiently for Temple to answer before supplying her own answer.

Alexis said, "Same old, same old. The party was at the Dobsons' house, right? Did everyone go swimming? I've always liked their house. It's so big, though, like they knew they didn't want to be around their kids when they became teenagers and had designed their house to have an under-twenty-one and an over-twenty-one wing intentionally. How old are their older kids? I know they're in college and stuff."

The girls sat in silence for what felt like an eternity before Temple said in just above a whisper, "One of the boys, Connor, I think, brought a friend from college home with him. He was cute, and he talked to me for a while. We walked around the house, and I stupidly thought we were just talking. I didn't think anything of it because they're in college, and I'm in high school. We sat by the pool for a while, watching everyone get smashed and thrown into the pool, and so many cannonballs. One of the cannonballs was right by where I was sitting. I was soaked…" Temple began to cry again, and Alexis held her hand, hoping to encourage her to go on with her story. Alexis looked into Temple's eyes to see the depth of her sadness. "I excused myself and went to Missy's room to grab a dry shirt. When I turned around Connor's friend was there, and it startled me, and put me on high alert. His friend accused me of leading him on all night, and he pushed me to the floor, and then he put his hand around my throat, and he choked me. I passed out for a bit. When I came to, my neck hurt on the outside, and my throat burned on the inside. I heard myself gasping, and my hands were secured above my head. I saw his face right over mine, and I felt him inside me," she groaned. "He was inside me. He was having sex with me. He was raping me, and…my virginity…it's gone. I didn't have a choice, and he hurt me. It was so bad. And I couldn't scream, and then he was finished. And he looked satisfied with himself. He buttoned his pants and left me there." She covered her face and sobbed. She turned toward Alexis a little bit, and the younger, smaller girl held her sister for all she was worth. Alexis smoothed Temple's hair and whispered how much she loved her. How they were going get through this. How Alexis was always going to be in Temple's corner.

"Alexis," she whispered, "he didn't use a condom. I am so scared." She pulled away to look her younger sister in the eye, and, upon meeting her gaze, Alexis knew she would need to talk to their mother. She would know what to do.

"Do you want me to talk to Mom? She can be as involved, or uninvolved, as you want. Tell me what you want, and tell me how I can help. I will never force you to do something you don't want to do. Would you like for me to tell you one of the things I would like to do, though?" Alexis asked. Alexis knew what she could do, but she had to be sure the punishment fit the crime, and she had to see what Temple wanted to do about everything before a definitely planned overstep on Alexis's part.

"Tell me what you would do," Temple croaked.

"First, I would put on my Pink Power Ranger costume." Temple smiled just slightly. "Nah. I wouldn't do that. I'd be too easily identified. But before this weekend is out, I would observe Connor and his friend.

They're going to go to the mall or something, maybe a restaurant. I don't know. What I *do* know is they aren't going to stay cooped up all weekend. At the first sign the friend is alone, I would ask him for the time. Then I would pretend to drop something and ask for his help finding it. I look too young, which means he's going to think I'm a child and not a teenager, and I won't disabuse him of the notion. But I'll tell him I found whatever it is we were hunting and ask him for a hand up. I will then return to standing and with him in my grip, I will throw him to the ground, and while still holding his arm, I will break it in three places. Then I will leave." My voice drifted off. "That's what I would do. I can and will if you give me permission."

"B-but what if he hurts you?" Temple stammered.

"He can't," Alexis stated confidently. "And he can't surprise me either. I already have a plan. But do you want to have Mom know what's going on? I kind of think we should let her know. She can help with some of the things I can't since I'm not your guardian, and I'm not over twenty-one."

"Could you go get her, Lex, but could you do all the talking, and could you tell her about the broken arm?" Temple's smile was wan at best, but even if she didn't want the broken arm, Alexis was going to break the guy's arm some time before the end of the weekend.

I'm relieved Alexis went to Sam and not to me. I think I would have rushed to the Dobsons' house and grabbed Connor's friend, turning his face into raw hamburger and requiring the kid be put on a ventilator. Sam eventually told me what had happened after the weekend was over. I'm not sure what I would have done had I known what Alexis had in mind. She did, in fact, find the rapist, and she did break his arm. He couldn't play football when he returned to school, which was a shame since he played division one and was being considered to be a top prospect as a wide receiver in next year's NFL draft. He would have had a bright future if he hadn't fucked my daughter.

Sam took Temple and Alexis to Planned Parenthood where she was thoroughly examined and given Plan B. Sam also found a therapist for Temple and Alexis, and they began therapy the following week. As a solution, I can't support vengeance, but as a dad, I would back Alexis 100% if she were ever brought to the fore.

And Sam? She had to act as if Alexis's plan were pure fancy and not a promise on behalf of her wronged sister. We knew we could stop Alexis, but we decided to give her all the free time she would need, and we told Pat to drive his sister anywhere she wanted to go for the rest of the weekend whenever she wanted to go there and to wait for her to return to the car.

I told this story to Clark a few years later, maybe when Alexis was a freshman in college. Clark did not seem surprised by the story and Alexis's involvement, but I did wonder if we did the wrong thing by providing special dispensation to Alexis when we had taught the kids to walk away from bullies and not take justice into their own hands. But the circumstances. God. Temple would want everything to fade away, and she would probably fade away, too. Because of Connor's friend's prodigious skill on the gridiron, he would probably get a free pass, and a rookie NFL contract for a few million dollars while my little girl would shrink and shrink inside herself. Alexis could be almost invisible, and she would only be caught if she allowed herself to be caught.

I asked Alexis maybe two years ago what happened when she broke the kid's arm. She said, "It all went like I planned, and while he was holding his arm, I said, 'You raped a girl on Friday night.' He looked completely clueless, so I said, 'Did you or did you not have sex with a girl on Friday night?' His face was all white from shock, but he nodded affirmatively. I said, 'The girl was my sister. You choked her, left marks all over her neck, and you tore her hymen.' He stuttered all stupid-like, 'Her what?' And I said, 'When you had non-consensual sex with my sister, you took her virginity.' And he said, 'I didn't mean to hurt her.' And I said, 'Well why then did you choke her to the point of passing out?' He was ready to pass out from the pain in his arm. Not only did I break it in three places, but I broke a thumb and an index finger to make it really hard for him to catch a football.

"I wanted to make sure he would have arthritis in his fingers and arms and think about how he stole a girl's innocence every time it rained and he felt rheumatic pain in his bones and joints." What was probably the most remarkable part of Alexis's story was how conversational she was in relaying events. It was akin to my asking her how much homework she had on any given school night.

Alexis had social media because all kids have social media these days. Hers was fairly sparse, though. She had links to a few philanthropies and her sorority. She curated the content carefully, only allowing very basic, surface information online. She had a link to GoodReads, and indicated she liked, "What We Do In The Shadows." She was simply a college student who did some fundraising and liked to read. When Clark told Sam and me about Alexis being perfect for Diamond Teams, we did a complete review of her, just like we would for any new employee, and she had a smaller digital footprint to clean up than almost all of our other employees did when we originally hired them. Meaning: Guy Brown might have a tough time learning about Alexis, unless he hired an investigator to follow her around for a few weeks; and even if he did, good luck. No one knew more about Alexis than what she wanted them to know.

CHAPTER 45
Kevin and Guy – *5 months ago*

Kevin registered for the conference in Indianapolis. Guy registered for the conference, and so did the others in their small group.

Kevin received an email from the conference sponsor asking for confirmation of his cancelation for the conference. Kevin simply stated, "I did not cancel my registration. Do you know if my hotel room has also been canceled?"

Ada, from the conference sponsor organization, flipped through the registration sheets in the accordion file on her desk. "I keep paper copies of everything, just in case my computer crashes," she said. "With all the hackers, paper is my source of truth."

"Oh, okay," Kevin said absently, while he pulled up his credit card app on his phone to see if there were any fee reversals showing up from the hotel where he was supposed to be staying.

"Aha!" Ada exclaimed, taking Kevin by surprise. "We arranged your hotel ourselves, and we haven't canceled anything because we wanted your verbal confirmation."

"Great," Kevin said. "I really appreciate your email about the cancelation. If there are any other changes made to my reservations or registration or anything, please contact me for verbal confirmation. I fully intend to participate in this conference."

After ringing off the call, Kevin left his office, walking down the street to grab a cappuccino to get him through the rest of the day. When he presented his credit card to pay for his drink, the transaction wouldn't go through. He tried a few times, holding his card this way and that. He tried using Apple Pay on his phone, and nothing worked. "Huh," he said. "I don't think I've had a card failure or anything like this for over fifteen years."

After the coffee shop incident, other strange little things began to happen. One morning Kevin had a flat tire. Another morning, his car battery was dead. One day he and Kate were overdrawn because an automated funds transfer was stopped. Kate contacted the bank and discovered someone had contacted them to say the transfer was an error and not to complete the transaction. The caller even knew their security questions and passphrases. Kate had to explain she and Kevin had been hacked. The bank offered her voice matching as part of their multi-factor authentication effort. She said great, and both she and Kevin had to read some stuff out loud, with their laptops as the intended audience.

Kate and Kevin went to California to visit Michelle. When they returned from the trip, tired and happy, they lay down for the sleep of weary travelers. They awoke to little bites on their legs. When they flipped the mattress over, they found bedbugs.

CHAPTER 46
Indianapolis Conference – *4 months ago*

Kevin checked a bag for the conference in Indianapolis, and, predictably, it was lost. Guy, too, checked a bag for the conference in Indianapolis, and, coincidentally, it, too, was lost.

While waiting for their bags, Kevin and Guy found each other in the hotel bar, "What are the odds?" Kevin laughed.

"Right?" Guy smiled. "I think I'm going to wait it out a little bit before I buy some new clothes. The lost baggage people are supposed to call me if they find my stuff."

"Same," said Kevin. "You want to go bowling? There's a bar a few blocks over with a couple bowling lanes in it."

They walked to the bar, bowled for a while, and drank a little more. Kevin said, "Tell me how you've been."

Guy responded. "I don't have a big social circle, and I find most of my social interaction is with our group during these conferences. Like-minded people and all that. I date some and recently started working on a strategy book." Guy paused a beat before saying, "Can I tell you something, and you promise not to think poorly of me or anything?"

"Sure," Kevin said. "Anything. What's up?"

"You know I have a four year-old son, right?"

Kevin nodded.

"There was a weird financial snag at his daycare/preschool, and the director threatened to remove him and plainly stated there were other boys and girls who could take Harris's spot. I made a single large payment to cover all of Harris's fees until he starts kindergarten in the fall."

The look on Kevin's face showed he knew nothing about the predicament Guy had been in.

"One day, I was waiting to cross the street, and there were a bunch of people surrounding me. I saw the daycare director in front of me. She didn't see me. The cars were going so fast through the intersection. And just for a moment, I thought how easy it would be to push her into traffic. No one would know it was me. There were so many people, it would look purely like an accident."

Kevin stared steadily at Guy to gauge whether or not he was serious, but Guy retained a sober countenance.

Guy paused. "What would you have done?"

While Kevin thought, he drew circles in the condensation left where his beer bottle had sat on the bar. "I would not take the nuclear option...ever."

First Kevin's and, moments later, Guy's cell phones rang. They both received updates from the airport about their missing luggage, which was no longer missing. Everything would be delivered to the hotel within the hour.

"I guess I don't need to go shopping after all," Kevin chuckled, "which is probably for the best. My kids hate it, when I do my own shopping."

"You look all right to me. Who buys your clothes?"

"My kids are in college, and they order things for me online. I hate going to stores and avoid it if I can."

Guy said, "I know you told me once where your kids go to school, but I can't remember off the top of my head."

Kevin swallowed his beer, "Michelle is at Stanford, and Dean is at Northwestern. They're terrific kids."

Guy said, "Stanford? I'll be guest-lecturing there and at Berkeley next month. I like going out there. It's a different vibe, different environment. It's nice. This will be my first time to lecture at Berkeley. Should be interesting."

"Michelle is in the business school at Stanford, and we have friends whose daughter is in the business school at Berkeley. How crazy is that? You might get to meet one or both of them while you're out there. Would it be all right to share your email with either of them? I'm sure either of them would love to pick your brain," Kevin said with enthusiasm.

They settled their bills, made their way back to their hotel to retrieve their luggage, then tucked into their respective rooms for the night. Guy's impression of Kevin not knowing what Kate did or her relationship with him was unchanged. He could not fathom how something so fundamental could be withheld from someone's spouse.

Diamond Teams placed personnel in key points throughout the food, lodging, entertainment, and conference spaces. Aside from one of Kevin and Guy's friends falling on some ice hidden beneath the snow, the conference went without a hitch. Kevin did exactly what he was supposed to do, and nothing seemed amiss.

Kate, Chris, Sam, Clark, and James were privy to all of Kevin's interactions with Guy, and they all felt confident things would take a turn once Guy made his way to California. Friends from an acronym agency monitored internet traffic from Guy's room and devices, and there didn't seem to be anything alarming immediately in the offing.

CHAPTER 47
The Parents
James Navarro's ranch – *3 months ago*

"Dad, can you help me get Blondie saddled up?" Kate asked. Sam, Chris, and Kevin's horses were already saddled, and they were working on getting themselves settled on their rides.

"Sure. Hold onto Shirley's lead for a sec."

James made short work of getting Blondie squared away. James liked to name his mares after female singers. Shirley was named for Shirley Manson from Garbage.

The five of them left the barn, taking a slow turn through James's property. The sun beat down on them relentlessly, not daring even a single cloud to mar the sky's perfection. James was the first to speak. "Both Michelle and Alexis are smitten with Guy Brown, but they are aware he means harm to one or both of them. Both girls want to slip something into his food or drink.

"Alexis says she's ready to go all 'Pink Power Ranger on Guy's ass.'" James shook his head smiling. He leaned forward, running his fingers through Shirley's mane.

"James," Chris said. "This is especially hard for all of us because it's our girls. I don't know how strategic I can be in plotting a course for them because it hits too close to home for me, and I think Sam feels the same way." Chris looked over to Sam who was nodding her head in agreement. Sam's horse, Gandalf, stopped to nose something around in the dirt, and Sam returned her gaze to what the horse was doing. Had she not been wearing sunglasses, they all would have seen her eyes welling.

"I understand the sentiment. When you all started this company. I knew there was the potential for someone to go off the deep end, and I felt exactly how you felt. My daughter, my sweet Kate, was out there sometimes making the rules as she went. What you all have done, though, has exceeded my wildest expectations. But now, you all get to occupy my position. Your girls don't get to make the rules, though. Well, at least, not the way you all did.

"You have so many different ideas the work groups came up with, though, and many of the ideas are viable and can be implemented without a lot of risk and with a minimal amount of personnel involvement. The more people you get into this operation, the greater the chance of detection—which is something critical you need to consider prior to putting a plan into action.

"What both girls want to know, though, is what Guy's plan is. How is he going to harm them? They know it would be painful psychically for everyone, and possibly physically painful for whoever his intended victim is. But they want to punish him in equal measure for what he has planned, no more and no less. They also want to remove any future threat he may pose. Mmmm. And I almost forgot, Michelle wants a key logger on all of Guy's devices if we can find them all. She wants all the passwords she can get her hands on. Both of the girls think with Guy being who Guy is, he has already documented a plan, and they want it. Personally, I think after learning his lesson with us the first time, he probably has more than a few plans documented."

CHAPTER 48

Guy – *2 months ago – Lecture week, Monday, Berkeley*

I'm lecturing at Berkeley first and plan to be there for a full week. Kevin passed my email address on to both Alexis and Michelle. Michelle is a strange one, if you look at her on paper. She has a few patents already, and she's pursuing a business degree, presumably to get some of her patents to market. She interned with a company in the UK over the summer, and her work was classified. She has a brilliant mind, but she is a problem solver, fixer, and inventor. Again, based on what I see on paper, I would expect her to be odd, however, she's quite charming from what I've seen on her social media.

Alexis is gregarious. She is going to be in the C-suite someday. She is calculating, astute, and five minutes ahead of everyone else in the room. There's not much about her online. She has a profile photo, incredibly basic bio, and a few posts from high school. I watched her for a while before my lecture dates were due to start at Berkeley. I wanted to get a better feel for who she is and see how she could best fit into my plans. I think I would structure my lecture a little differently than I normally would. Having a chance to interact with her was going to be the only way I would know which strategy I would employ for taking down all of Diamond Teams. This was going to be a lab practical of sorts where I could test out the theories in the book I had begun writing on power dynamics and identifying interpersonal strategies to leverage relationships. I planned to dedicate the book to Kate.

I broke Alexis's class into small groups and gave each group a different case study. I would get a good feel for their thought processes today, and then during tomorrow's class, I would go through the psychology, logic, and mathematical modeling to determine the best course of action. On day three, I would give them another case study, and then discuss the differences between their solutions from the two different cases and talk through how they might handle the cases from the first day differently. Going the route of smaller groups would give me the chance to interact with Alexis directly.

As the students made their way into the classroom, I asked them to pick up an index card from the stack next to the lecture podium. Every card was numbered. I asked the students with the number one to gather in the back left corner of the room; group two to the back right; group three to the front left; and group four to the front right. Alexis was in group three. I learned Alexis thinks just like I do. She must have already taken a good number of psychology classes and management science, too. What was she going to do after graduation? If I weren't dead set on ruining her, her parents', and Kate's lives, I would have hired this girl. After she picked up her index card, she approached me, extending her hand, "Hi. Alexis Kono. I'm one of the college students who has been emailing you in preparation for this amazing lecture. Kevin Baldwin gave me your email address. You know him professionally, I understand." I took her tiny hand in mine and greeted her formally. She continued, "I have so been looking forward to your lecture. I've read your dissertation and all of your articles, and I'm truly impressed by your career trajectory. Chief Strategy Officer is my ambition, too." She pinkened, and her earnestness gave me a rush. I wondered how quickly I could get her to trust me, to go somewhere alone with me. My plan for her was already in motion, and I didn't think it would take much effort judging from this first encounter.

Nearly everyone has friends. Nearly everyone has acquaintances. If you're not part of the group of 'nearly everyone,' money fills palms and creates pathways not requiring friends or acquaintances. Everyone has a use for money. I found some people who had uses for young women. They were a club who rented young women to anyone who could pay, generally kept them for a week or two, and discarded them when they were finished. I had been following the group for a while to see what the outcomes were for the young women, and, without exception, they were left virtually shell-shocked, husks of their former selves, and hollow. Not a single one was capable of living independently. Some had been rendered incontinent from the abuse. One had lost an eye. Another had been disobedient and attempted escape. She had lost a foot, but after her release, infection had set in, and she was now an amputee from just above the knee. As despicable as they were, this club would serve my purposes. In fact, I would be the person to deliver Alexis to Kate's door, leaving Kate the responsibility of reuniting Alexis with her family.

It was a shame, really, to look at the light in her eyes and all the potential burning inside of her and knowing I would be responsible for snuffing it out. She was asking if I would be free to join her and some friends for dinner while I was in town. I knew she felt comfortable with me based on the introduction via Kevin, otherwise, I was a stranger and wouldn't have merited the invitation. I accepted.

"Wonderful," she said. She wrote down the name of a restaurant on the back of one of the index cards, and we arranged to meet in the bar for drinks with her and some classmates before dinner. Tonight was all about trust building and nothing more.

CHAPTER 49
The Girls – *2 months ago, Lecture week, Monday*

"I met him and invited him to dinner with my group from class," Alexis said.

"You gave him the note and used the pen I gave you?" Michelle asked. During Michelle's internship over the summer, she worked with a team on nanotechnology. The ink on the note Alexis gave Guy contained nano processors able to lift data from any device within a programmed proximity. Alexis affirmed she had used Michelle's ink pen. "Great," Michelle said. "I'll start looking at the data we're able to pull from his phone. I'll get into his phone first then will be able to hack into his laptop and cloud accounts."

The girls had agreed, once contact with Guy had been made, not to refer to their parents or Diamond Teams by name. They called them the dry cleaners or the store or talked about lingerie. Anyone listening to any subsequent phone calls between them would hear two college students talking about a hot prof, going to the mall, buying some G-strings, and borrowing earrings or taking an outfit to the dry cleaners.

Alexis arrived at the restaurant first. She found all the exits, restrooms, and storerooms. She knew the bartender from school, and at least a couple of the wait staff were from Diamond Teams. She wore a long skirt and coordinating bandeau top in an Aegean blue and had pulled up her blond hair in a messy bun with loose tendrils framing her face and listing lazily along her neck. A couple other students from class arrived, but Alexis was the standout, physically and intellectually.

Guy was late, good-naturedly blaming himself for taking a nap after his lecture and sleeping through his alarm. In reality, he had been following Alexis, then checking in with the group he had arranged to supply a young lady. He spent some time going through the case studies from class and was awestruck by the detail and thought put into the work by Alexis and her group. Their solution was elegant, fully thought out, logical, compelling, and exquisite in its simplicity and ultimate outcome. They had even had the foresight to include some mathematical modeling to support their solution. Guy prided himself on seeing all the angles and solutions, but this was one he didn't see, and he loathed and admired in equal measure the genius behind it.

Once seated in the dining room in a large round booth accommodating the six of them, the students wanted to discuss the case study from class. Guy asked, "How did you all decide on the outcome you chose? I would love to know the thought process."

A junior named Brady spoke up. "I would be thrilled to take credit or even say we brainstormed and our hive mind conjured a solution, but the truth is…it was all Alexis. Once she offered up a solution, the rest of us jumped in to make sure it was viable, which we uncovered with our modeling. Lex, you want to tell Dr. Brown how you landed on the solution?"

Alexis, sitting next to Guy, had to turn bodily to be able to face him and make eye contact. She had the bluest eyes, reflecting the blue of her bandeau. Guy had a hard time focusing on what Alexis was saying because he was so focused on her.

Alexis said, "You know how there's always a 'do nothing' option?"

Everyone's heads bobbed up and down, including Guy's. Alexis went on, "Well, I like an option called, 'Do almost nothing.' It doesn't require all the responsibility be assigned to one person, has a defined goal, and the flexibility to be time-bound or not. I begin with all the what-ifs, and in my head, I start attaching numerical values to all the scenarios. I can usually work out mathematically what the best solution would be, and then we poke holes, redecorate, and begin modeling. I have found the nuclear option is hardly ever the best solution, and in many cases, the best solution is usually something a very small amount more than nothing. Mathematically, I've proven this and generated enough models with up to ten derivatives and my 'do almost nothing' option provides enough gentle flexibility for a robust, iterative process."

This girl. If Guy weren't bent on destroying her, her parents, her parents' friends, and their company, he would hire her or clone her. Alexis knew she had him. She could see it in his eyes, the enchantment. She had one upped him without rubbing his nose in it. She left her phone face down on the tabletop and could see it vibrating with an incoming call. Alexis's facial expression showed worry crossing her brow when she turned the phone over to see who was calling. "I'm sorry, everyone. I have to take this call." She engineered her way out of the booth, holding the phone to her ear, whispering, "This is Alexis." She made her way down the hallway to the ladies' restroom.

"Hi," said Michelle. "Wanted to let you know the store provided the full inventory. I think there's going to be a dry cleaning drop off toward the end of the week, probably a van and warehouse setup. There was a big discussion about website design today. How's dinner?"

"Waiting to place my order, but my guest is a stone cold fox, and I would love to screw the guy if he weren't trying to screw me…over," Alexis said on a very quiet laugh.

"Enjoy yourself tonight," Michelle said. "Tomorrow we'll get the dry cleaning and website business arranged."

Alexis returned to the table, wedging herself between Guy and a classmate. When she was settled into her seat, she put her hand on Guy's knee, not looking at him. She felt his eyes on her, and she made it a point not to look at him until their server came to the table to take everyone's dinner orders. She asked Guy in a low voice, "What are you going to have?" Their gazes locked, and he knew she was intimating more than dinner. He had not calculated she would be aggressive toward him. From all his research, he couldn't find much about her personality, and he had made the mistake of creating a profile for her based on what he found online. She seemed private, though, and he didn't like being taken by surprise and having his assumptions prove to be so off base.

Guy said, "I think I'm going to have something light and save room for dessert. You?"

Alexis moved her hand up his thigh just the smallest bit, smiles, and said, "Same." She ordered a beet and goat cheese salad with grilled salmon. "It's a big salad. Would you want to split it?" she asked Guy.

He thought, 'Why the hell not?' It had been a while since someone had been as overt as Alexis was, and he found he liked it. "Sure. Sounds great," he said. Alexis placed the order and requested an extra plate for splitting everything. When their salad arrived, he observed her small, deft hands working with the fork and knife, rendering a near replica of the original salad in its presentation on the extra plate. He noted she didn't miss a single detail. She wouldn't make a mistake unless she meant to make one.

After dinner, the group dispersed, but Alexis stayed with Guy. "There's a good ice cream place down the street. How do you feel about ice cream? We can walk back toward campus. I'm assuming you're in one of the hotels close to the university. I live in a sorority, so we can't really hang out there. Am I being too forward?" Alexis blushed. "Can you tell I'm a little nervous? I don't think I even breathed through all of that!" She gave a self-deprecating laugh.

Guy laughed. She was nervous. For all her bravado and intelligence and the air of her being comfortable in her own skin, she was nervous. He wondered if she was still a virgin, which caused him a momentary pinch of guilt, knowing what he was going to do to her. "Alexis, you are refreshing. Except for your nerves right now, you seem completely unapologetic expressing what you want, and your poise is…well, it's alluring."

Alluring. She liked 'alluring,' since it's what she had been aiming for throughout the evening. She wanted him to think of her. She wondered if he would have second thoughts about his plans.

They stopped for ice cream, then walked to Guy's hotel, hand in hand. "This is me," Guy said. He leaned down, cupping her chin, and placed a gentle kiss on her forehead. "I'm not going to lie. I would love to invite you to my room, but I'm your instructor, and there are dynamics at play here, and I'm nine years older than you, and this isn't the right time or circumstance."

"I can't say I'm not disappointed," Alexis said, "but I completely understand how you wouldn't want to leverage the power dynamic to create a negative impact." She made eye contact with him, and she knew she had a provocative glint in her eye when she said, "There's always the next few days, though. Then you're off to your next stop on the lecture circuit, right?"

"Something like that," Guy said slowly. How could she know about his book, or was she attuned to him in a way he couldn't see. Did he mention his book to her or her class? He was fairly certain he didn't mention it at dinner.

She backed away from him. "Tomorrow then." She wondered if he was too broken or too proud to abandon his focus on seeking revenge. She walked toward her sorority house, taking a moment to sit on a bus bench to look over her email. Michelle sent the scans from TSA of the contents of Guy's suitcase and carry-on. He had zip ties. Alexis hated zip ties, but she could free herself from them pretty easily.

The next day, she would go to class. She wasn't sure if throwing in the bit about leveraging power dynamics was too over the top and would cause suspicion or awe or confusion. Michelle had found his book notes and manuscript, and Alexis had quickly skimmed it. What he had was interesting, hardly groundbreaking, but the application was the most novel part of what he was introducing in his book.

Before he finished at Berkeley, they would go for a hike, and Alexis would bring a picnic lunch of beautifully made subs, a bottle of wine, and one or two pieces of fresh fruit. Guy would naturally be suspicious of the food or wine being drugged; however, he might be lured into a false sense of security if Alexis ate and drank everything she included in the picnic. He would know he was outmaneuvered once he found himself bound and gagged, waking up in an unfamiliar location, coming through the fog of sedation.

CHAPTER 50

Guy – *2 months ago, Lecture week, Tuesday, Berkeley*

Alexis. It's too bad she's the sacrificial lamb. Her brain is a work of art. In class, the four small groups' first case studies were all over the place, with Alexis's group's being presentation-ready. Today, going through the logic and mathematical modeling exercises brought almost everyone to the same plane of understanding. I looked at the class and made eye contact with Alexis. She wasn't taking notes. She either had a thorough understanding of the concepts, or she had her own method rendering the same results. I would have to ask her about her process.

I knew I was taking the nuclear option. If I followed her practice of 'do almost nothing,' the stalking business would still be hanging out there, I still wouldn't have been able to complete my project, I'd still be on a leave of absence from work, and Virginia would still deny me unsupervised visitation with Harris. I wondered how easy it would be for Kate to have the stalking re-buried. If she could do that, it would eliminate my most pressing problems. I wouldn't have my money back, and I would still be a failure in completing my project, and then there was the degradation of being taken down a peg. I was so scared, I wet myself. God! I'm sure they could smell the fear and urine coming off me in rivulets. Just thinking about the whole night caused a burning feeling in my gut of resentment, humiliation, fear, anger, and the desire for retribution. What magnified all my feelings were the loss of my job and son, and I would do anything to get those back. Building an allegorical case study might be an option. I'd have the top performers in the Berkeley class come together to see what kind of solution they would recommend. I think I would have the group come up with solutions for both sides of the case.

CHAPTER 51
The Case Study

Acme Supply Company is a conglomerate with interests in a variety of industries, with the overarching goal of using technology to make people's lives better and more secure. One of their lines of business sells premium widgets that have a unique GPS capability. In order to purchase the widgets, a contract for fulfillment and security deposit are required. The party purchasing the widgets must obtain government clearance to be cleared to make the purchase and must agree not to sell the widgets to certain third parties (e.g., weapons brokers, hostile nations, etc.) who would reverse engineer and weaponize the widgets.

Snuffy Smith Enterprises (SSE) receives government clearance and has produced documentation they plan to use the widgets in cars and also in memory care facilities. Unbeknownst to Acme, SSE has a very lucrative deal in the works with a hostile nation for the widgets, and SSE plans to sell all the widgets to them. When SSE signs the contract with Acme, the company has no intention of honoring the provisions and feels its rights to commerce and free trade are being violated.

Acme learns of the deception, refuses to sell the widgets, keeps the security deposit, and informs the hostile nation directly of SSE's intentional breach of contract. The hostile nation is angry with the managing director of SSE and has made financial, physical, and reputational threats.

- How could retribution by SSE be a viable option?
- If SSE undertook a strategy of retribution against ACME, what is ACME's best counterstrategy?
- SSE is facing total shutdown, what is SSE's best course of action given the facts of the case? Is there a scenario where they can remain in business?
- What's the best strategy for resolving things with the hostile nation?

CHAPTER 52
The Girls – *Lecture week, Tuesday night*

"Michelle, did you read the case study yet?" Alexis spoke quietly into the phone. "I think he wants non-emotional insight into the situation between the dry cleaners and him. He must realize he's too emotionally invested and not thinking rationally. He wants a certain outcome, but he thinks the only way to do it is through some kind of scorched earth path."

"I agree," Michelle said. "Do you want to know what I think?"

"Hit me."

"There's no finesse, no strategy, no higher thought involved here, OK?" Michelle said.

"OK," Alexis answered warily.

"Go on the hike. He's going to make his move on the hike. You're going to make your move on the hike. I will be there to back you up. I will scout it tomorrow and get you all the details. Dean is coming out here for part of his Spring Break and will be arriving tonight. He's awesome at hiking and has done a lot of wilderness stuff. Leave it with us."

"What do I do about the case study? Should I go ahead and put the solutions together, or should I be prepping for the hike?"

"Do the case study," Michelle advised. "You know you want to, and Guy will expect an elegant solution. Give him the solution, but make sure it's a gross departure from his scorched earth approach.

"You know how in 'A Christmas Carol' when the Ghost of Christmas Future arrives, shows Scrooge how his life could have been, and how his choices led him to loneliness and devastation? You need to show the devastation."

"I can do that," Alexis said, "because it's not far off base anyway."

CHAPTER 53
The Baldwin Kids, *Lecture week, Wednesday*

Dean and Michelle Baldwin, nearly Irish twins, were fourteen months apart, with Michelle entering the world with loud screaming and pounding fists and pulsing little feet. Dean arrived a little differently as an emergency C-section. Kate's contractions were non-productive and Dean seemed to be pretty content hanging out in the womb. When he was delivered, he squawked a bit but seemed to take in everyone in the room, focusing his gaze on his parents. The nurses placed the baby in Kate's arms once she was sewn up and the baby was tidied. Kevin was in the room for both births, and he teared up each time he witnessed the miracle of his children's departure from their mother's body. He knew Kate did not enjoy pregnancy, but he also knew from the moment she knew she was expecting how much she loved those progressing balls of cells which were the amalgamation of their love.

Dean was a little late to talk when he was a toddler because Michelle talked for him, but once he started talking, he was quick to refute or support Michelle, as appropriate. Michelle loved to dream, and she shared her fantastical ideas with Dean, and he always knew no matter how far-fetched her ideas were, she could find a way to make them into reality. Dean watched out for Michelle. He saw every hazard, both human and non-human, and constantly looked ahead, calculating risks and steering them toward safety and the security of home and their parents.

As the Baldwin kids got older, they remained close, even though they pursued their own interests and had their own groups of friends. They played a game they devised, which they called, "Inventor." They would invent something. It could be tangible or not, realistic or not, useful or not…something, anything. The whole game took place in their 'shop,' and a corporate spy named 'The Minotaur,' would start hunting for the Inventors or the Invention. Initially neither of them wanted to be The Minotaur, and they made Kate be The Minotaur. Sometimes she won, sometimes she lost. When Kate lost, Dean noticed she often chose to lose. She was observing something about their gameplay, and he decided to observe her decision-making and gameplay as well. He would raise an eyebrow to Michelle, and she would know immediately they were going to try to lose to see how Kate would try to beat them to the loss. And then they would play again, and when they knew Kate was out to win, they would try to outplay her. Eventually, Michelle and Dean felt the best role in the game was The Minotaur, though Michelle loved to do the inventing. They created their own game board which looked like the HVAC blueprint of their home, and the goal was to get the invention out of the shop without having a faceoff with The Minotaur. If the inventor had a faceoff with The Minotaur, there were a series of three tasks to be completed. When they were in middle school, one of the tasks was always The Gettysburg Address. In junior high and high school, they changed gears requiring the recitation of a Shakespearean soliloquy or the preamble to the constitution. One time they made Kate recite all the lyrics to 'Hollaback Girl,' which to their surprise, she did with ease. They should have known better. Their grandfather had a horse named Gwen.

Eventually, Inventor moved from being on a game board to being outdoors. The whole family would pack up and go to a park. They would take a topographical map of the area and plot the boundaries of the game, and one parent or both kids would take the role of The Minotaur. No one in the Baldwin household was a stranger to primitive camping or preying on savvy, aware family members. The best games were when their uncle and grandfather and family friends, the Kelley-Konos all got together. There would be multiple minotaurs and inventions, and they could team up or destroy one another. If destruction was the goal, then there would be a faceoff. After they finished a game, they would all sit around and talk about where they were hiding, how they planned their routes for escape, if they had to lie to get information.

The kids didn't know their game was similar to what Kate, Sam, and Chris did in their jobs. The three principals of Diamond Teams loved the perspective of fun their children injected into evading, escaping, or preying.

When Michelle picked up Dean from the airport, she hugged her brother, handed him a topographical map of the park known for having really good hiking trails but also untamed wilderness, and said, "Look this over while I get us out of the city—it's going to be a little over three hours to get there. We're going to be playing 'Inventor' while you're here, and we're The Minotaur. We have to plot everything today, and we are heading somewhere you're going to love." As they walked to the car, Michelle texted Alexis.

Michelle: Inventor game prep, tomorrow. Dean's here. We're heading to the pin right now. We'll get situated and see you in the morning.

Alexis: Cool. Drop a pin, and I'll meet you there.

Michelle: Greenlight on hike?

Alexis: Yep.

Michelle: Cool.

Leaving the airport, Dean casually asked, "So how is the Pink Power Ranger?" When they were children, Alexis was always the Kelley-Kono kid he wound up playing with, since they were the same age and grade in school. Their moms were close, and the girls seemed like cousins to one another, but Dean had harbored a crush on Alexis since the time he could walk. He knew what was at stake with this game of Inventor, and he would give every ounce of energy he had to ensure a win for himself, Michelle, and Alexis.

Alexis would send email to Guy to let him know they would need to get an early start on Saturday, to plan for a full day and around eleven miles of hiking in Yosemite National Park. The next few days would be good days, she decided, pocketing her phone.

Dean sent a group text to his parents, grandfather, and uncle.

Dean: Arrived in San Francisco. Michelle is taking me to Yosemite. Playing "Inventor" this weekend. Sending location when we arrive. Love to all!!

James: Get me a t-shirt and brochure.

Clark: Send me some photos.

Kate: Stay hydrated.

Kevin: Drink water, not booze!

Dean paired his phone with Michelle's car, searching for the perfect song to kick off their sibling road trip. Red Hot Chili Peppers. "Road Trippin." The Baldwin kids sang along, "Just a mirror for the sun," while they headed East.

CHAPTER 54
The Parents and Extended Family

Later, the same day, Kevin, Kate, Chris, Sam, James, and Clark sat around their respective computers to discuss what Michelle, Dean, and Alexis were doing in Yosemite National Park. James started the conversation. "How does everyone feel about them playing Inventor?"

Kate responded, "I feel fine about the game, but I'm not sure about Yosemite. People die or get lost there. Do they have provisions in case they get lost? Do they know how to get out?"

Chris said, "I feel pretty confident in their ability to navigate the park, or at least the part where they're going to run the game. Remember Kevin and I took the boys out there for a week about, what, five years ago?"

Kevin nodded and stated, "Both of the boys did fine. Kept their cool, made good decisions, stocked their packs appropriately. I'm thinking we should text the kids a checklist or something. If they need to pick anything up, they have a little time to get what they need. Alexis is taking a backpack with her, isn't she?"

"She is," Sam said. She was drinking what looked like a very large tumbler of Diet Coke. As she raised the cup to her lips, they could all see her hand shaking. Chris sat next to her, his hand on top of her free hand, squeezing gently. No one wanted to see their children involved in something where there could be potentially catastrophic consequences. They all knew what Guy planned to do with Alexis if things managed to go his way, and they had an inkling of what the kids had planned for Guy if things went their way. James was the only one who knew the kids' end game with Guy, and he thought there was a solid chance they would be successful. Yosemite was a mighty big park. James would be there for backup or extraction as needed. He knew the parents were all capable individuals, but their emotions would add unnecessary risk to everything. Clark was staying close to Yosemite and would be on-call if James thought there might be a need to get someone else to assist, but his gut told him Alexis, Dean, and Michelle would be all right. James' phone alerted him to a new message.

Clark: You sure you don't want me to shadow you or the kids in the park?

James: Can't have you shadow the kids, especially Alexis. If Guy sees you, he will recognize you.

Clark: Right. Please don't hesitate for even a moment if there's the smallest chance you or they may need me. I am so close to the park, I can be there in an instant.

James: I know, son, and I appreciate you. Your sister does, too.

CHAPTER 55
Guy – *Lecture week, Thursday, Berkeley*

Yosemite National Park. What a great place for a hike. Alexis said to be ready early and to plan for a full day. She would pick me up on Saturday morning at 5 a.m., getting us to Yosemite around 8 a.m. She didn't like to waste a minute of the day, I guess. Her message indicated she already had an eleven-mile hike chosen.

In the grand scheme of things, my best play would be to drug Alexis when she came to pick me up. She wouldn't come to my hotel room, though, after the speech I gave her the other night. I could invite her to breakfast in the hotel restaurant, but they didn't start serving until 6 a.m. It wouldn't hurt to ask her to arrive at 6, have breakfast, then hit the road. It would throw off her plan by two hours. Still. I could give it a go. Getting to Yosemite would introduce too many variables outside my control. Taking my phone out of my pocket, I sent her an email. If I had to go to Yosemite, then I'd go to Yosemite, and I'd get this thing done. I really didn't want to have to carry her eleven miles back to the car. She'd be dead weight, and it would be such a drag.

I could keep myself occupied on the drive going through the case studies I gave to the class, evaluating their answers, looking for any insights. I could work on my manuscript. Alexis and I could talk, too. I worried about talking because I genuinely liked Alexis and talking, having a dialogue with her, opened me up to liking her more platonically, and on a deeply buried level, I didn't want to subject her to what I had planned, but it was a calculated move against Diamond Teams. My thoughts seemed to jumble, and I knew I was spiraling, every time I tried to tease Alexis apart from Diamond Teams, who her parents were, and the relationship with Kate.

But the fact remained: I was spending this time with Alexis, not Harris—my son wasn't an option because of Diamond Teams, and I had no idea if and when I would get to resume visitation. I sure as hell didn't want to do anything about the bench warrant, but I couldn't run away from it since it seemed to be the main thing standing between Harris and me, and my job and me.

I'd be leaving Stanford at the end of next week, and I wouldn't be going back to my job. I wouldn't be going back to anything. I'd be going back to my book. I would have to hire a lawyer to sort out the stalking business. When I was finished with Alexis, I would have burned the bridge between Diamond Teams and me, and there would be no assistance they could offer to squelch the stalking issue.

I needed a plan, a set of plans. Plans if my plans didn't work or I couldn't go through with my plans. Plan A – breakfast at the hotel. Best case scenario would be Alexis agreeing to a later starting time. Plan B – lunch at Yosemite. We would be about three hours into our hike by the time lunch rolled around. If the trail was rigorous, we'd be around three miles into the hike. It wouldn't be so far if I had to drag or carry her back to the car. Inconvenient, yes, but not impossible. I'd drive us back to Berkeley, and rendezvous with the man who had arranged taking Alexis for the time he and his group needed her. Plan C – upon our return to Berkeley. I would take her to dinner, drug her, take her back to her car, and make the delivery, and cap off the evening in the hotel bar when I was finished. Looking at the options, Plan B seemed most likely to yield success, variables and all.

I checked my email, looking for Alexis's reply, and sure enough, there it was. I was going to have to go with Plan B. Alexis said since she was doing the driving, she didn't want to have the two-hour delay tacked on to the back end of the day when we would be heading back from Yosemite. Fair point. I conceded easily. After lectures were finished for the day, I planned to make sure I had everything I would need for a long hike, and drugs--Klonopin, Rohypnol, Benadryl, Valium. There were decisions I needed to make about the drugs. I needed to keep Alexis sedated or compliant until I could get her back in the car. Once we returned to the car, then zip ties would do the job for the rest of the ride back to Berkeley. A pillow and blanket would make it look like she was napping in the backseat in the event I was pulled over for whatever reason (crazy things could happen) or encountered curious bystanders when we inevitably would need to stop for gas. For now, I needed to make a list of everything I would need for the most probable outcomes and hope I had already procured everything. If I had missed anything, I would need to make all the remaining purchases and get everything packed nicely into a hiking backpack. I had the rest of today and all of tomorrow to be sure I had prepared adequately. Failing to prepare is preparing to fail.

CHAPTER 56
Alexis – *Lecture week, Thursday*

My mother once told me a story from when she was a teenager. Back before cell phones were part of our landscape, she would get into her car, pop a cassette into her car's stereo, and drive the hour from her small hometown to the mall in the nearest larger city. For the time she was away from home, she was a speck in space. Anonymous and floating around, like a dust mote dancing on a sunbeam, and completely free of anyone who might know her. For the time she was away, she was just a soul, living out her existence, without expectation, and she could go anywhere, really. She was a dot on a scatter diagram, no real meaning without all the other dots, and impossible to control or catalog, only part of the collective whole, unreachable and untouchable. I loved the story, the implication of the fierce independence, and the idea of being unseen while in plain sight. I wanted to operate the same way, but with cell phones, someone could always find you, and I understood the benefits of being able to be found in an emergency situation. To date, I had never found myself in a situation where I needed help, but there was always a first time, I suppose.

My dad. Chris Kono. He's a bear of a man. I could imagine him standing on the prow of a Viking ship, and my brother Pat was a near carbon copy. My sister Temple was a blend of my parents, but I took after our mother and resembled Tinkerbell. I don't think I became cognizant of the fact I was so much smaller than other kids my age until I was in eighth grade or so. Most of the girls had stopped growing around puberty, and it seemed I was still waiting for a growth spurt. When my first period happened, I realized there would be no growth spurt. It was a disappointment. I looked at Temple and how her height and body had bloomed into the most graceful, lithe, and elongated frame, and I had counted on the same happening to me. I realized my mother was my blueprint.

Like Temple, my mother is lithe, fluid, and comfortable in her skin. But when I look at photos of her with Pat and Temple, it stuns me to think she gave birth to these two kids who are so much bigger than she is. When I see photos of the two of us together, we're two peas in a pod. We make sense. A small woman with a small daughter. Even now, on the brink of adulthood, we would easily be reunited if we were separated in a mall or an amusement park or something. We make all the sense in the world. Temple and Pat would easily be reunited with our dad. They make sense.

My desire, though, is to move through the world being seen when I want to be seen, and being anonymous and invisible, a shadow, a wraith, able to move freely when I feel I need it. I don't know if I have entirely succeeded in creating this type of existence, but it's definitely an aspiration. If I had to choose a superpower, it would be invisibility for sure.

When I was little, before my parents found the miracle of ADHD medication for me, my mind bounced around constantly. It was like a door was wide open for thoughts and ideas, and they were always crashing through. I couldn't stop them if I tried. I saw the picture of the Dutch boy who plugged the dike with his finger to stop the water from rushing through. All the water coming through was ideas, thoughts, plans, and strategies. For me, instead of the breach being the size of a finger, it was the size of a garage door. Every idea had merit, and I wanted to capture them all, and it was impossible. My frustration gained traction to the point I felt I physically had to chase all the ideas down, and I knew it wasn't feasible. How could I catch the wind? How could I collect the ocean? I would get caught in a loop of ideas and thoughts and frustration. So much frustration, and for a while I acted out. My mom saw what was going on, and we went to a child psychiatrist who ordered genetic testing to see what the best option for ADHD medication might be for me. And so it went.

The ideas? They still came all the time, but I had coping mechanisms now. I always carried a small notebook and pen in my bag. There was great succor in being able to capture fleeting thoughts, whether or not they were worthy or of merit was secondary. It was simply the act of knowing what was going through my head wouldn't be lost forever, like a fishing net, I suppose. It was quick, easy, and no one knew I was doing it, except my family. Quieting my brain allowed me to take in new information and learn, and I loved learning. I'm not sure what I'll do after I graduate from college next year, but I'd be fine staying in school for another four years, learning and melding my knowledge with some of the ideas from my notebooks. In my mind, true science fiction isn't fiction. It's a depiction of what might one day exist, and it seems, to me at least, to be the thoughts and dreams of someone with ADHD, just like me. We only have to wait for the world to catch up.

My parents let me try all sorts of sports and activities to corral my energy and harness my attention, and it made me strong physically, mentally, and emotionally. I had a strong sense of what was right, wrong, and the gray area, and I had made peace with the fact we sometimes had to operate in the gray area because right and wrong could be relative, and choosing absolutes was closing off a part of the brain, and for someone whose brain was churning out thoughts and ideas constantly, it didn't feel right to close a valve of potential value. I loved swimming, gymnastics, and karate. When I was younger, I thought martial arts and gymnastics might be enough for the Power Rangers to come find me and ask me to join them. Of course in reality, this was never going to happen; but I did find I could use all the skills I learned to help others who couldn't help themselves.

The guy who raped Temple? I check his social media occasionally, and he's not playing football. He went to law school, lives in a small town, and is married. They have a baby girl. I hope she never meets someone the likes of her father—at least not the version of him from college, the arrogant, entitled asshole who took what he wanted with no regard for anyone else, their boundaries, their wishes. Not everything ended with broken bones or physical pain. Sometimes I would have a crucial conversation (I went through crucial conversations training), and things were easily sorted and put to rights. Sometimes I would place all the dominoes in a line, and let the person know just the tiniest push on their part could send every last domino to the floor, and we came to an understanding and course correction, averting the disaster.

Every now and then, someone would attempt to mess with me at a party or a bar, and a gentle prod solved the problem, quickly, quietly, and easily; and the someone saved face. Usually, after something like this happened, I became invisible to the person, and I have to admit, being given a cloak or invisibility, or a scrap of it, seemed like I won. As long as winning (or losing) was on my terms, it was a win to me, and I liked winning.

Guy Brown. I liked his brain—the part of his brain which wasn't trying to tear apart everything my parents and Kate had worked to create. Michelle hacked him, and we knew what he planned to do with me, and yet he still pasted a smile across his face and ingratiated himself to me. We could never become friends, ever, because he was never going to be sincere.

Guy actually thought he had a right to kill someone. Because I liked how his brain worked, I tried to work through how he could come to this conclusion, like a mathematical proof. Finally, I had to remove all possible variables, stripping the situation to the barest possible components before I finally found the solution. The woman who he had wanted to kill wasn't the point at all. First and foremost, he wanted to see how it felt to take a life and see how it felt wielding the metaphorical sword. Priority two was to get away with it. No great moral outrage on his part. It all came down to vanity, pure and simple. His vanity puzzled me for a moment, but only a moment. He had always been the cream rising to the top, and over time, his self-regard and vanity ratcheted to a vantage point where he thought he could do whatever he wanted without any repercussions because he was entitled. Vanity. Bleah.

Our parents' business was a game. It was intended to be a game resulting in self-discovery and team building and strengthening. When I was in grade school, I complained and complained how it was such a drag to pack all of my things every day to go to the pool to swim laps, and how inconvenient it was for someone to have to drive me each morning before the sun came up. Wouldn't it be nice to have a pool, or a lap pool, or one of those swim spa things with the resistance flow for swimming for a couple hours every day? I worked this angle every single day for six months. I did odd jobs for Mom inside the house, and our baseboards never looked better. I was too little to use the lawn mower, but I asked how to use the weed whacker, and I did everything I could to help Dad outside the house. I announced I was going to get a paper route to earn money for a lap pool, and I think this is where my parents truly saw my commitment, and they were none too keen on my riding a bike in the wee hours of the morning.

We agreed I would be the caretaker of the lap pool. The pH strips and chemical tests were my responsibility. If I needed help with the levels when they were outside normal limits, and we needed to shock the pool, then Mom and Dad would gladly assist. We also agreed what jobs I would keep inside and outside the house, and I was pleased to have an active role in bringing the lap pool to our home.

The workmen came, dug out the ground for the pool, and then there was so much cement. All around the pool was new sidewalk. The concrete guy told me the concrete needed to cure, and I could help by spraying the new sidewalks every day with cool water for two weeks or so. I had my mom take me to Lowe's to find the perfect nozzle for our hose. It was green and had a dial on it with a bunch of settings for all the different flow rates and spray patterns. I think the only thing to make this nozzle cooler would have been if it were pink; but I sprayed the new concrete every day, and after two weeks, I considered it cured. I loved it when I pointed the spray in just the right direction that the angle of the sunlight hitting the water droplets created a rainbow. The rainbow was one of the things I looked forward to finding every time I worked on curing the concrete. All this concrete curing is what I felt my parents' work did for their clients. The curing process kept the concrete from cracking and devolving prematurely. It enhanced the integrity of the matrix poured over the space. What my parents did was so similar but with people. Corporate America, in my opinion, needed some curing, and I was proud of what my parents were doing to contribute to even the tiniest improvements.

In my few interactions with Guy Brown over the past week, I found him to be highly intelligent, guarded, and charming. He displayed no outward signs of deceit, and knowing what I knew he planned to do with me, his complete lack of a 'tell' bothered me. During classes and during the evening at dinner, I watched him carefully. I didn't bother taking notes. My focus was on this guy, this aberration, and then I realized what he did when he was off kilter. I asked a few questions to see his response. I tossed him some easy questions, some difficult. I came on to him. Sure enough, his go-to reaction was placing his hand in his pants pocket. It was such a casual gesture, to all outward appearances, it seemed natural. But it wasn't. Guy was an animated speaker, and subduing his natural inclination to move around, gesticulate, and punctuate his words with movement was what gave him away. I wondered if he ever watched videos of his lectures to look for his responses to inquiries.

When I was in high school, I joined the debate team. I watched replays of my performance, and I quickly observed my physical response to anything making me unsure or uncomfortable. I consciously worked to stop. I continued watching videos for the next few years to ensure I didn't slide back into old habits or didn't create some new tell I would need to erase. If I give a presentation, I rehearse it often enough and watch video replays. I anticipate questions and have answers prepared. On the off chance I receive a question I didn't forecast, I don't ever waver, and carry on with the same aplomb. I always know my material.

With the exception of my family and a few close friends, no one knew more about me than I wanted them to know. Keeping this layer of insulation was what made me a fierce and dangerous competitor. It certainly helped me in karate. It helped me with Guy Brown. I think he thought he could read me, and I did not disabuse him of anything he thought he had picked up. What a tool. He was hot and all, but he was a dad! And he was crazy. And he was homicidal. I'm twenty-one. I do not want any part of Guy Brown's situation and mental shit show.

But with a little help, I would save myself, my parents' company, and we would take Guy Brown's token off the game board. Michelle had a brilliant solution, and we were going to work through the mechanics, and by the time I went to sleep on Saturday, we would reach the finish line. I would sit through his class this morning then drive out to Yosemite to start the Inventor setup. What a great game, and what a fabulous location.

CHAPTER 57
The Kids – *Friday, Yosemite National Park*

Alexis, Dean, and Michelle met in a camping area inside the park. The morning found the three of them sipping coffee and sitting on logs around what had been a small campfire the previous night. Michelle brought two pieces of cardboard out of her tent. Both had maps taped to them and were decorated liberally with solid and dotted-lines, arrows, and Post-its. The three of them gathered around the maps, each equipped with red, green, and black markers.

"Rules of game play," Michelle began. "We all agree we will stay within the bounds marked in red on the map. It's a safety thing. We're biting off a tiny bit of the 761,000 plus acres of this park."

Alexis and Dean nodded their heads in agreement.

Alexis leaned toward the second map and made a large 'X' near a lodge and trail head. "I'm parking my car here tomorrow. You should be able to track my phone. Check every fifteen minutes, starting at 6:15 a.m. to make sure we are progressing toward the park. If I appear idle for more than fifteen minutes, then things are NOT all right."

"Right," said Dean. "We call Grandpa and Uncle Clark. Depending on where you are one of them can intercept you and Guy. But Guy doesn't know anything about your practice of karate. He also doesn't know you are a physically formidable opponent. I don't think it's a terrible idea to put a tracker in your shoe. Of course, the technology is only as good as our ability to get a cell signal."

"Here's where I come in," said Michelle brightly. "I've been working on a cell signal booster. It's one of my projects for the Department of Defense. The tech is mine, but their application of the tech is classified. Give me an hour to work on it. I thought this might be a possibility, and I brought some trackers with me. Do you want one for your car, too? This feels very 'Spy vs Spy.'"

Alexis nodded. She marked the map with a green dot. "Here's where I'm planning to stop for lunch." Tapping the map with her marker she said, "He's going to try to drug me during lunch. I'm going to let him think he's been successful. I don't know if he's going to throw me over his shoulder, give me a piggyback ride, or drag me along with one of my arms around his neck and one of his arms around my waist. His progress will be pretty slow, and he will have to take several breaks because I *will* be dead weight."

Dean reached across from where he was sitting, and taking Alexis's hand in his, he tried to look sincere and said, "I hate to be the one to tell you this, but if he has you on his back or over his shoulder, you are going to have to pee your pants. It will make his journey so much worse."

"Good one," Alexis said. "I like it."

Michelle marked the map with a red star. "Here's where you have some options, and we'll be able to help you either on the way to or from your lunch stop. Remember the boulders we saw near the ravine? It's a good natural rest stop. It's also a scenic overlook. You're off trail here, so it's not an area normally traveled or monitored. We have loads of options to place obstacles, and I think this is our best option."

Both Dean and Alexis agreed. They quickly packed up their camping gear, doubling back to their vehicles but stopping by the area with the boulders. Michelle and Dean carefully maneuvered around the boulders, looking for natural cover, thinking through the best approaches to the Guy Brown problem. Michelle pulled a small wire out of her backpack. "This is the answer." Her face was positively aglow.

She continued to explain her plan to Dean and Alexis, and they both smiled, quickly warming to her idea. When they returned to their cars, Michelle called James, relaying their plan. He liked it. He liked it a lot and felt it was elegant in its finesse and lack of outright brutality. It was a far cry more humane than what Guy had planned for Alexis.

CHAPTER 58
Guy – *Saturday*

Oh, my GOD. This girl is a morning person. Her cheeks are naturally rosy, her eyes shining bright, and I think there might actually be a glint on her teeth. Her hair is back in a low ponytail, and she's wearing a baseball cap. She is effervescent. Energy comes off her in waves, and I imagine it will peter out on the drive to Yosemite.

"I made a kickass play list for the drive," Alexis gushed as she led me to her car. "Is it ok to put your backpack in the trunk? Is there anything you need immediately? I brought some homemade granola, in case you're hungry, and I have a thermos of blond espresso. But I'll warn you to drink it in moderation. It's super-charged with caffeine."

Oh, my GOD. She shared she had already downed a couple mugs of espresso before she left her sorority house this morning to pick me up. "How long have you been awake?" I asked her.

"Hmmm. I don't know. Maybe only since around 4 a.m. I like to be prepared. I made a checklist, and I wanted to make sure I had everything. I don't want to wind up in the middle of nowhere and realize I left my Epi-pen at home."

"You have an Epi-pen? What's your allergy?" I asked her.

"There are a handful of things, but I had an anaphylactic reaction to a bite from a red ant when I was little. They aren't everywhere, but it would be stupid to be somewhere like Yosemite and not be prepared. You know? So many microclimates and ecosystems—you just really have to be prepared for anything."

"Do you always have this much energy in the morning?" I asked her.

"I do," she answered. "Usually, I swim for two hours or so to burn through some of this *excess*. I have severe ADHD, and physical activity in the morning helps me get focused for the day. What about you? Do you do any kind of anything?"

"I run, go to the gym, and I journal for twenty minutes every morning. Then I set my day. It's something I've done since I was a kid. I keep a notebook, separate from my journal, and I write down three things I want to accomplish. Some are tasks, and some aren't. Then I think through what's mission-critical for the day and create a checklist. I also list the things that would be nice to get through but aren't mission-critical. As the day progresses, I check things off. At the end of the day, I review my progress.

"I focus on the accomplishments and not the deficits because tomorrow is another day, and I get to try again and, chances are, I'll get the things done I couldn't finish today."

"Guy," Alexis exclaimed. "What a phenomenal approach. You need to write a book about that!"

"It would be a good book," I told her. "In fact, I picked up a lot of the fundamentals from another book. It was a bestseller in the early 1990's."

She nodded thoughtfully. "I brought doughnuts. You should have some. We're going to hike eleven miles today, and it will be a while before we stop for lunch. I also cooked some bacon and made some bacon sandwiches. Everything is in the cooler or the basket in the backseat. I also brought car bingo, in case you aren't in the mood for my rompin' stompin' playlist."

"Uh, wow," I said. She packed a lot of words into these single breaths of speech, and she spoke quickly, which meant I had to pay extra attention to everything she was saying.

She turned toward me, looking me in the eye, while we waited for a stoplight to cycle through. "I wanted to apologize for coming on to you the other night. It was inappropriate, and I don't want you to feel you have to be on your guard with me. I respect you and your boundaries, and, I'm only twenty-one, and you're like thirty or something, and it's an age gap. I get it. Really. We'll be friends. OK?"

"You have nothing to apologize for," I said, "I was really flattered. I don't get out a whole lot, and I've been directing a lot of my energy into my book. But again, nothing to worry about. Water under the bridge." I paused before asking, "Would you be terribly offended if I caught a little sleep for about thirty minutes or so? I have been knackered this week from the time zone difference. Going west is always a tougher adjustment for me than going east."

"Oh," she paused. "Sure! Of course. Will it bother you if I listen to music or a podcast or something? Will you be able to sleep through a little background noise?"

"I can sleep through virtually anything," I replied, pulling off my jacket and molding it into shape to support my head against the window. Sleeping would give her a chance to settle down and would put an end to the yammering and awkward attempts at dialogue. Maybe by the time I awoke, we could talk about normal things, and I could avoid playing car bingo, which sounded horrible. I have no idea where the poised, self-possessed young woman from class had gone, or the coquettish young thing from dinner. It was like there were three versions of Alexis, and I wasn't sure which was the real deal, but I was leaning toward the highly intelligent and perceptive woman with the keen eye who seemed to strip me bare from the inside out from my lectures. I closed my eyes, my mind zoning in on the road noise. She had the thermostat turned up to 76, and the warm air blowing gently onto my forehead and eyes made sleep irresistible.

I dreamed about her, about putting her in the trunk of a car, about taking her home with me, locking her up, keeping her as a pet. I pictured Cameron Diaz in the cage in "Being John Malkovich," and in my dream, having a pet female human seemed natural. But in dreams, we don't address practicalities of life like showering, toileting, clothing, parenting, or simply being human. My dream took me down a strange path where I was the pet in the cage, and I couldn't get a good look at my owner's face. They kept feeding me boiled cabbage, and then I could smell something. In my dream, I leaned my head at an angle to get a good whiff of my armpits. They were fine, but I couldn't shake the smell. I realized it was food. We were stopped. Alexis was pumping gas, and there was a bag on the console. She had picked up a breakfast sandwich for me? I knocked on the window, startling her where she stood, watching the meter run up on the gas pump. She pressed her hand to her heart, and gave a small, embarrassed smile. I watched her. Her movements were smooth, assured, and fluid. She was comfortable in her body. I wondered if she had been a dancer as a child and adolescent.

When she got back in the car, she seemed more like the Alexis I had known in class. "I picked up a sandwich for you, in case you were hungry," she said, starting the car and pulling away from the filling station. She was looking straight ahead, focused on driving.

"Thanks. How long was I asleep? Did I snore?" I asked. Now I seemed to be the jumpy one of the two of us. I hated the idea of my snoring. "Really, though. Thank you for the sandwich. I was so afraid of oversleeping this morning I didn't get a solid night's sleep." I stretched and yawned. She chuckled.

"You'll love seeing the park early. There's so much you don't see if you miss the earlier morning hours," she mused. "How often to you get to see the natural world wake up? It gives me peace. I love it." She fumbled with the thermostat. "I hope you'll love it, too," she said quietly.

We drove on talking about the park, the hike, how she had enjoyed school on the West Coast, how I enjoyed lecturing about strategy, what it was like for me to get through school at such a young age. The remainder of the drive passed quickly.

CHAPTER 59

The Kids – *Saturday, Yosemite National Park*

Alexis parked the car exactly where she had planned to park. She and Guy each took their backpacks, hoisting them on their backs, and Alexis also took a small spiral bound pad and pen, which went into her front pocket. Guy looked at her curiously because it seemed like a strange thing to need to have on a hike. Alexis responded to his expression, "I've been carrying this little pad with me on hikes for years. I like to catalog interesting plants or animals or make note of something remarkable and singular that I see or experience on a hike. Things I don't ever want to forget." Guy nodded his understanding.

"I take it you know the route?" Guy asked.

"I do—not backwards and forwards, but I've mapped out where we're going, when we can stop for bio breaks, lunch, those sorts of things. I've even figured out where the best photo ops are. I have a hard copy map, and then I also have it on my phone. Even if I can't get a cell signal, I can still figure out where we are or will be."

"I am genuinely impressed!" Guy said, slowly shaking his head back and forth. "Are you always this prepared?" Alexis began leading toward the trail head, and Guy

"I told you earlier about my ADHD. One of my coping mechanisms is preparation. I can't solve a Rubik's cube to save my life, but I can keep rotating the thing and come up with a thousand things I need to do to get through my homework, presentations, whatever. And I have to make lists. And I almost always have some kind of notebook and writing implement with me, and I also use the voice memo function on my phone."

"Ah. I think I guessed you were over-caffeinated this morning or had become very nervous about this trip, in spite of the ADHD," Guy shared frankly.

"I didn't get to exercise this morning, so I'm pretty much full bore for a while. I like to think of the physical activity like the sun burning the dew off the grass in the morning. It takes me a little bit to sink into being myself, but then I'm all-systems-go." She looked at the map on her phone, scouted both directions then said, "Anyway. Enough about me. Let's see some nature. I did this hike a few years ago, and I hope it's as breathtaking as I remember."

They walked side by side. Alexis didn't want Guy Brown anywhere where she couldn't immediately see him. She knew not to trust the shiny wrapping paper he wore for the public. It was just as easy to wrap a wasp's nest in pretty paper as it was to wrap a Cartier watch.

Alexis had the small wire from Michelle wrapped inside the barrel of her pen. It would send a micro-current just strong enough to interfere with Guy's cochlear implant, eliciting a migraine. He would more than likely be incapacitated before they ever stopped for lunch.

Michelle gave them 90 minutes of hiking time before starting the projection of the current. They had to be far enough into their hike that turning around and making it back to the car in short order wasn't a viable option. After 90 minutes, they could turn around, but it would still take them at least 90 minutes to return to the confines of Alexis's car. Their route was off trail, close to an incredible scenic overlook. And of course, Alexis wanted Guy to have a photo. It was a must—something to prove he had been to beautiful Yosemite.

Dean and Michelle maintained a position close enough to Alexis and Guy's route to amp up the current, causing Guy's balance to suffer severely. With his head throbbing and his balance impaired, Guy stumbled and slipped. Alexis helped him up, but she couldn't support his weight. They hadn't brought any walking or hiking aids, and Guy told her he could tough it out. She asked him if he needed to stop, sit a moment to gather himself. Nothing on the route was a surprise to Alexis, especially not the boulder she was delighted to show Guy. "Why look! There's a nice boulder. Rest there."

Guy ambled to the boulder and tried to perch himself atop. The pain in his head became more intense, a constant pounding, reverberating against the inner walls of his skull. He felt his heartbeat from inside his eye sockets. He attempted to lie back on the boulder, to recline his head. If only he could recline his head. He made a vain effort to become comfortable on the boulder, and with his altered sense of balance, he rolled off the boulder. Alexis said, "Whoopsy daisy." Guy tried to regain his footing and retake his position on the boulder. He fumbled around, circling the boulder for the best approach, not paying attention to the terrain around the boulder. He found the sweet spot, but it was on a vulnerable side for him. His ankle turned, making an ugly cracking noise, and Guy crumpled in a heap, and he was not able to gain purchase on anything. He rolled ten, twenty, thirty, forty, fifty feet down the steep embankment, getting caught on old tree roots which had found themselves lying above ground. The roots seemed to lash Guy's forehead and while he raised his arms to protect his head and face, he did nothing to grasp at the roots to stop his downward momentum, which took him farther down the embankment another fifty, then one hundred feet. Alexis heard him calling for help, and she answered in the affirmative. Alexis didn't call for help, though. She sent a text to Dean and Michelle and James.

Guy's 'accidental' fall eventually concluded at the bottom of a deep ravine. He passed out from the pain in his head. He didn't notice when Alexis had put a transmitter similar to the one in the pen into Guy's pocket when he was sleeping in the car. When they were certain Guy was unconscious, or at the very least, incapacitated, Dean, Michelle, and Alexis carefully hiked to the bottom of the ravine. Guy had no idea he had been assessed and observed for injuries. He had cuts and abrasions on his face and exposed skin. He had a broken orbital, multiple broken ribs, fractured wrist, ankle, clavicle, and a punctured lung. There was so much blood. Head wounds were messy, for sure, but he was unaware Alexis had slipped some blood thinners into his breakfast sandwich and coffee, and the blood wouldn't clot, at least not quickly or normally. The broken ribs and fall made short work of his lung. Guy was breathing, though. It didn't sound pretty, but he was breathing. Dean removed Guy's backpack. It survived the fall remarkably well. He found zip ties and drugs, lots of drugs. Drugs meant for Alexis.

Dean, Michelle, and Alexis marveled over the drugs. "Jesus," someone said. They left Guy without much in the way of supplies, should he need to stay in the ravine overnight, should he regain consciousness. In his current state, it would be irresponsible of them to allow Guy to start a fire. He would not be able to contain it or put it out if he lost consciousness suddenly, and after his fall and all the injuries he had sustained, there was a high probability he would have been unable to manage much of anything. They left him some pain reliever and an apple. With the broken wrist, he wouldn't have been able to open a can or anything. Leaving canned food with Guy would have been a waste. Michelle took a video of the area, from the bottom of the ravine, and progressing up to the boulder where Guy's fall had begun. She ensured the coordinates for the location were captured and could be monitored via satellite. She sent the information to James.

The three young adults proceeded to the marked trail, speaking little, pondering what they had done and what they hadn't done. They spent very little time thinking over the morality or ethics of their acts. Guy might have survived, or he might not have, and it was up to him. They watched the satellite feed periodically over the next several days, then they stopped. Diamond Teams continued to monitor the satellite feed, but the lure of the feed was intoxicating to Dean, Michelle, and Alexis.

Dean returned to Northwestern, Alexis to Berkeley, and Michelle to Stanford. The guest lectures scheduled for the following week were canceled. James and Clark traveled to see each of the three to debrief and provide any counseling as necessary. For all three of them, life returned to normal.

CHAPTER 60
Chris – *2 months later*

Sam and I joined Kevin and Kate, along with all of our kids, James, Clark, and his family in Palo Alto for Michelle's graduation from Stanford. It was a perfect day. We rented a large home through Air B&B and made a wonderful long weekend of it. It was such a nice trip, we decided to make our way up to wine country and take the following week off.

Michelle had decided to go to graduate school at MIT the following year. She was working on some nanotechnology which had earned her a full ride to pursue her graduate degree. Dean and Alexis, both rising seniors, decided to try dating—each other. If they could make a long-distance relationship work, then why not? They were both very mature in telling all of us if things didn't work out, they wouldn't make it weird for all the rest of us. I had to chuckle. What about if things did work out for them? We would be family, and I kind of already felt like we were family. The two of them are talking about working for Diamond Teams after they graduate or opening some kind of self-defense business or both. I liked to kid around with Sam (and only Sam) they could lead hikes where their clients never returned to their regular lives.

Sam and Kate were working out their exit strategies from Diamond Teams. Clark and I would transition into their roles, and we would then begin working to fill our former jobs. Were they leaving big shoes to fill? Hell, yes. The two of them were finesse personified.

I asked Sam what she planned to do in her next chapter, and she said she thought accounting for the mob might be fun and different. I clutched at my heart, and she swatted me and said, "Really?"

Kevin told me Kate wanted to become a cheese monger. "She doesn't even eat cheese!" Kevin said. "She complains about all the fat content in cheese, and said if Courtney Love doesn't eat cheese, then she's not eating it either."

"Huh," I said in reply. "I didn't know she was following Courtney Love's dietary recommendations."

"Making cheese," Kevin said. "I don't know whether to believe her or not. Do you think this is her new Cirque du Soleil bar lie? I think I'd be less surprised if she told me she wanted to raise wolves."

"I guess we'll have to wait and see."

While we were in wine country, I said, "Hey, Kate. I heard Cirque du Soleil was looking for some new talent. They said one of their stars had broken her pelvis. Do you want me to give them your name?"

Kate flipped me the bird and replied dryly, "Ha. Ha. Ha."

Guy Brown. He was the big unknown. We weren't sure where he was in the world. The satellite footage didn't show him at the bottom of the ravine, but it didn't show any movement either. We just sort of lost him. It's possible a bear got to him or a mountain lion. Who knows? He hasn't turned up near his son or ex-wife. He hasn't shown up at his parents' house or the homes of any of his siblings. Things were never cleared up with the bench warrant, and the Chief Strategy Officer role at his former company was filled a month ago. I've been monitoring everyone's credit reports, and the only weird things I've seen were a subscription to PornHub on Clark's credit card, which he categorically denied doing, and a subscription to 'Cat Fancy' on Bruce's credit card, which he also denied, but he said Leeza wanted to keep the magazine.

Leeza and Chun came to Clark and me with a brilliant idea. They wanted us to invite prior clients to participate in the Commando game orchestrated by Diamond Teams, only offered once annually. We're massaging the details, but Kate and Sam think there's a lot of merit in the undertaking, and only doing it once a year would preserve the cachet.

James decided he would stick around through the Sam-Kate transition and offer assistance, just like he always has, until Clark and I are settled in our roles, but he's ready to be a full-time rancher and grandpa to all of the kids. He says he wants to raise horses and grandkids, and eventually great-grandkids. Great-grandkids! Making Kate and Kevin grandparents, but whose children—Michelle's or Dean's?

I think I'm going to take my bride, the woman of my dreams, the smart, cool girl who has owned me since I was sixteen, on a second honeymoon, and when we return, there won't be great pomp and fanfare, and there won't be a magical glimmer bathing everything around us, and we'll still be grownups, and we'll still have these lives we've built on our own and together, we'll take things a day at a time—like regular people do every single day.